Risking It All
for a Hitta

Risking It All
for a Hitta

Ducati

www.urbanbooks.net

Urban Books, LLC
300 Farmingdale Road, N.Y.-Route 109
Farmingdale, NY 11735

Risking It All for a Hitta Copyright © 2025 Ducati

ISBN 13: 978-1-64556-700-4

First Trade Paperback Printing April 2025
Printed in the United States of America

10 9 8 7 6 5 4 3 2 1

This is a work of fiction. Any references or similarities to actual events, real people, living or dead, or to real locales are intended to give the novel a sense of reality. Any similarity in other names, characters, places, and incidents is entirely coincidental.

Distributed by Kensington Publishing Corp.
Submit Orders to:
Customer Service
400 Hahn Road
Westminster, MD 21157-4627
Phone: 1-800-733-3000
Fax: 1-800-659-2436

Risking It All for a Hitta

by

Ducati

CHAPTER ONE

TOKYO

The sound of my heels clacked loudly as I walked down the long, narrow hall. The closer I got to the door, the more rummaging I heard. All I could think was, *yeah, motherfucker, I'm here now.* As I was about to turn the knob, I heard, "Shit, shit, shit! Fuck! Bitch, move!" It sounded like someone had fallen or hit the floor. I had to laugh, because while I had been sitting around waiting for the other part of my pay, this fat motherfucker was banging one of the many strippers who worked in his club. Uncle or not, I wanted my money, and since I knew he didn't have it, I was about to end his fucking life. Two things I didn't play about were my sister and my money.

I burst through the door and pointed my gun directly at him. "What's up, Unc?"

"Oh, God, uhhh, Tokyo, I was just about to call you!" he stumbled.

"Yeah, once you got done fucking her, I'm assuming? Or maybe after another one of your tricking-ass trips you can't stop taking these bitches on? How the fuck, if you don't mind my asking, can you have time to fuck and afford these trips, but your ass can't send me my money on time? Shit's mind-blowing if you ask me."

The young girl tried to run past me, but I grabbed her by the hair. She turned around and covered her breasts with a loose shirt as she reached out for him.

"Baby girl, shit don't get that hard for you to have to fuck this slimeball-ass snake for an extra piece of change. And what you covering ya titties for? You're a stripper, right? Let me see those motherfuckers." I ran my gun along the side of her face as she slowly put her hands down, letting the shirt she had fall to the floor. I laughed and let her go.

I walked over and sat my thick, round ass right on his desk. As I stared at him, I could only imagine how my father would feel. I hauled off and hit him across the face with the butt of my gun. He stumbled back, falling against the wall. When I cocked it, his eyes widened, and it seemed like my pussy got wet, too. Putting fear in a man always gave me that tingly feeling in the crotch of my panties.

"Why haven't you paid me the rest of my money? You knew what it was once you hired me, my nigga."

"Just give me a few seconds to get it for you." He looked back and forth between me and the safe that sat on the ground in the far corner of his small, smelly office. I wasn't stupid by far. I knew he didn't have my money. I also knew he never kept any money in that safe, only a small .22. I waited for him to put the code in and turn the latch. After licking the barrel of my gun and smiling, I aimed it at his back. When he grabbed his gun, I shot him. He spun around and started carelessly firing all through the office.

I ducked behind his desk, laughing. I loved a good adrenaline rush. When I heard the gun start clicking, I got up and walked over to him.

"So this is how you wanna play it? You could have just simply paid me my shit instead of trying to trick on these bitches in here. Now look at you in here about to meet your fucking Maker. How the fuck do you think your death is going to make my father feel?" I cocked my head.

"Tokyo, please," he panted, "all I need is a little more time and I'll have your money. I promise!"

"I've been waiting on my money for almost three weeks now. Had you had been anyone else, I would've been smoked your ass after twenty-four hours. This shit ain't a game! I kill motherfuckers for a living, literally! Plus, do you really think I'd be stupid enough to let you live after I just shot your big ass in the back? It's over!" I stood and aimed at his face. He threw his hands up in an attempt to block the shots. I fired the whole sixteen into him. Bullets tore through his flesh like a knife cutting butter. Blood, brain matter, and chunks of his face splattered all over the wall and my pedicured toes.

I went into the tiny dimly lit bathroom and snatched a towel down off the back of the toilet. Running hot water on it, I sat on the lid and started cleaning my feet and stilettos off. Walking out the door, I didn't bother shutting it. When I got back up the hall, my uncle's bodyguard was still watching out for anyone who may have tried to come up.

"Thanks, Big Black." I patted him on his back and kept it moving.

"Hey, you still gonna hit me up for that business meeting? And what about my money?" he called out.

"Meet me around back in an hour."

He was out of his rabbit-ass mind if he thought I would hire his ass after he had sold out his own boss of twelve years. He was sadly mistaken. When I got back downstairs to the bar, Miss Cynthia, an older stripper, called out to me.

"Hey, Tokyo girl! Where you been?" she attempted to yell over the music while running over to me in her panties with her big double D's bouncing freely. I sat at the bar and waited on her to join me.

"What's up, Cynthia? What you up to?" I hugged her.

"Girl, not shit! Ready to get the hell out of this place. My damn bunions are screaming for dear life!" She wiggled her feet.

"What can I get for you, little momma?" Susan, the bartender and Cynthia's only daughter, asked.

"I'll take a Blue Mother Fucker and a shot of tequila."

"And make Momma a drink too!" Miss Cynthia added.

"Coming right up." She started filling two cups with ice. "So why you ain't been around here lately? I was beginning to think you skipped town type shit."

"I've been very busy here these last couple of weeks on the go, you know, with my father having cancer and all."

"That's really sad," she said as she shook her head. "Your uncle been telling us about that, too. How is he holding up?"

"As good as he can. They have him on oxygen now and all these different meds. I just got him another at-home nurse. The last one was stealing food and shit out of his crib when he was sleeping. So you know I had to beat her ass." I smirked.

"Girl, you is too violent," she laughed. "Was your uncle upstairs?"

"No, I don't think so. I knocked on the office door and didn't get an answer."

"That's strange." She looked down at her watch. "Usually he'd be here by now to collect from all of us."

After a few more drinks and some past-due catching up with Cynthia and her daughter, I noticed the young stripper I caught in my uncle's office rushing out with a gym bag. I said my farewells to Cynthia and her daughter, and then left to go pay Big Black what I owed him and head home. Crossing the street, I jumped in my Suburban truck and hit the button to dial home. My sister picked up on the third ring.

"What's up?" she smacked into the phone.

"That fat fuck is out of here." I sighed.

"I told your ass he wasn't going to have it. I told you so. Now you owe me two thousand for losing that bet."

"Yeah, yeah, I know."

"Well, I guess this means we'll be going over to Dad's tomorrow."

"Yeah, let me hit you back." I hung up the phone and pulled into the back alley. I sat in my truck playing *Bubble Pop* on my cell phone until Big Black came creeping out the back door and started speed walking up to my window.

"I sure am glad that fucker is dead," he giggled as he shook his head.

"Me too. Here's your money." I smiled, reaching under my seat for the loaded gun. When I pulled it out, I put the tip directly on his nose.

"Goddammit!" He closed his eyes. "I knew I shouldn't have trusted you."

"Nah, my nigga, it's the other way around. Who's to say after I paid you, you wouldn't rat me out? I mean, let's be real. You sold my uncle out for four hundred dollars."

I could've sworn this nigga pissed his pants and let a tear fall right before I pulled the trigger. Boom! I cut my truck back on, rolled my window up, and pulled off. I hit the button to dial home again to finish my conversation with my sister. She hated when someone didn't finish a conversation with her. I didn't know what it was. As I turned the corner, the young stripper chick I snatched up was standing in a phone booth. I slowed down and took a gun out of my glove compartment.

"I was about to say, your ass better call me back!" India got jazzy with me.

"I know, but never mind that. We'll just talk once I get home. I have to handle something real quick." Disconnecting the call, I rolled my window down. She looked like she was panicking on the phone.

"Hey, li'l momma, you all right?" I called out to her.

She turned and looked then hung up the phone. As she raced toward my truck, a look of shock washed over her face once she saw it was me. Before she could run, I fired two quick shots into her head. She dropped to the ground like a sack of potatoes. I had to get rid of her ass, because besides Big Black, she was the only other person who knew I was the last person in my uncle's office. I shook my head and lit a blunt. I sped off laughing and cut my music on and all the way up.

When I pulled into the driveway, the living room light was still on. I got out and hit the alarm button to my truck. I didn't need my keys as I walked right into the house. No one knew where we lived, and that was just the way I liked it. Not even India's supposed man. She was on her laptop doing some online shopping as usual. I knew it was for Bryson's conniving ass. I couldn't stand the ground his greedy, wannabe gangster, money-hungry ass walked on. Something about him just didn't sit right with me. I personally felt like he was using my sister for her money. But there wasn't shit you could tell someone about the person they were in love with.

CHAPTER TWO

INDIA

I glanced up and made a "pay me my money" gesture with my hand toward Tokyo when she came through the door. She flipped me off and went into the kitchen. I heard her go into the fridge and start going through the mail. It had totally slipped my mind that my credit card bill was still in there.

"Aye yo, India, what the fuck is this?" she asked, walking back into the living room. I looked up at her and then at what she had in her hand. I closed my eyes and shook my head, cursing to myself.

"I'll take care of it in the morning." I shrugged.

"The fuck you mean you'll take care of it in the morning? I want to know why the hell eighty thousand dollars is missing out of your account and you're in the negatives by damn near a grand!" She spoke a little louder than she needed to.

I stood up and cut my eyes at her. "I said I'll handle it, so why you trippin' on me?"

"Probably because that's your fucking school money! What did you spend that on, and Lord forbid your silly ass say Bryson!"

I hesitated for a moment. "Look, we don't keep secrets from each other, so I'm going to tell you flat-out. Me and Bryson decided to have a baby, and the procedure that I needed cost sixty alone. The rest was for him to send to his mom because she's sick. That poor woman." I shook my head. Tokyo looked like she wanted to punch the fuck out of me. I could also tell me mentioning a baby was about to send her over the edge.

She just stared at me for a moment. I could tell she was still stuck on the wanting a baby part. For years, all me and my sister had was each other and our father. We didn't need friends because we stayed with each other at all times. Then one day I started college, met the love of my life, and made him my boyfriend. Tokyo hated him and didn't trust him. I wasn't trippin' though, because she was like that with everyone.

"Wait what? You mean to tell me," she began, massaging her temples, "this bitch-ass nigga has two kids already he doesn't take care of and you're about to give his deadbeat ass a third? No! You ain't doing that shit. Talking about a fucking baby, your ass better adopt a fucking dog! He gon' get you knocked up like the other two wealthy mammies and leave you high and dry!"

I could feel my blood beginning to boil. She looked like she felt sick. What the fuck was wrong with her?

"Tokyo, watch what you say. You ain't about to sit up and disrespect my man like that." I raised my hand.

"Disrespect? Bitch, you ain't seen disrespect yet!" she freaked out.

"Look, all I'm saying is chill the fuck out! What the hell has been having you on edge so much lately?"

"Don't worry about it. I don't even feel like talking."

"That's yo' issue now, you always bottling shit up. Evil-ass bitch." I sat back down and started scrolling on my laptop again. I was about to buy my man a few more outfits and some more shoes for our trip that he wanted to take me on, even though I was the one who paid for it in advance. I loved Bryson, and if I was going to be looking good, I was going to make damn sure my man matched me.

Now I know what you're thinkin', and no, I wasn't no sugar momma, and I wasn't buying his love. I just liked spoiling whomever I was with. It'd always been that way, even with my sister, who I was sure was giving me the look of death. I glanced over the top of my laptop, and true enough she was!

CHAPTER THREE

TOKYO

I felt like I wanted to flip the fuck out on her, but there was a huge lump in my throat. This was my little sister by two minutes! She was the only thing in the world I had. My damn twin, I mean, a direct spitting image of me. My ride or die, and now some lame-ass, nickel-and-diming motherfucker was slowly but surely stealing her from me? I couldn't have that, hell no. Call it what you want, but my twin belonged to me and only me. I wasn't about to share her with someone else, let alone a baby! I instantly started thinking of ways to kill Bryson.

I guess it was written on my face because next thing you know all I heard was, "Bitch, you bet' not dare do what I think you're thinking about! That's crossing the line and would be so fucked up to hurt me like that, Tokyo. I know that flicker in your eyes."

"What flicker?" I glanced at her.

"The same one I get in my eyes when I'm about to do something really fucked up."

When she said that, it instantly reminded me of our father. That's how he could always tell when we were up to no good. I had orange bright-looking eyes that would turn red when I was sad, pissed off, or being sneaky, and India had green ones that got brighter when she was happy and turned like a dark-ass evergreen color when she was mad. That was the only way to tell us apart, and if you didn't pay attention to that small detail, nine times out of ten you wouldn't know which one of us you were even talking to.

"I'm not going to do anything to him. It is what it is." I bit my tongue and walked away, heading for my room upstairs. I needed to take a shower and just breathe for a moment. India followed me to the staircase.

"So that's it? Nothing else to say? No congratulations or anything?"

I looked over my shoulder and gave her a dry, "Congrats."

"Oh, wow, seriously? You're upset and acting childish." She threw her hands up.

I just kept walking. When I got into my room, I snatched off the body-fitting red dress I had on and tossed it into a corner. Taking my heels off I did the same. I felt myself getting more and more worked up. I rushed into the bathroom and cut the shower on. Taking off my bra and panties, I stepped in, trying to let the pressure of it soothe me and calm my nerves. It didn't work, because out of nowhere everything hit me at once. And I do mean hard. I started bawling like a baby. This wasn't fair! I was losing my dad to cancer, my sister to a no-good nigga and a soon-to-be baby . . . who would I have then? And the more I cried, the more furious I became.

I stood in that shower, mad at the fucking world, hitting myself in the head and kicking the walls until the water ran cold and I almost busted my ass. I was even more pissed off I had cried. That was just something I never did. My dad always said that wasn't right, especially for a woman. I just never had a reason to until now. Stepping out, I dried my body and walked back into my room. Slipping on a long black T-shirt, I put on my house shoes, grabbed my blanket, and went back downstairs. India was on the phone ordering our pizza. It was a Friday night, and no matter what, we always spent it together watching movies and talking about our week. That was something my father started with us when we were younger. My mother never participated because she was always too busy chasing her next high and cheating on my father. I couldn't stand her and was happy she was dead. I got so sick of her always making my father and sister cry and taking us through the most that one night I copped some drugs and put some bad dope into her purse knowing she would use it. A few days later me and my sister came home from school and there she was, sprawled out in the middle of the floor with a needle hanging out of her arm. I didn't call 911 either. I was praying the shit hadn't just knocked her ass out and had actually killed her. Nothing happened until my father got home from work. How someone could love someone so disrespectful, evil, and toxic was beyond me. That was my first kill, my first body—my mother, and the shit felt great. I loved seeing that look of emptiness in a dead person's eyes.

Sitting on the couch, I picked the remote up and cut the TV on. India finished with the call and threw a pillow at me.

"I don't feel like playing right now." I surfed through the channels.

"You know, if you had someone of your own, you wouldn't be so upset. I know I wouldn't get mad at you. I'd be happy for you." She placed a hand on her thick hip.

I ignored her and kept doing what I was doing. She walked over and stood in front of the flat screen.

"Move, India! Damn!" I shouted.

"If you want to watch TV that bad, then make me move," she challenged. I had to laugh and shake my head. She always chose to get on my nerves when she knew I was upset.

"I can't stand yo' ass for real for real." I smiled.

"I know, that's why you're sitting down."

"Whatever."

"Girl." She walked over and plopped down on the sofa. I kept my eyes on the TV, and she kept bumping me until I finally gave her my attention.

"Awww, come here, my little tinka butts," she said in a baby voice, reaching out to hug me.

"Don't fucking touch me, traitor." I pushed her off.

"How does it make me a traitor? Because I want to be with someone and have a love life? I don't see why you won't give a guy a chance. I'm starting to think your ass is gay!"

"Yeah fucking right! You wish. Honey, I'm strictly dickly, and besides, I don't need a man. I'm smooth on my own." I rolled my eyes.

"Now how would you know what the hell you are if you haven't even had any? Fuckin' virgin talking about what she think she is." She stood up and started switching through the room and snapping her fingers making jokes about my sex life. Well, the one I should've had.

"Girl, you finally gave a lame your V card and now you know about sexual preferences?" I cocked my head.

"Uh, sister girl, I'm just saying you ain't getting no younger, so give a nigga a chance and give up that thang before it pack up and leave yo' ass!" she joked with a smirk.

"I am perfectly fine the way I am. Nigga and drama free, not having to answer to anyone or worry about what he's doing when I'm not around. Call it what you want, but I like my peace and sanity. That's why all the guys back in school wanted me, because they knew I had something precious I was holding on to." I started laughing.

"How the fuck would you know? More than a majority of the time they didn't know if they were looking at you or me! Your ass was rarely at school anyways! Plus, on top of that, they were scared of your crazy ass!" she exclaimed.

I rolled my eyes and looked at the TV screen as it switched to our security camera views. The pizza man was walking up to the door. India grabbed a few dollars from her bag and went to open the door before he could ring the doorbell. When she did, he stepped back and admired her thick thighs.

"Gaaat daamn!" he exclaimed.

My sister turned around and gave me "the look." I knew it was showtime. I seductively walked up behind her and slid my arm around her waist smiling at him.

"Holy fucking shit! Twins!" he screamed, almost dropping our pizza.

On the inside, I was rolling my eyes and thinking, *this fucking clown-ass nigga,* but on the outside, I was licking my lips.

"You like what you see?" India asked, raising her shirt a little, exposing a little more of her thigh.

"You wanna come in and eat with us?" I kissed her on the shoulder.

The poor boy looked like he was about to have a damn heart attack.

"Hell yeah!" he yelled as he attempted to walk through the door.

"I don't fucking think so!" India snatched the food and pushed him back, then tossed the money and walked off.

"In your fucking dreams, lame!" I slammed the door in his face.

We both busted out laughing until I heard him shout, "Tricking-ass bitches!" I whipped around and grabbed a snow globe off the mantle and rushed to the door. As he was halfway back to his car, I reared back and threw it as hard as I could, hitting him straight in the back. He fell on the sidewalk, screaming curse words.

"Ya old-ass mammie is a tricking-ass bitch! I should shoot yo' gullible dirty sourdough-smelling ass!" I flipped him off as he jumped up and ran to his car. India was laughing with a mouth full of pizza as I walked back up to the door.

"Bitch, you crazy as fuck!" she said with a laugh as she fell against the doorframe.

"His bitch ass got me fucked up! He got the right fucking one tonight! Fuck around and get his shit blown the fuck off."

"Okay, okay, calm down, Rambo." She shut the door behind me. We started watching *Austin Powers* and ate our food. After the second movie I got up and poured us both a nice cup of wine. We ended up drinking two bottles before our father's number flashed across our flat screen.

CHAPTER FOUR

TOKYO

"Oh, shit, bitch, it's Daddy!" she said, attempting to fix her hair and shirt.

"So what? Pick up the phone!"

"Bitch, it's been hours now. You know what the fuck he calling for this late! It's goddamn three in the morning!"

It had honestly slipped my mind because it was just another job to me. I grew a little nervous thinking about my uncle and what my dad would say.

"Well, what you gon' tell 'im?" I looked at the TV, then at her.

"The fuck you mean? You the one who killed the man! You pick up!"

"Nah, nigga! You said you were going to talk to him! Don't back out now!" I grabbed the cordless phone and shoved it into her. She pushed it back at me. We did this whole back-and-forth thing until the phone stopped ringing. Next thing you know my cell phone started vibrating on the living room table. We both just watched it. It stopped, and then India's phone started going off. She walked over and took a deep breath, then answered.

"Hello?" she answered and put the phone on speaker.

"Hey, baby girl," my father coughed into the phone. He sounded so tired. "You know I wouldn't be calling this late disturbing you girls unless it was important."

"Oh, no, Daddy, it's fine. We were just watching a movie. What's the matter?"

I picked up a pillow and threw it at her. She flipped me off and moved closer to me so I could hear better.

"Well, some detectives just left not long ago. Uh, there is no easy way to say this, but someone killed your Uncle Marvin tonight at his club."

"Oh no!" she exclaimed, faking her emotions.

"Yeah," Daddy went on as he coughed even more. It sounded as if he was trying not to cry. "I told him to leave that club mess alone a long time ago. And I know he was doing illegal things on the side, too, and messing with them young girls. Now it done finally caught up to him," he sighed.

"Well, do they know who did it?" She looked at me and rolled her eyes. I threw my hands on my hips and started smiling.

"No, but they think it was a robbery, said something about an open, empty safe. They are going to finish contacting and questioning everyone who was there tonight. Do you know if Tokyo was there?"

"That nigga ain't have no goddamn money," I mumbled.

"No, sir, not to my knowledge." She shoved me and looked at the ceiling. Her eyes started to water, because one thing she didn't do was lie to our father. It sucked, but shit, I never intended to bring family in my line of business. Oh, well.

"Dammit, how am I going to break this to her?" There was a brief pause before he said, "They were so close."

"They really were. I'll go get her so you can talk to her." She shot me a dirty look as I covered my mouth trying to muffle my laugh.

"No, that's okay, and don't cry, baby girl. Just bring her over here tomorrow so I can break it to her."

"A'ight, I'll make sure that's the first stop we make."

"Okay, well, I love you girls, and I'll see you tomorrow."

"Love you too. Good night." She hung up the phone.

"Bitch, really? Since when were me and him close? The only reason I frequented that damn club was because it was a nice cover for my clients."

"Ugh, shut up, Tokyo, I can't believe I just lied to him like that." She shook her head.

"Well, either way, you knew it was coming. Bitch, plus you lied to him about what yo' loser boyfriend does for a living." I grabbed my blanket.

"Yeah, well, that don't count, and I ain't doing that shit no more. Don't be having me break the father-daughter code for you." She threw another pillow.

"Bitch, you already did, and throw something else, I'ma throw you! Plus, daughters lie to their parents all the time." I shrugged.

"Yeah, but not us!"

"Well, it's a little too late for that 'us' shit." I shut up, not realizing what I said.

"What you mean? You done lied to him before and you ain't tell me?"

"I mean, it wasn't anything major. A small little white lie." I started thinking about my mother and what I had done. Not even my sister knew I had done that. She loved my mother too much, and I just knew things wouldn't be how they were now had I told her that all those years ago. That was something I planned to take to my grave with me. I trusted my sister, but that was a thing I knew she would look at me differently for. And before anyone else's, her love for me mattered more than anything in the world.

India squinted her eyes at me. "Tell me." She sat so close to my face I could feel the air coming out of her nose.

"For one, back the fuck up." I nudged her. "And for two, no! I ain't telling you that."

"So really, we're keeping things from each other now?" I gave her a blank stare. "My nigga, your ass already knocked up and you just now telling me today."

"Really? Get over it! Quit acting like you don't want to be an aunt to myyyy baby. Besides, I had to wait until I thought you were ready. Which, now that I think about it, seemed like it was still the wrong time."

"Well, I feel the same way about that small little lie. Plus, why the hell you drink all that wine if you pregnant already, India?"

"Like I said earlier, if you had someone, you wouldn't be so hard up about that. I love Bryson, and you should try to like him a tad bit more. He's really cool, plus I'm still on my first cup. You drank it all. It won't hurt the baby. I mean, hell, Momma was on drugs with us and look how we turned out." She smiled, holding her hand out.

"Girl, that ain't a goddamn compliment. You know that'll never happen. I'm telling you he's sneaky! I can't put my finger on it, but trust me, I know I'm right. I guess you just gon' have to see it for yourself." I grabbed the remote and pressed play for the movie.

CHAPTER FIVE

TOKYO

The next morning, me and India got dressed and ready to head to my father's. I was more than a little irritated because she caked it on the phone with Bryson the whole time. His voice was mad annoying doing all that fucking bickering, so I said fuck it and blasted the music, making her end the call. When we pulled into my father's driveway, his new nurse was just walking into his house.

When we walked in, I could smell the cinnamon buns my dad had in the oven. That was my favorite thing to eat when something was bothering me, and my father would always fix them before giving me or my sister bad news. We walked into the kitchen, and he was drinking a cup of apple juice and taking his meds for the morning.

"Hey, Daddy!" me and India said in unison and went to give him a hug.

"My girls, I've missed you two so much." He hugged us long and hard.

"So," I said, breaking our embrace and pulling out a chair, "what's the news you have to tell me?" I beamed, putting on my innocent smile.

My dad looked at India, then back at me and dropped his head. "Well, baby, I know you loved your uncle and all very dearly. But something happened last night." His voice cracked.

Me and India locked eyes, and then I focused back on him.

"What you mean something happened? Is he all right?" I reached across the table and grabbed my father's hand. When I saw a tear fall, an itty-bitty tiny piece of my heart hurt for him. I kind of felt like shit for making my dad cry.

"Baby girl, someone killed him last night at the club, and they took some money out of his safe or something." He started crying so hard he couldn't finish his words.

"What?" I jumped up out of my seat, knocking the chair over and making my father pause mid-cry. India dropped her head on the table. I knew that petty bitch. She wasn't crying. Her ass was laughing at me.

"Baby girl, I'm so sorry." He reached for my hand.

"Fuck sorry! Do they know who did the shit?" I banged my fist on the table. My sister stood up and ran out of the kitchen like she was crying, but when I glanced in the living room, she was holding a pillow to her chest, silently laughing. Now some may feel that we were a little fucked up, but I'm sorry, it was what it was to me. I walked over and held my dad and shed a couple of fake tears.

After a few more minutes of us talking and my dad reminiscing on the good times he and his brother used to have, I was over the shit. Changing the convo, I asked, "So where is this new nurse I saw come in earlier?"

"Oh, she's probably upstairs in my room getting it set up for the night."

"Well, let me go up and introduce myself, seeing she doesn't look like the same one I just hired for you."

My dad looked at me sternly. "Tokyo, she's really sweet and nice, so be kind and behave yourself!" he warned.

I smiled sweetly and walked straight out of the kitchen and went upstairs. When I reached my father's room, she was making his bed up and fluffing his pillows.

CHAPTER SIX

TOKYO

"Aye, wassup." I leaned against the doorframe.

"Oh, hello. You must be India." She walked around and stuck her hand out. I instantly sized her ass up, because I didn't like being touched.

"Nah, I'm Tokyo." I gripped her hand quickly and didn't let go.

"Ohhh, okay. You're the feisty one?" she laughed nervously and tried to get me to release her hand.

"Nah, I'm the fucked-up one, so let me tell you this." I gripped her hand a little tighter and stepped closer. "Steal anything, hurt my father, or make him feel the least bit uncomfortable, and the next time you see me will be the last time you see anyone."

She snatched her hand back, and I laughed at her.

"Well, Tokyo," she said, cocking her head, "I like your father and taking care of him. He's a very sweet man. So, trust me, you don't have to worry about anything happening like what happened with the last nurse." She walked to the side of his bed and started prepping his nighttime meds and laying his pajamas out.

"That's good then. How old are you?" I questioned.

"I'm fifty-two. Now how old are you, if you don't mind my asking?" She glanced in my direction. I didn't know what it was, but I instantly liked the fact that she didn't let me intimidate her. Those were automatic cool points.

"I'm twenty-eight. You got kids or some shit?"

"Well, yes, I have two sons. One is thirty-one and the other is thirty-five."

"Oh, so you started out young, I see. Is that why you chose this line of work?"

"No, not really. I come from an okay upbringing and my boys, they make more than enough to stunt on a few. I just like to work taking care of people. Do you have any kids?"

That question instantly had me stuck, but oh, well. "Fuck no, I'm a virgin. I love money too much, and I'm not about to get tied down with some random nigga's kid. I'm smooth on that. Either way, it was nice meeting you. I gotta roll." With that being said, I headed back downstairs.

When I reached the kitchen, Dad was icing the cinnamon rolls, and India was stuffing her face with one already made. As soon as I thought I was about to grab one, there was a loud knock at the door.

"I'll get it," Dad's nurse yelled, coming down the steps.

"Thanks, honey," he called back and then instantly bit his bottom lip. Me and India just stared at him. That was a first. I automatically knew something was up. Me and my sister's "twin senses" started tingling.

India looked at my dad. "Honey, huh?" She licked the icing off her fingers and snatched a paper towel, wetting it.

"Yeah, I caught that too," I chimed in.

"Well, she is a really sweet woman, and I like her." He sipped more of his apple juice.

"Dad, you haven't had eyes for any woman since Mom died. What's so special about her?" India eyed him suspiciously.

"Well, she's really caring." He smiled.

"No squat, she's a nurse. Next?" she asked with a smirk.

"Well, I'm a grown man, and I have needs, and everyone needs somebody to love. Your mother, Lord rest her soul, died almost fifteen years ago. I feel like I have the right to move on." He looked back and forth between the both of us. I didn't care about the way he felt about her. It was all beyond me. Wasn't my field.

"Well," I said, standing up, "I have to get going. I've got business to tend to. Let me know what else is going on and when you plan to start making arrangements." I shook my head.

"I will, baby girl. I love you and keep your head up."

As soon as I turned around, there were detectives entering the kitchen.

"Tokyo Miles?" the short, blond lady flashed her badge.

"Yeah, what?" I put my hand on my hip.

"My name is Detective Washington, and this is my partner, Detective White. Do you mind if I ask you a few questions about last night?"

"What about last night?"

"Well, a few people were killed at your uncle's club, including him. He was in his office, and his bodyguard was found in the back alley. What blows my mind is that a block away one of the strippers was found dead also. Do you happen to know anything about that?"

"Now hold on, Detective." My father tried to stand.

"Nah, Dad, she's good." I looked back at her. "I don't know anything about last night. I went there to go see him and he wasn't in his office, so I left after having a drink or two with one of the girls."

"So, you were there last night. About what time was this?" the fat man asked, writing on a notepad.

"Yeah, motherfucker, didn't you hear what I just said?"

"Watch your mouth please when talking to the law," Detective Washington interjected.

"Fuck the law." I shot her the bird.

"Excuse me, what the hell did you just say?" She inched toward me.

"Aye, bitch, you don't even wanna see her on that level." My sister came and stood beside me.

"Oh, look, twins." The fat one smiled.

"Oh, look, the Pillsbury Doughboy." India smirked.

"Carlos Miles, you have some really rude daughters. Tokyo, why are you so defensive?"

"Probably because I don't like pigs, especially ones trying to get in my business. Now anything else?"

"Well, not right now." She looked back and forth between all of us.

"Well, good. India, let's roll before my temper gets me into trouble."

We said our final goodbyes and turned to leave.

"I'm not done with her. Something tells me she knows a little more than she is letting on. I can feel it in the pit of my stomach," Detective Washington said to her partner.

"Well, now, if you have nothing more for me, could you leave my home please? Thank you."

CHAPTER SEVEN

TOKYO

As I drove us back home, a message came through on my burner phone.

New Number: Red Toyota Camry, 9th Chestnut 3rd level parking garage. Duffle bag in the trunk, keys on the hood. Text when you get it.

Wondering who the fuck it could be, I dismissed the thought as I closed the phone and threw it on the back seat. As we pulled into our driveway, I kept my eyes on the dark green Impala with tinted windows that sat on the corner. We knew every car that frequented our street, and that run-down shit stuck out like a sore thumb.

"You see that shit?" I checked the rearview again and cocked the gun I had stuck under my seat.

"Mmm hmm." India looked back, doing the same.

We exited the truck and made our way in our home.

"Fucked-up thing is, I've seen that car somewhere before. I just can't recall it." India put her gun on safety.

"Well, I haven't, but if they want smoke, then they gon' get a whole lot of it." I walked over to the window and peeped through the blinds, but the car was gone. I all of a sudden had this uneasy feeling in my gut.

I headed to my room and changed into an all-red jogging suit with some matching red Nikes. I told India I would be back a little later, then headed out. She chucked me the deuces and put a plate into the microwave.

When I got to the location, I sat in my car for a few minutes before getting out three spaces down from the Camry. After opening the trunk and making sure all my money was inside the bag, I carefully read over the notes left in it. There was also a picture of a Hispanic-looking female. She was really pretty.

"Miss Maria, you better be dressed to die tonight. I'm coming for that ass, shorty." I smiled at the picture and continued to read. The notes said she would be attending a birthday party at a well-known club downtown, Club X, tonight, and that's when I had to off her ass. It also said to dress in all white. I was a meddling-ass person when it came to my business, so whoever ordered me to off someone had to give me a reason. I wasn't a petty-ass cheap hit woman. Anything I did always ran someone $600,000 or more. I mean, let's be real, court costs and lawyer fees were not cheap.

The reason they wanted her gone was because she was known for setting up drug dealers for her father or robbing them. Well, I guess she had set up the wrong one this time.

CHAPTER EIGHT

INDIA

Pulling up on Forty-first and Cecil, I smiled hard, watching my man make his little serves. It wasn't much that he made weekly, but at least he was doing something to make sure he was getting through college. Every now and again I also helped with his payments. I sat back watching as he pulled his phone out of his pocket and took a quick call. I decided to call him myself.

When the phone rang twice, he glanced at it and then hit the ignore button on me.

"Really, motherfucker?" I cut my car off and got out. It was kind of cool today, so I threw my jacket on, quickly making my way across the street to him.

"So you just gonna ignore my fucking call like that?" I asked him with a smile.

Bryson damn near jumped out of his skin looking at me.

"Oh, shit, hey, baby. What the hell you doin' here?" he asked as he watched his surroundings.

"You said you wanted me to spend time with you today. Remember?" I put my hand on my hip.

"Yeah, but I ain't mean right now. Plus, you know I don't like you popping up on me."

I rolled my eyes and smirked. His phone started ringing again. He took it out and looked at it then at me.

Whoever it was wasn't feeling the fact he had ignored their call because his phone started dinging back-to-back from texts.

"Who the hell is that?" I questioned, looking him in the eyes.

"Never mind all that. Let's roll out." He looked around, grabbing me by the hand and leading me to my car. He was acting real strange all of a sudden. This wasn't my Bryson.

Getting in the car, he told me he wanted to go grab something to eat at Burger Boys before heading to his crib. We swung by there, and then I made it to his crib with the quickness. I had to pee, and I was horny as hell. As we walked in, his older brother Mike was on the game.

"Nigga, roll out real quick." He bumped him off the couch.

"Damn, fool, I'm in the middle of a fucking game." He never took his eyes off the TV.

Bryson walked over and snatched the controller out of his hand. "Nigga, I said roll! You act like you live here!"

His brother stood up, sucking his teeth, and snatched his jacket off the armrest of the couch and left, slamming the door behind him.

"Baby, what's wrong? Why you acting like that?" I walked up and wrapped my arms around him. He made me release him and sat on the couch. He rubbed his head and closed his eyes, sitting back. I walked over and sat next to him, slapping him in the chest.

"Look, India, I'm real stressed out right now. Everything that I'm doing and that we are doing is costing a shitload of money. And I ain't making enough right now." He looked away.

"Baby, what are you stressed about? I have more than enough money to take care of us. I always got you. What is it that you need?" I rubbed his leg.

He looked at me then at the ground. "I need to send my mom some more money for her meds. I ain't got three grand right now. Shit, in the last week I only made fifteen hundred." He continued looking at the ground. Next thing you know, his phone started ringing again. He checked it, then put it back in his pocket.

"Who was that?"

"My mom calling. I don't feel like talking to her right now." His phone rang again.

"Well, I'll give you the money, and if she's calling back-to-back like that, maybe something's wrong." I tried to grab his phone, but he snatched it back and put it in his other pants pocket.

"Oh, really, we're doing that now?" I cocked my head.

"Baby, I'm horny. Make daddy feel better, please?" he pouted, giving me the puppy-dog eyes. I sucked my teeth, smiling as I stood up and began to undress.

"No, I want some head like last time." He began unbuckling his belt.

"And I want some dick like last time." Bryson rolled his eyes and began to get naked as well.

"If that's how you feel, then maybe I should just go." I grabbed my pants.

"Dude, yo' big ass is so fucking sensitive now. Bring yo' ass over here." He stood, grabbing me by the waist, and began to kiss me deep and slow. I wrapped my arms around his neck and could feel his already-hard dick pressing up against me. He then began massaging my breasts and running his hands over my curves. I slowly turned around and bent over the couch.

"Aw, yeah, is that how you want me to hit?" He smiled.

"Yes, baby, but don't be too rough. We got a baby on board."

"Yeah, I know." He slid his dick into my already-wet pussy and pushed deep until it was all the way in. I dropped my head and began working my pussy slowly back and forth on him. He then picked his pace up as he reached in front of me, grabbing my breast. I began to grind my hips, trying to match his stroke. The shit felt so damn good I was already about to climax.

"Oh, shit, pregnant pussy really is wetter." He sped up as my juices coated his dick and nappy pubic hairs.

"My pussy is always wet." I threw it back harder and harder on him, working up another nut.

"Yeah, but shiiiit, not this wet." He tried to turn me around and lay me on my back.

"Really, nigga?" I folded my arms.

"Baby, shut up." He positioned himself between my legs, ready to taste me. I wasn't too stoked on that. I mean, I loved the boy and all and the dick was good, but li'l baby's head game was the worst. I always had to think of someone else when he would give me head and grind on his thick lips that he didn't use to suck my clit. He started licking my coochie like a kitten licking milk out of a bowl.

I looked up as his phone began to ring in his pants pocket again. I tried to ignore it, but it started ringing again and again. This shit bothering me was going to make it even harder for me to bust.

"Baby, give me some more dick. This time rough." I pulled his head up.

Bryson climbed on top of me and shoved his dick back in.

"Like this?" He took it out and shoved it back in again, this time harder than the first.

"Yessss," I hissed as he put my feet on his shoulders and fucked me missionary like it would be the last time.

When we finished, he got up and went into the bathroom to get a warm, wet rag for both of us. His phone started ringing again. I slid off the couch and grabbed it out of his pants. It was an unsaved out-of-town number. I heard him cut the water on, and then it rang again. This time I answered.

"Hello?" I answered as I lay against the couch.

"Who the fuck is this?" a female snapped through the phone.

"Bitch, who the fuck are you? I'm Bryson's woman." I rolled my neck and looked at the number again.

"Bitch, where he at? I ain't got time for this weak shit. Put Bryson on the phone now!" she yelled.

"Bitch, go eat a dick!"

Just as I was about to hang up, she screamed back, "I eat his all the time!"

"Yo, India, what the fuck?" Bryson rushed over to me and snatched the phone. "Hello?" he said, then looked at the screen.

I stood up asshole naked and threw my hands on my hips. "Bryson, who the fuck was that bitch?" I screamed.

CHAPTER NINE

TOKYO

Since I was going to have to go to the club, I needed someone to go with me. I knew my sister wouldn't because she would be stuck somewhere under Bryson's ass. I had no friends, so I had to choose between our hairdresser, Cynthia, or her daughter. It was hits like this that made me miss my sister doing it with me. Pulling back up to our house, I pulled out my cell phone and called Cynthia.

"What's popping, sugar?" she squealed into the phone.

"Hey, I was wondering if you were busy tonight. I need someone to go to a birthday party with me at Club X."

"Aw, yeah! I'm down for that shit! I'm free! What time you want me to come get you?"

"How about we just meet somewhere—" I started.

She cut me off. "Nah, I know damn well you trust me by now. It ain't like I'ma tell someone where the hell yaw asses live at! Shit, I don't like a mu'fucka even being able to contact me unless it's a trick. And you ain't trickin'." There was a brief pause.

"Well . . ." I hesitated. "You're right. I guess if I had to tell someone, it would be you. Well, I'll text you my address when I wake up. I need a quick nap beforehand."

"All right. I'll see you later."

"Yeah, and wear all white please."

"Girl, I'm a goddess. That's all I wear unless I'm shaking this ass for some cash."

We hung up, and I went to lie down. My head was banging. Wine was never my friend after a night with my sis. She never got migraines from the shit, but I did. When I woke back up, it was going on eight o'clock.

"Shit!" I sat up on the side of my bed and stretched. I grabbed my cell phone and texted Cynthia the address, telling her to be here by eleven o'clock. I went downstairs to get some water and to unlock the door. Walking back up the stairs, I heard my cell phone ding, indicating a text message. It was India letting me know that she wouldn't be coming in tonight because Bryson didn't want to be alone. I rolled my eyes, tossing it on the bed, and walked into my walk-in closet.

I don't know why but when it came to picking out an outfit I always started with my heels first. Grabbing some gold-strapped white six-inch pumps with diamonds on the heel, I sucked my teeth as I thought about what outfit would set those off. I stood up and started going through the different colored one-piece cat-looking suits. I had plenty of white ones, but which one?

I decided on the strapless one with no sleeves.

"Yes, doll," I said as I held it close to my body as I walked over to my full-length mirror and checked myself out. I then grabbed my favorite scented bodywash, Caress Sheer Twilight, and my vanilla-scented candles. I went into the bathroom and turned the shower on. Lighting the candles, I began to inhale and exhale slowly and deeply. Undressing and stepping into the shower, I repeated that breathing technique until I could then smell the scent of my candles. Vanilla always helped to soothe and calm me so I could think clearly before a hit.

After getting dressed, I fixed a drink before doing my makeup. In the midst of heading up the steps, I saw headlights turning into the driveway. Cynthia had a nice-sized Suburban truck, and she was blasting Cardi B's "Press." I laughed and kept going. She could let herself in. When I got in my room, she called my cell. I told her to just come up. I needed a few more moments.

I threw my drink back then started with my makeup, deciding on some cherry red lipstick, a little eyeliner, and mascara. That was all I needed. I could say that my mother gave me and my sister some hellafied features, Lord rest the bitch's soul.

"Awww, shit, girl, look at you! Ass on phat phat in that fit. You showing off those curves tonight, ain't ya?" Cynthia danced her way into my room, holding a bottle of E&J.

"Oh, no, ma'am, look at you, Miss Thang!" I snapped my fingers in a circle. She almost had on exactly what I had on but she did all-white heels with her shoulder-strap one-piece.

"So, whose birthday party is it?" she asked as she took a seat on the edge of my bed.

"I honestly don't know him. Some guy named Python. Just received a random invite by text."

"Damn, is that how you young people do it nowadays? Shit, I ain't get one!" She took a long swig out of the bottle.

"Well, I'm going to assume that's how it goes when someone knows you're the type to only do VIP."

I walked over to my dresser and grabbed the picture of Maria and stuck it into my purse. I also put my gun in with my ID, money, and lip gloss. Going into my top drawer, I grabbed my small but very sharp pocketknife and slid it in between my breasts.

"Girl, I'm glad I ain't the only one packin' a knife. I don't trust these hoes at the club nowadays. They be in there ready to fight for any damn thing stupid." She stood up.

CHAPTER TEN

TOKYO

We chose to drive my truck and left. Cynthia kept complimenting me on my ride and also saying it looked like it belonged to a dope dealer of some sort. She also tried to pick my brain on what me and my sister did for a living to be able to afford the home we lived in and the cars. I just kept laughing and changing the subject to money. She loved talking about money.

Pulling up to the club, I found a parking spot not far from the entrance. The line to get in was wrapped around the damn block. Whoever this Python guy was had to have a serious rep in the city. Only thing about that was I had never heard of him.

Stepping out, me and Cynthia took our coats off and left them in the truck. I threw my purse over my shoulder and did a final check on my makeup before locking my doors and heading to the door. Shit blew my mind when I saw Boon, my deceased uncle's second bodyguard, working the door for security.

"Fake bitch." I smiled, walking up to him.

"Hey, Tokyo baby girl, how you doing?" he asked as he lifted the rope.

"I'm good. It ain't take you long at all to find another gig." I grabbed Cynthia by the hand to let him know she was with me.

"Hey, you ain't in here for no bullshit tonight, are you?" He eyed me suspiciously.

I rolled my eyes. "Of course I'm not. I was invited to this party actually." I kept it moving quickly. It had honestly just pissed me off that he had asked me that. I was going to have to take care of him sooner or later.

The inside of the club was lit! There were gold and white balloons everywhere and lights flashing all over. Guys and girls were on the dance floor getting down to Cash Money's "Back That Ass Up." It was crazy that no matter where or how old that song was, it always got everyone up and moving.

I bopped my head, making my way through the crowd and toward the steps that led up to the VIP area. A guy asked me my name when we finally made it up there. After confirming I was in fact on the VIP list, he let us through. I grabbed a table toward the steps so I could look out over the dance floor and the rest of the club trying to spot Maria.

She was a really pretty girl. It just blew my mind that she was the type to set niggas up to get robbed or would in fact steal the money her damn self after a night of fucking your brains out and drugging you. I was about to have to put a stop to it. A real question that was bothering me was, why couldn't this person do it themselves?A waitress soon came over, holding a notepad and dressed in all black. "Hello, ladies, what can I get you tonight?" She smiled sweetly.

"Aw, shit, nothing. I'm good." Cynthia patted her purse. I shot her a dirty look and shook my head.

"We'll have two bottles of Cristal and six shots of Rémy on the rocks, and could you bring some cherries with that?" I reached in my purse and pulled out a $1,000 bill and placed it in her hand. She looked at me then the money with wide eyes.

"Your total is going to be . . . uh, I can't break this right now," she said nervously.

"I'm not asking you to." I winked at her.

"Well, in that case, I'll be back very shortly with your order." She switched off.

CHAPTER ELEVEN

TOKYO

As I was just starting to unwind, a group of six guys entered the VIP. All were dread heads except one. I assumed that he was the leader walking in back of them. My mouth watered for some reason looking at him. His whole demeanor screamed he wasn't the one to be fucked with. He had to be at least six foot seven inches tall. And I could tell he was ripped under the white V-cut sweater he was rocking. When we made eye contact, I could've sworn he winked at me! My eyes got kind of big as I turned my head away from him. I had never laid eyes on any man and felt what I felt looking at him.

Even under the dim lighting in the club I could tell he had some of the brightest hazel eyes ever. They actually set off his mocha-colored skin. Taking a second glance and looking him up and down, I tried to focus in on the tattoo on his chest and neck. I couldn't tell if it was a snake, dragon, or lizard, but I knew I had seen that exact tattoo before. He had a full beard that was thick and as black as night, and full pink lips. I had to again break my stare because he smiled at me with a dope-ass set of pearly whites as his crew and him made it past me, occupying a few tables in the middle. Damn, it was the birthday guy himself, the man of the hour, Python.

The waitress came back with a tray filled with our drinks, and a second girl behind her carried our bottles on ice. We instantly took the six shots to the head, no chaser splitting them. I only did that because that big-ass man eyeing me like that made me nervous. I needed to stay focused on the mission at hand. Glancing back to the dance floor, I noticed a group of rowdy girls making their way up the stairs to the VIP. There she was, plain as day and tipsy as fuck—Maria.

I sat up straight and pretended not to notice when her crew made their way right over to the middle tables and started flirting and dancing with the group of guys with the birthday guy. I needed to find a way to get to her ass. As if on cue, she tapped a girl on the shoulder and made a smoking gesture while laughing and grinding her ass on Python, who seemed to be paying her no mind at all. He was occasionally watching me.

When she got a lighter from a chick whose makeup looked a hot fucking mess even under the lighting, she walked to the end of VIP to some stairs that led to the bathrooms and the back of the club. I got up and prepared to follow her.

CHAPTER TWELVE

TOKYO

"Hey, Cynthia, I'll be right back. I need to use the bathroom. You good?" I asked as I smoothed out my outfit and pushed my breasts up.

"Helllll yeeeah, girl! Go piss! This my song!" she slurred, snapping to the beat of Soul 4 Real's "Candy Rain." I glanced back, and Maria was already making her way down the steps. The whole time that I walked, I felt his eyes on me. Trying to get past the people on the stairway, I watched Maria dart into the bathroom. When I got in, she was snorting a line of coke off her wrist.

"Shit, girl, I needed this." She leaned back up against the marble sink.

"Girl, trust me, I know. I hope yo' ass plan on fucking Python tonight! 'Cause he is looking mighty fine with his big-dick ass!" a short, dark-skinned girl said as she high-fived her.

I went into an empty stall and acted like I was using the bathroom and continued to listen to their conversation.

"Girl, that nigga is extra dumb!" she laughed. "While we were fucking last week, I had my brother and his boys creep in and steal some of his money and dope," she said without a care in the world while checking her makeup over in the mirror. I became furious as I continued to listen and watch her through the crack of the bathroom stall. She finally pulled out a pack of cigarettes and walked out the door. I rushed out and quickly washed my hands and exited the bathroom without drying them.

Walking out the back door, I was damn sure relieved when I saw no one else out back. Maria was standing by the dumpster, smoking. I ran my hand over my breasts, making sure my knife was in place as I walked over to her.

"You're really pretty. You mind if I bum a cig from you? I think I dropped mines somewhere in the club." I fake stumbled in her direction.

"Sure, *chica,* and you're not so bad yourself." She smiled sweetly and reached in her bra.

When she did, I quickly checked my surroundings and pulled my knife out. She was so high she didn't notice. When I got close up on her, the back door to the club busted open, and two drunk guys came out laughing and falling against the brick wall. I quickly grabbed Maria by the neck and kissed her to play it off.

"Well, damn! I wish I was fucking them tonight!" one guy said as he turned to go up the alley toward the parking lot. The other guy stood there for a while and just watched. It kind of shocked me that Maria didn't fight off the kiss, seeing that I was a total stranger. I slowly turned her back toward the onlooker while giving him a show. He hit his Black once more, smiled, and began to leave. I felt my body go numb and a cold feeling wash over me as I took the blade in my hand and stuck it in her throat as I continued to kiss her. This was a new feeling, and I enjoyed it.

Spinning her back around, I quickly shoved her in the corner of the dumpster, making sure her blood didn't get on me. She clasped her hands around her neck as she struggled to breathe with eyes as big as saucers. I looked over my shoulder making sure we were still alone, as I made my way closer to her yet again.

"You fucked over the wrong person, little lady," I said with a smile as I stood over her. I grabbed her by the hair and dug my knife as deep as I could into her neck and slowly slid it from one side to the other as I watched her choke on her own blood as the life left her eyes. I stepped back, watched her take her last breath, then went back in the club.

CHAPTER THIRTEEN

TOKYO

I stuck my blade back between my breasts and walked into the empty bathroom. I washed my hands off. Doing a once-over and making sure I had nothing on me, I deeply inhaled and made my way back to VIP. When I got up there, Python was nowhere in sight, but one of his boys was all in a drunk Cynthia's face, cheesing and rubbing her thigh. I shook my head and laughed, grabbed the Cristal out of the ice bucket, and drank straight from the bottle.

After a few more swigs of the bottle and a couple of songs, I was feeling myself. I wanted to dance. Killing someone always put me in a good mood. It was like an illegal stress reliever. Me and Cynthia made our way onto the dance floor bopping and singing along to Beyoncé's "Before I Let Go." By the end of the song, that's when the screaming started. People started running all over the place and shoving one another. I was about to make my way toward the door when Cynthia yelled that her purse was still in VIP.

She grabbed my hand, and we rushed into that direction, fighting against the crowd trying to get out of the club. Once we retrieved it, to make matters more hectic, gunshots rang out. I looked back trying to see where they were coming from. I should've kept my ass moving because as soon as I did, I felt something tear through my shoulder.

"What the fuck?" I grabbed my arm.

"Tokyo! You a dead bitch!" I heard a female voice yell. That made me turn around with the quickness. Another shot hit my shoulder two inches away from the first hole. That shit made me stumble back and finally hit the ground. My head was spinning as I tried to get up. What the fuck was really going on? When I was able to finally focus and gather myself, a furious Python had hit the chick who yelled at me and apparently shot me hard in the side of her head.

Cynthia helped me up to my feet. "Do you know that bitch?" she asked as she looked back and forth between us. "Jesus goddamned Christ, you bleeding bad, girl!"

She sat me on a stool. The club was completely empty by now, and I could hear sirens outside, and then I blacked out.

CHAPTER FOURTEEN

PYTHON

I rushed over and scooped a bloody Tokyo into my arms. She was barely conscious and bleeding more than those wounds should've caused. I was hoping that bitch hadn't hit a main artery.

"Man, lock those fucking front doors and let's roll! Now! Somebody grab that big bitch and take her to my crib, too!" I ordered.

My crew did as they were told, and I jetted out the back. Carefully placing Tokyo in the back of my truck with her older friend, I jumped in the front and backed out of the alley quickly. I needed to get her to my crib and quick.

"Hey, where you taking us? She lives in the other direction in Woodcrest!" Her friend hit the back of my seat.

"Fuck!" I hit the steering wheel. She lived closer than I thought to where we were. "What's the address?" I asked while calling a good friend of mines who handled shit like this for me. I had been shot plenty of times, and when I shouldn't have made it, the nigga always came through for me, saving my ass. Plus, with the shit I did and the shit she did, a hospital wasn't an option. At least not in my eyes.

"I don't think I should give you her address! She doesn't like anyone knowing where she lives!" she cried, holding Tokyo.

"Bitch, you want her to bleed the fuck out or not?" I glared at her in the rearview.

She gave me the address as I told my doc over the phone to meet me there and quick. Speeding down her street, I would've never thought she would live in a white-ass neighborhood like Woodcrest Hills. I hit the brakes hard, threw my truck in park, and jumped out. Grabbing her up, I shook her a little to make sure she was at least still responsive. She didn't budge, so as I headed toward her door, I squeezed her shoulder and arm to wake her.

"Ow! What the fuck?" she yelled weakly, trying to kick and squirm. I damn near busted her front door down off the hinges, getting in and laying her on the couch.

"Go get me some towels and some hot water!" I looked back at her friend, who was in shock. She rushed off to do as I asked. Even bloody and passed out, shorty was still a bad one. I applied pressure to her arm and prayed Doc would hurry the fuck up. As I tried to keep the wounds from bleeding more, I heard tires screeching. My nigga came rushing in, taking shit out of his bag.

He pulled out two needles and two small jars, one with a yellow label and one with a green one.

"What's that shit?" I watched him closely.

"One is for pain, which will also knock her completely the fuck out for a few hours, and this one is to slow her heart so it doesn't pump the blood as quickly. It'll help slow the bleeding until I'm finished. Now back the fuck up and let me work."

I walked off and started looking through her crib. She was neat as hell, seemed like she ain't have any kids but maybe a roommate. I assumed it was her friend who was with her. Walking into her kitchen, her friend was ending a call with tears running down her face.

"You live here with her?" I sat at the table and started going through the mail.

"Nah, hell nah." She pulled out a flask and took a long drink.

"She got a roommate?"

"You sure are meddlesome." She smirked. As I was about to give the old bitch a piece of my mind, I heard the front door bust open again.

Looking in that direction, my fucking jaw dropped. Rushing in was a chick that looked exactly like Tokyo. I got up and walked in the living room to get a better look. As long as I had been watching her, I never noticed she had a twin. Then it made me think. Had I actually even been following and keeping tabs on the right one all these years?

"What the fuck happened to her?" she yelled and rushed in my direction. As I was about to tell her, the crazy bitch hauled off and punched me in the fucking chin.

"Bitch, are you out of yo' goddamned mind?" I towered over her. The shit kind of turned me on, because she kept the same energy and didn't back down. Everyone I came in contact with feared me.

"Nah, bitch, are you? What the fuck happened to my sister?" She drew her fist back, ready to strike again.

"Shorty, so help me God, if you hit me again I'm going to break your fucking neck with my bare hands." I gritted my teeth.

"Well, talk, motherfucker!" She rushed to her sister's side.

"She was at the club at my party. Some shit popped off and some bitch shot her."

"Who was it?"

"How the fuck am I supposed to know?"

"I done seen that girl before somewhere. I just need a little time to think," Cynthia chimed in.

"Well, hurry the fuck up, because the way I'm feeling, my sister ain't about to be the only one in this bitch bleeding from a gunshot wound. Bet that!"

"You ain't gon' do shit when it comes to me, so I ain't trippin' on nothing. This ain't the snake pit you wanna get caught in, my nigga." I sat down on the all-black love seat, looking her dead in the eyes.

She stood up and cocked a gun. "Who the fuck are you anyway?"

"You two have fun with this shit. She's going to be all right," Doc interrupted us. "When the stitches heal it won't be pretty, but it won't be ugly either. Here are some pain pills for her. Make sure she rests that arm though for a little while, and then make sure she moves it around and exercises it daily."

"Thanks, Doc." I took the pills and read the bottle, then threw them at her sister's feet.

"My nigga, you dead-ass testing me right now." She glared.

"When Tokyo wakes up, tell her to be expecting my call around noon. Plus she needs to be dressed. We got shit to talk about and handle." I stood up ready to leave.

"I ain't telling her shit. And furthermore, she ain't going nowhere with you. Nigga, we don't know you!"

I walked toward the front door. "You heard what the fuck I said." I stuck my hand in my pocket and grabbed the burner phone out and tossed it on the chair before I left.

CHAPTER FIFTEEN

PYTHON

When I got back to my crib, my boys were still there. I loved the control I had over them niggas, even more the respect they showed me. Getting out, I popped my neck twice and thought about my next move. How was I going to handle this situation with Tokyo? I walked in and my maid/aunt, Miss Nelly, greeted me.

"Hello, handsome, the guys are downstairs already. I cooked you a late meal and already did the laundry for the next week. Anything else you can think of before I leave?" she asked with a smile as she walked toward me.

"No, ma'am, go head home and get some rest for me." I kissed her on the cheek. "You gonna need it tomorrow."

"All right. Be here around noon."

As I stepped down into my basement, the room grew quiet. All eyes were on me as I looked every single last one of them niggas in the face. I felt myself getting pissed off as I inhaled and exhaled deeply.

"You niggas had one fucking job tonight. One fucking job! And that was to make sure that goddamn party ran smoothly! How the fuck did this bitch"—I pointed at the big girl who was tied up in a corner—"get in my fucking club with a gun?" I roared.

Them niggas looked back and forth between each other not saying shit, which pissed me off even more.

"Speak, niggas!" I yelled again.

"Man, Python, look," Buckey, one of the semi-older cats spoke up. "I was on the front door with the big nigga. I ain't have shit to do with that. She clearly came from the back door." He shrugged.

"Yeah." I stroked my beard. "Tell me this though, who was in charge of watching the back door?" I looked around. Yet again nobody said anything. If these niggas had only known what I was thinking at that moment, they would've been speaking a thousand words a second.

Then finally, the new young nigga who had just started working for me spoke up.

"It was me. I had the back door. But I had to use the bathroom though. That had to be when she got in." He glanced at me, her, and then focused on the floor. I just stared at him, because that shit didn't make sense to me. It was supposed to be two on each entrance. Plus I wasn't feeling how he didn't wanna make eye contact with me.

"Who else had it with you?"

"Man, Python, that li'l nigga lying. He followed yo' ass and yo' niggas up to VIP, and when I saw him he was rubbing on some old stripper bitch who worked at that old-head nigga's strip club who got smoked a couple nights ago," Worm, another one of the guys, told. That nigga always peeped everything, but he told too god-damned much on the other niggas. That's why they didn't fuck with him like that, ole snitching-ass bitch nigga.

"So you just lied to me?" I questioned.

"I'm sorry. If I tell you what's really going on, can you just let me go so I can go finish it?" He looked up with tears in his eyes. Now I was fucking intrigued, but shit clicked fast in my head.

"You left that back door unattended on purpose, didn't you?"

"Yes, sir."

"Why?"

"Because somebody needed to kill that bitch Tokyo for killing my big sister!" He let more tears fall.

"How old are you, kid?" I walked over to him with my hands behind my back.

"I'm twenty-one." He sniffled. "I want that bitch dead, and my cousin was gonna handle it!"

"Aw, okay, you calling shots and ordering hits now? That's wassup." I smirked. Out of nowhere I picked him up by the neck and slammed him into the ground. I picked him back up by the neck, and he kicked and swung and scratched at my arms, trying to make me release him. But it was too late. I began to squeeze his throat until his nose started bleeding, and then I dropped his weak body on the floor.

As I took off my shirt, Worm said, "Aw, man, come on. Python, he's just a kid. Don't do that to him."

"Shut the fuck up, nigga! You talk too goddamned much!" I pulled my gun out and shot him in the face.

"Oh, shit!" a couple of the guys said in unison as I walked over to the boy who was backing up toward his tied-up cousin. I picked him up again, this time in a bear hug, and tightened my grip harder and harder until I heard his ribs breaking. His body started to go limp as I made sure to squeeze until all the air left his lungs and more blood came out of his mouth, nose and ears. Then I dropped him on the floor and stomped his face until it caved in.

"Get rid of this body," I panted.

"Cool, what you want us to do with her?" Buckey nodded in the chick's direction.

I walked over to her. "Now who is this cousin that this Tokyo chick killed of yours?" I snatched the tape off her mouth.

"She . . ." she stuttered. "She worked at Tokyo's uncle's club. Her name is Brittany. She called me crying, saying Tokyo had put her hands on her. She said Tokyo was there to kill that man. He was panicking and . . ." She sobbed some more.

"So Tokyo killed her own uncle?"

"Yeah! I know she did. She's fucked up like that. She killed my cousin. I know she did. I heard her voice call out to her when she I guess tried to hang up the phone. Then I heard two gunshots." She sniffled as snot ran over her lips.

"That's wassup. Tell me this, shorty. Have you told the police or anyone else about all this?" I looked her dead in the eyes.

"No, not anyone. I wanted to handle it on my own," she answered honestly. "What are you going to do to me? What are you going to do?" She started crying harder, looking back and forth between me and her now-dead cousin.

I stood up and looked down at her. "I'm gonna tie up this loose end," I said before I started kicking and stomping her. Blood splattered all over my Timbs and pants. I didn't care about the mess anymore. She started shaking real bad on the ground and choking on her own blood as I walked away to get a shovel. As I went back to her, her eyes began to flutter and roll to the back of her head. I placed the tip of the rusted iron in her mouth. Then I stomped my foot down on it hard, taking the top part of her head clean off. Her body jerked on the ground for another two minutes. I smeared the blood across my face and stared at the top part of her head, and then I kicked it across the room. The guys stood there in shock as usual, watching.

"Fix yaws' fucking faces. This shit ain't nothing you niggas ain't used to," I panted as I snatched my sweater off the rusted table and walked off. I was ready to kick back and eat. A nigga was starving. Plus, I had to check on Tokyo. I needed her fine ass in tiptop shape for the future. I needed her for a hit I was going to pull. A major hit, and what better way to get it done than to send a man's greatest weakness, a fine-ass woman?

CHAPTER SIXTEEN

PYTHON

The next morning when I got up, I called to check on Tokyo. Her smart-mouth-ass sister picked up and said she was in the shower about to get ready, then hung up. I knew eventually I was going to end up smacking the shit out of her. I called my man Buckey, who was also my part-time driver.

"Aye, I need you to go pick up Tokyo at her crib for me and meet me at Ray's Chicken Shack on Eighteenth in thirty."

"Cool, I got you, boss." He hung up.

I grabbed a fruit smoothie out of the fridge and went to go take a shower. But before I did, I called my mother to make sure she was okay and didn't need me to send her anything. I needed to spend time with her sooner or later. Once I was done, I dressed and rolled a blunt. Lighting it, I grabbed my keys and dipped out, making my way to my meeting. When I got inside the joint, there were just enough people in there but not too crowded. I grabbed a menu off the table and waited for a waiter.

A few minutes after receiving my order and beginning to smash, I almost choked on my fucking fork when Tokyo came walking in throwing her ass like she owned the fucking world.

"Gat damn! She's even finer in the daylight," I said to myself. She glanced in my direction and then made her way over to me.

"So is that how you dress for a business meeting?" I asked, checking her thick thighs and ass out in the Adidas two-piece she was wearing.

"Well, seeing the fact that this painful, ugly shit on my arm didn't heal overnight, I guess so." She smirked, taking a seat.

"Smart ass." I smiled at her.

"Yeah, whatever. So what's up? You need me to hit a lick for you? I'm gon' tell you now I ain't cheap with my shit." She sat back, attempting to fold her arms. The pain of it kept her from accomplishing that move.

"Well, clearly I ain't a broke nigga. I paid you more than enough to off that sneaky-ass Puerto Rican bitch Maria." I shoved a forkful of greens in my mouth.

"So you the one who hit me up? How the fuck you find out about me?" she questioned, sitting up closer on the table.

"I have my ways, but to keep it real with you, I been checking on you and checking you out from time to time over the years. You met me back then when you were around thirteen or so." I continued to eat.

"So you been stalking a bitch for some years, huh?" She picked up a menu.

"I ain't stalk shit. I just kept my eyes on the prize. I knew what you were up to that night you copped from me. Ain't no female as young and that fine as you on drugs. It was either your mom was sending you to cop from me or you was up to some shady shit." I finally glanced up at her. She now had a puzzled look on her face. Then it was like something clicked in her head.

"So you know about my mom?" She ran her tongue across her teeth.

"Man, hell yeah, I'd always sold the best drugs to her and whatever nigga she would be with. So when you copped from me, I knew it was for her, but when word got back to me that she had overdosed on a bad pack, I instantly knew your evil ass had something to do with it."

"So why you ain't say nothing?"

"Didn't have to. Plus, at the time you were too young. But I knew eventually one day I would need you, and you were young and not afraid to take a body. Fucked me up at the funeral when I saw everyone crying except you. I put ya digs together and it clicked."

"Yeah, well, and? The bitch had it coming. So what's up, what business you need from me?"

"You know the bitch I had you knock off? I need you to do me a favor. Her father is a big-time drug lord in Puerto Rico. We were doing business together, and then next thing you know he sent that bitch my way and she robbed me for everything in my crib that I had just copped from him."

"Okay, but what that got to do with me?"

I rolled my eyes and gritted my teeth. "Either you down or you ain't. I know you make your money, but what if I told you that from this hit you could walk away with a couple million?"

She looked me square in the eyes and thought about it. Then she finally agreed.

"So when?"

"Well, I'll tell you this, you won't be going alone. Me and my niggas will be going too. We gon' take everything he has once you put him down. We can discuss the details at a later time."

"A'ight cool, I'm out."

"How you gonna leave? My nigga brought you to me. He ain't gonna be back for a while. You can ride with me for a bit." I closed my container and wiped my mouth.

"I drove myself here, I don't trust nobody to be riding with strangers."

"You say that, but you here with me." I sat back.

"That's because money is involved."

"So money calls, and you just come running?"

"Yup, now what you wanna do?"

"Get in yo' whip and follow me. Plus that bitch you killed the other night at your uncle's club, that was her big cousin who tried to kill you. But don't worry. I took care of that bitch."

"Is that right?" She smiled.

"Yeah. I wasn't about to sit back and let some bitch take you away from me."

"Take me away from you? Nigga, I don't belong to you." She raised a brow.

"I ain't saying it like that, but let's keep it real. You will eventually. I always get what I want, Tokyo."

"Yeah, well, like I assume you know, I don't date and ain't looking forward to it. When do we start planning shit for this hit? And am I just going to set him up, or am I killing him?"

"We'll discuss this later. Eat so we can head out." I pulled out my phone and started scrolling.

CHAPTER SEVENTEEN

TOKYO

We sat in that restaurant for a little while longer discussing not too much of nothing as he watched me eat. For him to say he wanted me made me have this funny feeling in the pit of my stomach. I tried to shake it but couldn't. All this "man" sitting in front of me made me feel some type of way. But I was never one to mix business with pleasure, so I tried my damned hardest to put all that shit to the back of my mind. I just had to know though, because all that man had to be spoken for.

"So you single?" I asked, eating the last of my chicken.

"Yup, I don't trust these bitches. They out to get my money instead of getting their own. Which is what made me want you, Tokyo, on my team, that is. I can make you my right hand. I know motherfuckers fear you like they fear me. Ain't never run into a female like that before." He looked out the window.

"Well, as mean and as heartless as I am, I'm sure my mom made a pact and fucked the devil. Because my twin is nothing like me." I shook my head.

"Shit, I can't tell. Shorty punched me in the fucking face when she first saw me."

"Well, I can't blame her."

"I'm just saying, I started to smack the fuck out of her," he chuckled.

That instantly pissed me off. Business or not, nobody threatened India. I stood up and pulled my gun out and put it in his face.

"Don't ever, in your fucking life, ever make threats toward my sister, and I mean that shit. I don't give a fuck who fears you, but I don't. And don't think for a second I won't blow your ass away in this place and walk out like ain't shit happened."

This nigga actually sat back and laughed, until I cocked that motherfucker. Then he stood up. I looked up at him with the gun still pointed at his face.

"Do it then, Tokyo. Pull the trigger." He pressed my barrel closer to his head. This nigga had a serious death wish or something because Lord knows I wanted to, but he had just turned me the fuck on. I busted out laughing and shook my head, putting my gun away.

"You're a real piece of shit, Python."

"Nah, baby, you just can't fear death in this line of work. I see that your sister is a soft spot for you though."

"Yeah, she is. Now let's roll. I'm ready to get to business."

We left, and I followed him to his crib. When we got there, there were already two trucks parked in his driveway. I assumed they belonged to him.

When we got inside, I had to admit that he most definitely knew how to decorate for a single-ass bachelor.

"Nice place," I said as I scanned the pictures and art paintings on the wall.

"Thanks. My aunt helped decorate for me. I don't know shit about all this. Plus, you had a nice place yourself. I was feeling all the black, red, and gold. But follow me downstairs to the basement."

When we got down there, there was an older lady on the floor scrubbing up what seemed to be dried blood. She looked up and smiled as Python walked over to her and kissed her on the cheek.

"Thank you, Auntie. Where are the fellas?"

"They are in the back of here in your business room."

Now to say he had a nice big crib would be an understatement. His basement alone could've been a whole other crib by itself!

"Oh, yeah, Auntie, this is Tokyo. Tokyo, my aunt, Mrs. Nelly."

I walked over and shook her hand, then proceeded to follow Python farther into the basement. When we entered through the big steel door, there was literally a big-ass wooden table that seated at least twenty people in the middle. I assumed the chair that resembled a throne was his. There were about fifteen guys in there who all shut up when he came in. Then they all laid eyes on me.

"A'ight, my niggas, straight up. This is Tokyo. She's going to help with that Puerto Rico hit. Also, I'm making her my right hand, because after the way you niggas fucked up, I can't fuck with yaw fucking this up or me over."

I walked around the table, looking at all of them as they checked out my ass as I walked by. I sat right down in Python's chair. He chuckled and laid a hand on my shoulder.

"That's my chair, shorty."

"Sit somewhere else. I'm already comfortable." I raised a brow, flirting with him. He nodded and began to rub his beard. The other guys must have been shocked, because their jaws dropped as Python sat on the edge of the table.

"We gon' have to make this hit soon, within the next month. We already planned out the majority, but we gotta run this shit all into Tokyo. No matter what, when it comes down to it, we protect her by any means. She gonna be the one to seduce that old perv nigga while we take everything up out that bitch. Yaw know that shit going to be heavily guarded. But I ain't worried about it with a team full of hittas. Tokyo gon' be the one to take the nigga out. When she does that and we grab the shit, we get her outta there by any means! And safely."

The meeting lasted about four hours. Python wanted to be extra sure that I understood my role and how to play about everything. I was quick to catch on and remember, so after that I was ready to vamp out.

Walking upstairs, I checked my phone and saw that India had called more than a dozen times. I had to hurry and hit her back before she would lose her fucking wig. That girl was too damn paranoid, but I wouldn't expect anything less.

"Aye, Tokyo, you seeing anybody?" Python asked as he grabbed my arm.

I turned around and looked at his hand, then at him. "For one, no, I'm not," I said, jerking away, "and for two, I don't like to be touched."

"Feisty-ass thing. I knew you wasn't anyway. Why though is what I wanna know."

"I think that's for me to know and you to find out one day." I smiled.

"Oh, I more than intend to. I know you got a fire shot on you, too. I can tell by the way you walk and act." He laughed, looking at my breasts without a care.

"Yeah, well, you must have a fire shot of dick. I hope you ain't that big for nothing." I cocked my head.

"You trying to find out?" He grabbed himself.

"Nigga, no." I rolled my eyes and walked out.

When I got home, India's car was in the driveway. I walked in on her cursing while listening to Keyshia Cole's "I Should Have Cheated.""Hey, sis, what's wrong with yo' ass? Baby got you emotional?" I laughed.

CHAPTER EIGHTEEN

INDIA

"That funky-ass nigga Bryson is what's wrong with me. Some bitch called his phone yesterday! Talking shit." I turned around from washing the few dishes we had in the sink.

"What the fuck you mean?" Tokyo took a seat. I could already see the color of her eyes changing.

"He claimed it was his cousin just messing with me, and at this point I don't know what to believe. He been acting real strange here lately. I don't know. Maybe I am overreacting. He claimed she was just mean and nasty like that and I had nothing to worry about."

As I was about to go into full detail, there was a knock at the door. Me and Tokyo both glanced at it and then got up. She cocked her gun. When I opened the door with my sister on my heels, I was shocked to see Bryson standing there with an armful of flowers, some candy, and a teddy bear.

"Bryson, how the hell you know where I live?" I tried to play it off. Truth be told I had brought him through a couple times when I knew Tokyo would be out of town.

"Don't worry about all that." He smiled, and then his smile vanished when he saw Tokyo behind me holding a gun and giving him the look of death.

"Nah, nigga, how the fuck you find out where the hell we stay?"

Bryson smirked, then focused back on me. "Here, baby, I'm so sorry for the other day. I know you don't believe me, but I swear that was my cousin just fucking with you."

I couldn't help but smile as I took the gifts and let him in. Tokyo stood in his way though.

"Hi, Tokyo," he said as he walked past her.

"So, I sent the money to my moms. She gonna be straight. Now we ain't gotta worry about her blowing me up for a while." He took a seat on the couch.

"I wanna know how the fuck he found out where we live. India, don't fucking lie to me, have you brought this snake-ass nigga to our shit before?" Tokyo asked as she put her hands behind her back.

"Look, maybe just once or twice. Sis, I'm sorry. But we been together for a while and I trust him." I gave her the pleading eyes. Tokyo sucked her teeth and walked off. I caught Bryson looking at her ass as she walked up the stairs.

"Well," I said as I sat down next to him, "I guess I forgive you, baby." I leaned in for a kiss.

Bryson rubbed my belly and said, "I can't wait for my little man to get here for real."

"How do you know if it's going to be a boy? I want a daughter!" I laughed.

"Yeah, yeah, yeah, I know. But I'm sure it's going to be a boy. You mind fixing me something to eat, babe? Plus, can I use the bathroom?" he asked as he looked around.

"Sure, and you already know where it is." I stood up, heading for the kitchen.

I fixed him a nice, thick, dressed ham and cheese sandwich and snatched a beer out of the fridge. When I took it back into the living room, he still hadn't made it back yet.

"Damn, what that nigga doing, taking a shit?" I laughed as I picked up the remote and cut the TV on.

A few minutes later, Bryson came walking back in the living room with a big smile on his face.

"You know you done pissed the devil off."

"She'll be all right. And you pissed her off, not me, by popping up. Baby, you knew better."

"Well, hell, she already don't like me no ways. So, I decided to get under her skin." He laughed as he looked at his ringing cell phone. It was the same number as the day before. I ignored it, fuck his ugly-ass cousin.

"Boy, you don't wanna go swimming in that ocean of sharks when it comes to her. Baby, don't do this anymore. It was a nice gesture, and I forgive you, but just call next time okay?"

Bryson stood up. "I'm yo' nigga not hers! And I gotta call before I come over? India, you her sister, not her fucking daughter! This place is just as much yours as it is hers! The fuck?" he exclaimed as he began to button his jacket back up.

"Baby, where are you going?" I stood, attempting to grab him. He smacked my hands away.

"Until you can start acting like a grown woman and not some bitch child, I won't be back over at all. As a matter of fact, don't even call me until you get that shit taken care of. And I mean that shit. Holler at me when you ready to grow the fuck up, India." He turned around and left as quickly as he came. It confused the shit out of me, because he was just here to apologize, and now this?

Once he walked out and slammed the door, I ran to my room crying. What the fuck was really going on? What was going so wrong and so fast? Maybe this baby thing wasn't such a good idea. Ever since we had agreed on it and then had it confirmed that I was indeed pregnant, Bryson had changed on me. What was wrong with my man?

CHAPTER NINETEEN

BRYSON

When I got outside to my car, my phone rang again. I picked up with the quickness.

"Hello? What's up?"

"Nigga, why the fuck you ain't answer when I first called?" Bianca, my wife, screamed through the phone.

"I was handling business. Calm down, damn. Did you get the money I sent you?"

"Yeah, I got it. Thank you, baby. That's all I was calling to say. I can't wait to go shopping for our trip!" she squealed.

"I know. I'm gonna have to go handle something in a few and I won't be able to call until tomorrow. I'm about to hit another nice li'l lick for us. And then I'll be coming home for a while, okay?"

"Yes, baby. I miss you so much! I can't wait to ride that dick and that face," she teased.

"Now you know I'll let you ride my dick but yo' big pregnant ass ain't sitting on my face until you drop my twin boys," I corrected her.

"Yeah, right, and I ain't that big! I'm only five months!"

"Baby, you big with them twins. But anyway, I love you and I'll talk to you soon enough, okay?"

"Yes, you be careful."

"Cool, rub ya belly for me."

When I got off the phone with her, I called my brother Red.

"What's up, nigga?" he answered on the third ring.

"I did it. I left a window unlocked and the back door to the basement cracked open. We just gon' creep in tonight when they go have dinner with they daddy and scope shit out whenever they leave. Then we dipping. We can hit the lick on the weekend when I know they gon' be gon' over they dad's. They supposed to be planning her uncle's funeral or some shit, so we'll have enough time to get in and get out with no problems." I smoked on a loose cigarette.

"Cool, nigga, that sounds like a plan. I wonder why them bitches don't keep they money in a bank," my brother said.

"That's the thing, they do, and I already cleared India's shit into the negatives. Now I'm about to take whatever it is her and that bitch Tokyo got hidden in that house. Dumb-ass bitch India talk too fucking much." I smirked.

I was pumped as hell about that money in that house. She ain't tell me where it was, but she slipped up and told me it was there. I was about to take these bitches for everything they had. I didn't know what that bitch did for a living, but I was sure she was going to have to work overtime to get all that back. India said they was always careful and never put anything all in the bank at once. I knew from dicking her down and questioning her that they had well over $2 million cash hidden somewhere in that crib.

I knew it had to be in the basement, but knowing Tokyo's overprotective ass, bitch probably had the shit in her room or some shit. Maybe even buried in the backyard.

Later on that night, I called India to apologize and find out what her and her sister would be doing later and faked like I wanted to see her. Her goofy ass told me exactly what I needed to be true. They were supposed to be going out to eat with their father and some out-of-town family members around eight thirty.

When my brother met me at my crib, I was high as hell off some new shit motherfuckers had been smoking on called purple haze. When he walked in, he was dressed in all black.

"What's up, bitch-ass nigga, pass that shit!" He sat next to me on the couch.

We smoked and talked about all that money that would soon be in our possession. I was happy as hell because I needed that shit to give my wife the wedding she deserved and to get prepared for the babies I had on the way. I wasn't worried about India. All the bitch would be able to do was go to child support on my ass like the other two bitches I knocked up and used. Funny thing was, she ain't even know my real name. Bitches could be so dumb when they were "dickmatized."

CHAPTER TWENTY

BRYSON

When me and Red crept up the block, I saw India's car already leaving. I slid down into my seat so as to not be seen. Once the headlights passed, I looked to make sure Tokyo's car wasn't there either.

"Let's wait a couple minutes, then head in." I looked behind us and rubbed my patchy chin.

"Nigga, fuck that. Let's go now! We ain't got time to waste, bro, the fuck?" Red said as he got out of the car and quickly walked to the house. I followed suit.

"Nigga, it's the window in the backyard." I grabbed his hoodie and made him follow me.

When we got to the side of the house, I picked up a loose brick and threw it in the backyard, trying to see if they had any security sensors. Nothing happened, so I quickly slid around and began to slide the window open. Once I did, I climbed in and waited a few seconds to see if I heard anything. It was dark as hell in there. I guess Tokyo had left before India.

Red climbed in next, and we both signaled to split up and check shit out. I went straight for the basement. When I got down there, I didn't see a safe or anything in sight. I moved pics and all to see if they had anything hidden behind them. Nothing. There were two big-ass rugs hanging up against the wall. I thought maybe something could be behind them, and what do you know it was two large-ass vaults! Of course I ain't know the combo to them, but I bet that's where the stash was. Because I couldn't open them, I then made my way back upstairs. Red was searching in drawers in the kitchen.

"Dumb-ass nigga," I whispered, "we looking for two mill! They ain't gonna have it in a fucking drawer, dumb-ass! I saw two big vaults downstairs, but we ain't got a way to open them right now. Come the fuck on with me upstairs and let's look for something else!" I crept toward the stairway. When the stairs creaked, I instantly froze.

"Nigga, what you stop for? Ain't neither of them bitches here. We just watched them leave!" Red pushed me up the steps. When we got up there, there were five different doors.

"You take the two at that end of the hall. I'll take these three. Let's make it quick. Don't move shit out of place. We just scoping, remember? If anything, take something that won't be missed or obvious," I said, taking my mask off.

"Nigga, you a liar. Whatever the fuck I see that I like, I'm taking that shit!" Red protested.

"Bitch, now ain't the time to be on no goofy shit. That's how shit always get fucked up. Do what the fuck I said! Damn!" I said a little loudly.

When I walked into the first door, it was a big-ass walk-in linen closet. I shut the door and tried the next. It was India's bedroom. I started checking the closet and under the bed. When I opened the second door, it was a bathroom that connected to the other room on the other side that I was sure was Tokyo's room. When I entered, it was dark. Only the moonlight shined through the window.

All of a sudden, I had this uneasy feeling wash over me. I tried to shake it but I couldn't. I walked out the door about to go get my brother Red, when I felt something cold press against the back of my head.

"Red, quit fucking playing!" I whispered as I whipped around. I almost shit myself as I looked into the eyes of Satan herself, Tokyo.

"Oh, fuck." I put my hands up.

"Tsk, tsk, tsk," she said as she shook her head. "You just don't know how I've been praying for this moment." She smiled wickedly.

CHAPTER TWENTY-ONE

TOKYO

This dirtbag-ass nigga was creeping into my and my sister's home, trying to rob us. Lord knows I hated my period, but the fact that it had come on earlier today saved me from going to dinner with my pops and sister. Which also helped me to catch a fucking thief. Now the question was what to do with his dumb ass.

"Dumb-ass nigga, I peeped when your goofy ass threw that brick in the backyard. Where is that fat fuck who came in with you?"

"He dipped back out. He got scared," he stuttered.

"Nigga, you lying!" I gritted my teeth. I wanted to hit his ass with my gun so fucking bad!

"I said the nigga dipped the fuck out!"

"Cool, let's go!" I kept the lights out and made him lead the way down the stairs and to the basement.

As we reached the bottom part of the steps, I heard the guy say, "Man, these bitches ain't got no fucking money down here! And what vault was you talking about?" while smacking on a bag of chips.

"Bitch, you eating my favorite damn chips, too?" I yelled, startling him. He dropped the bag and threw his hands in the air. These had to be the dumbest two niggas in the history of robbing a motherfucker. I shook my head and pushed Bryson into the wall.

"Since you niggas wanna be here so bad, y'all's asses ain't never leaving!" I kept my gun pointed at them while I got some rope from the cabinet by the vault. "Tie that nigga up now!" I tossed it at Bryson.

"Fuck you. I ain't doing shit!" He threw it on the ground. Then it hit me. Two niggas were going to give me problems. There was no way I was going to be able to tie one up without the other pulling some goofy shit. I reached behind me and pulled my cell phone out of my back pocket. The phone rang three times, and before I knew it, that soothing-ass voice said, "Hello? What's up, Tokyo?"

"Hey, Python, you remember where I stay, right?"

"Yeah, why? What's going on?"

"Well, I got two niggas over here who I'm assuming wanna play with me. And I just don't think it would be fair if it was two on one in this game." I smiled wickedly, holding the phone.

"Oh, yeah? Say no more. I'm on my way." He hung up.

"Who the fuck is Python?" the fat one asked.

"Oh, shit. Oh, shit. Aw, hell nah!" Bryson looked like he was about to panic.

"Bryson, you must know him?" I inquired.

"What the fuck she talking about, cousin?" The fat guy looked at him.

"Remember that nigga I copped from trying to get on and never paid back?" he asked with big tears falling.

"Aw, damn! You never paid that nigga back his money? That big-ass nigga with the fucking dragon on his chest and neck?" His cousin almost squealed like some fucking pig.

"Yeah!"

"You dumb-ass nigga!" The chunky guy ran closer to Bryson and started swinging on him. I shook my head and stepped back while they wrestled and tumbled on the floor like some damn idiots. Picking up my bag of chips, I sat down and watched until I heard my phone receive a text. I wrote Python back and told him to just come in and come down to the basement. When he got down the steps and stepped into the light, all movements ceased. Bryson and his cousin stood there frozen while watching him stroke his beard.

Python looked at me and then at them. "Stand up."

They both did as they were told and didn't dare make another move.

"Yo, Python, man, look, I ain't know this was your girl. I'm sorry," Bryson tried to plead.

"She's not. But didn't you—"

The chunky brother cut him off. "Hell yeah, he copped from you and didn't pay you back! I ain't have shit to do with that, man! That was all him. I don't know you folk at all. I just need to leave! I won't say shit. Nigga shouldn't have tried to rob a mu'fucka like that. He should've paid you yo' money back." He inched closer to Python, speaking a thousand words a minute.

"But aren't you two here to rob me and my sister?" I cocked my head.

"Aw, yeah?" Python smiled while taking his gun out. "What you wanna do with these niggas, Tokyo?"

"Well, I don't care what you do to the fat one, but this nigga Bryson, I want him. I'm going to keep him." I stood up and walked over to tie him up. He cried and cried and cried until Python knocked his ass out. Then he shot his cousin.

"I'll get rid of this body for you, but only if you promise to go on a date with me." He turned around while holding the body.

"I don't care too much for fast food and all that. Cook something at your crib and it's a deal." I rocked back and forth with my head down.

"Cool, this weekend. Saturday. Be at my crib by five and we'll spend the rest of the day together. Have fun." He glanced at Bryson, who was now crying again. I walked over and got him up. We walked to my vault, then I put the code in and pushed him inside.

"Your sister will never forgive you. Just let me go! I'll never do this again! I swear please!"

"I knew there was something up with you when I first met you. You should've picked someone else to fuck with."

"She'll never forgive you. She'll choose me over you any day! That's why you don't like me. Be honest!"

I walked to the door of the safe and was about to shut it, when he said, "You gonna make her raise a baby by herself? She will always hate you for this." He dropped his head.

"No, she won't, because she'll never find out." I shrugged and began to shut the big door.

CHAPTER TWENTY-TWO

JACOB PHILLIPS

I couldn't wait to get off work. These fucking people in this nasty-ass restaurant had gotten on my last god-damned nerves with their nagging and complaining! As I was headed to the register to count down and get ready to clock out, that's when she walked in. She was beautiful as hell. She had to be about five feet seven inches tall with black wavy hair. Her figure was more than perfect as I scanned her body. I noticed that she had a small pudge. When she made her way over to my register, I noticed that this chocolate sista had the most mesmerizing set of green eyes ever.

"Hey, please before you close down, can I put a small order in?" She smiled at me but then it faded. She looked like she was confused for a moment.

"Sure, what can I get for you, beautiful?" I rubbed my neck.

"You look familiar as hell. What's your name?" she questioned.

I tapped the nametag on my shirt. She folded her arms and then asked if I had a brother or something who looked like me.

"You know, for someone who's trying to put in a last-minute order before we close you sure are wasting time." I looked down at her. Then it hit me. She had to have seen my brother before.

"Yeah, sorry about that. Uhmmm, can I get three pieces of fish, no slaw or tartar sauce, uhmm, and a small side of greens and a medium side of mac and cheese." She reached in her purse.

"Sure." I rang her up. "That'll be $16.50."

"Okay, cool."

As I put her order in, I noticed that she kept eyeing me. It kind of made me nervous to be honest. I started rubbing the back of my neck again, which was a habit when I was nervous or feeling uncomfortable. She walked back over to the register.

"I'm sorry, but I can't help it. You look like someone I've seen somewhere before. I can't call it, but I know I have. And I know it wasn't here."

I squinted my eyes and smiled. "Well, I do have two brothers I'm looking for."

"Oh, why though? How do you not know where they are?"

"My mom split us up at birth. I'm looking for her also."

"Wow, that's crazy. I couldn't imagine giving my baby away." She looked down and rubbed her belly.

"Well, everyone is not the same." I folded my arms.

"Yeah, you're right about that. You're a really big guy." She smiled, looking me up and down. "And nicely fit, too."

"Damn, lady." I had to laugh. "You just bold with your shit, aren't you?"

We talked for a few more minutes before exchanging numbers and I gave her the food she ordered. I was beyond excited for the simple fact I knew she hadn't seen me anywhere before, but she had seen my brother Desmond, aka Python. That instantly let me know that sooner or later I would be running into that motherfucker.

CHAPTER TWENTY-THREE

JACOB

My name is Jacob Phillips, but some people back home in Alabama know me as J.P. I was here in Kentucky to find my brother and our piece of shit mother who gave me away and kept him. But before I handled any of that, I had questions that needed to be answered. Besides, I also had a plan, and that was to off Python and take everything he had. I was going to be him. I was going to become him. Trust when I say it wouldn't be hard because no one besides our mother and my foster mom even knew I existed.

Walking out to my car, I checked my cell phone and saw that I had five missed phone calls from my foster mother and some text messages. Before I could put the phone back into my pocket she called again. I really didn't want to answer but I knew she would pitch a bitch if I didn't.

"What?" I answered.

"You nothing piece of shit! Don't fucking 'what' me!" she yelled. I could tell she had been drinking.

"Yes, Mother?" I gritted my teeth.

"That's more like it. Before yo' ass come in here, stop by the store and get me some more tequila. And I need some cigarettes, and don't forget to play my damn numbers before it's too late." She hung up.

I clapped my phone shut. "I hate that bitch!"

Going through this shit made me hate my birth mother even more. All because she gave me up, I grew up living a shitty filthy life and getting the fucking skin beat off my back every time I blinked or breathed too damn hard. I didn't have any real money, and I was struggling bad. I drove a beat-up car that damn near cut off on every red light I stopped at. Plus, to make matters worse, I still lived with the woman who hated my guts and used me all those years for a check from the government.

Don't ask why I didn't leave when I was old enough to get away, because truth be told I didn't know shit. I wasn't the smartest man in the world, but I wasn't dumb either. I just didn't know anyone and I had no family to my knowledge. Until I went meddling in my foster mother's room looking for a condom and found the adoption papers with my name on them. The bitch didn't even have the decency to change my damn name or anything.

When I questioned her about it, she took a lamp and slapped me upside the head with it and yelled, "The bitch ain't want yo' ass, and she threw ya ass to the State and ran off to Kentucky to start a new life!"

I wanted to find her and my brother, but the more I tried to search for them the more pissed off I became. The only reason me and my foster mom were here now was because I told her I had found them and they were wealthy and promised me and her money. That was enough for us to relocate here so I could do what I needed to do.

When I pulled up to the run-down projects known as Lakeview Apartments, there were people outside drinking, gambling, getting high, arguing, and fighting as usual. Kids ran around with no shoes on and no adult supervision without a care in the world. We lived in the taller building of those projects on the seventh floor. The elevator didn't work, so every day after work I had to walk up seven flights of piss-smelling stairways, stepping on used needles and sometimes junkies.

When I put the key in and turned the latch, my foster mom, known as Lynn, was dancing to Al Green's "Love and Happiness" and smoking on a long cigarette. She laid eyes on me and then the bag in my hand. She walked over to me and snatched it out of my arms. "Give me my shit!" she snapped, then switched over to the couch and plopped down.

I shook my head and walked to the far back of the apartment where my room was. I snatched off my apron and pulled off my work shirt, and I sat down on my bed and contemplated my next move. I pulled out my cell phone and called the girl who gave me her number. India picked up on the third ring.

"Hey, big guy, finally off work?"

"Yeah, finally. What you up to?"

"Nothing much, about to finish eating then get back to my schoolwork."

"Oh, yeah? You're still in school?" I asked, puzzled.

"Well, yeah, I go to the University of Louisville. I'm studying to become a surgeon," she said.

"That's what's up. A smart girl." I lay back on my small twin bed.

"So, tell me about yourself. I mean, I know where you work, but are you in school? Do you have any kids or anything?"

"Nope, no children, no woman, and no school. I had to drop out to take care of my sick foster mother," I lied, looking toward the door.

"Oh, damn, I'm sorry to hear that. What's wrong with her if you don't mind me asking?"

"She's mentally unstable sometimes and on a lot of meds," I half lied again.

"Damn, that's deep. You're a good person for doing that though. So about what you told me earlier, do you have any information at all about your birth mother or brother?"

"Nah, not really. I mean, I have her name and his name. But that's it."

"Well, that's actually all you need. Why don't you just Google them or something?"

"You know, I never really thought about that." I honestly hadn't, but I didn't own a computer, so I was going to make it my business to go to the library tomorrow instead of work.

"Well, glad I could help."

"Hey, you wanna hang out sometime? I mean, I don't know anyone here and I have no friends or anything. I just get sick and tired of working and coming home being alone." I sat up.

"Well, sure. I don't see that as a problem. When is a good time for you? I'm usually free on Wednesdays and every other weekend."

"Whenever you want to is fine by me. Quick question though?"

"What's that?"

"It won't be a problem for the father of your child, right?"

There was a brief pause. "Hell no. I'm sure he's preoccupied anyway. He's been acting really strange here lately ever since I got pregnant, which was a decision me and him both made."

I sat on the phone and listened to her tell me about their situation and some chick calling his phone cursing her out. We talked about our lives growing up and she told me that her mother had overdosed when she was 12 or 13. She also told me that she had a twin sister, which I found to be real unique seeing that I was searching for my twin brother. We made plans to meet up over the weekend and go to the movies. I was glad it was payday Friday. Otherwise, she would've had to pay for the date. We finally got off the phone around five in the morning, and I dozed off.

CHAPTER TWENTY-FOUR

JACOB

I was sleeping well as hell until a few hours later, Lynn came busting in my room and threw a bucket of cold water on me.

"What the fuck!" I jumped up, falling into my dresser and then into the wall.

"Rise and shine, bitch nigga! Go pay them goddamn bills and go pick up the laundry from Miss Betty on the third floor!"

She walked out and slammed my door.

I swear to God one day I was going to kill that bitch! I punched a hole in the wall and then fell to the ground. I was sick of this shit. I needed to make something happen and quick. I was going to have to speed my plans up and fast. I changed out of my wet clothes and went to go do as I was told.

When I got the clothes, I didn't bother putting them up or nothing. I just simply walked in, sat them by the door and walked back out. Lynn was on the couch passed out drunk with a lit cigarette dangling from her mouth. If the shit fell and started a fire, I wouldn't miss the whore. I said a quick silent prayer walking down the hall for it to fall and cause a fire before I got back.

After paying the LG&E and the house phone bill, I went straight to the library. The lady at the desk told me

I needed a library card in order to use the computer. So, I signed up for one and got down to business. I looked my brother up first on Google, but nothing showed up but white men who were all around the age of 50 or 60. When I looked my mother up, where she worked showed up and a past address but nothing more. I wrote the address of her job down and the name of the company and left.

I pulled up to the brown brick building that read HOME NURSING AND NURSING HOME Center. She was a damn nurse taking care of people, but couldn't take care of her children? I banged my fist on the steering wheel. Looking into the rearview mirror, I checked myself over. I was in need of a shape up and a beard trim bad. Thank God for the long, good, curly hair she gave me, because I was still able to pull it off. I stepped out and smoothed my clothes over and went to walk in the building.

It smelled like old people and hand sanitizer all through there. I spotted the front desk and walked over to the chubby red-haired lady with bright, long acrylic nails on. She threw her finger up while she was on the phone before I could even say anything.

After a few moments, she finally ended the call. "How may I help you?"

"Uh, yes, I'm looking for my mother, Sherryl Phillips. Did she happen to come in today?"

"Yes, she did, but she already left to head to the Miles residence. Would you like me to call her?"

"Uh no, ma'am, that won't be necessary. I just wanted to surprise her today with lunch, that's all."

The lady looked me over and then smiled. "Well, she may need a good surprise to lighten her mood. I'll write the address down for you so you can head on over. Don't you tell her it was me either. Plus, aren't you her baby boy?" she questioned while getting a piece of paper out.

"Yes, ma'am, I'm Ja . . . I mean, Desmond." I smiled back.

"Well, hell," she said, looking around after handing me the paper, "you even finer than the pics she showed us."

"Thanks," I said as I turned around. I was about to walk out the door when I heard the nurse's voice speaking loudly on the speakerphone.

"Hey, girl, your son just left. Don't say nothing and act surprised but he's about to head over and surprise you with lunch today." She beamed happily.

"Really? He came there? I can't wait to see him. I ain't seen that boy in a month of Sundays he's always so darn busy. Thanks," she excitedly said and hung up.

CHAPTER TWENTY-FIVE

INDIA

I had been calling Bryson nonstop because I had a doctor visit today at three in the afternoon. He still hadn't answered any of my calls or texts or returned them. I was beyond pissed off. Maybe he was done with this. Maybe my sister was right. I wanted to cry. I had gotten so upset I thought about an abortion, but I knew that was something I could never do. Besides, this baby didn't ask to be made. Me and him planned this and I was too far along. I was beginning to feel like a damned fool.

I got up off the couch and walked upstairs to Tokyo's room. Making my way closer to the door I heard her on the phone.

"Bitch, when I see you, I'm going to cut your fucking titties off and hang them on ya dead mammie's door, whore!" she yelled, then busted out laughing.

"Who the hell you talking to?" I walked in. Tokyo jumped up and put the phone behind her back.

"Nobody, just some bitch I was prank calling." She smiled. I knew that was bullshit because she looked like she was up to no good.

"So now people paying you to prank call folk?" I rolled my eyes.

"Not exactly. I'm just doing it to help someone out." She smiled.

"Well, Bryson still isn't answering his phone and I have an appointment today to check on the baby. Can you go with me? I don't wanna go by myself, please?" I begged.

"Sure, little sister, anything for you. Let me get dressed." She stuck the cell phone in the drawer, and I walked out.

I made sure to drink plenty of water before we left, because I knew they would ask for a urine sample when I got there. This was all so new to me, and when I should've been sharing these moments with Bryson and happy, I was in fact sad and angry riding in the truck with my sister as she swerved in and out of traffic like a bat out of hell while blasting rap music. She seemed more happy than normal. This was a side of Tokyo I'd never seen before.

When we pulled up to the clinic, there weren't very many parking spaces out front. We ended up having to park around the corner and paying for a parking spot. When we finally made it inside the building, I looked at my watch and saw that I was ten minutes late to my appointment.

"Are they going to see you with you being late and all?" Tokyo asked, snatching up a magazine.

"Yes, now hush and sit down," I shushed her.

I signed in and was handed a urine cup. As I was turning around to go to the bathroom, Tokyo took out two sticks of gum and began smacking loudly on them. After filling the cup up and placing it inside the cabinet, I washed my hands and went back into the waiting room. Tokyo was bopping her head, popping her gum, and flipping through the pages of a magazine called *What to Expect When Baby Comes*. I sat right next to her.

"Ooh, girl! They say you can shit on yourself if you eat before giving birth!" she said as she eyed the page closely. I had to laugh.

"Yeah, I know. That's if you get a C-section or some shit. They tell you don't eat twelve hours before then."

"Oh, my God! Your breasts are going to be leaking milk, too!" She continued to read. "What the fuck is a mucus pluuuggg?" Her eyes widened, and she looked at my middle part.

"Seriously, Tokyo?" I shook my head.

"Girl!" She flipped another page. "You better hope yo' pussy walls snap back after you drop that mu'fucka!" She shook her head. A lady close by cleared her throat while staring at us.

"Bitch, the fuck you looking at?" Tokyo snapped. "Clear your throat again and watch me handle yo' ass in here! Meddling and shit."

I dropped my head. "Tokyo, please, just for once be calm and be cool. Please." She looked at me then back at the magazine and was quiet the rest of the time that we waited. Finally, an hour later a doctor came out and called my name.

"India Miles?"

"Yes, right here!" I stood up, grabbing my purse.

When we got in the room, she handed me a gown and told me to undress from the bottom only. I did as I was told and lay back on the bed. When she came back in, she cut the machine on and the TV screen they had plastered on the wall.

"So has everything been okay so far?" she asked.

"Yes, ma'am, as good as expected. No morning sickness at all though. Is that normal?" I looked over.

"Well, yes, it is. Sometimes it won't start until your second trimester. Other times it can start before you even know you're carrying. Sometimes never at all." She lifted my gown and poured the cold jelly onto my lower belly. She then hit a few buttons on the keyboard and turned a few knobs that made a picture pop up.

"Okay, now, let's see how baby is doing in there," she said as she moved the wand and pressed it closer into my belly.

The next thing you know, I saw something tiny on the screen and funny shaped.

"Okay, there the baby is . . ." She dragged out her words as she looked closer at the screen.

"What's wrong? Is everything okay?" I looked back and forth between her and the monitor. Tokyo stood up and walked closer to me, grabbing my hand as she looked too.

"I ain't no expert when it comes to this, Doc, but why are there two little thumping things in there?" Tokyo twisted her neck.

"Well, that's because there are two babies in there." The doctor smiled and patted my arm. "Congrats, mom. Would you like to hear their heartbeats? You can now because you are officially twelve weeks today."

"Yes, ma'am." I began to cry. Not only was there going to be one baby, but I had to fend for two by myself.

"Sis, don't cry. I got you, okay? We gon' make sure these babies have the best fucking life money can buy! Fuck Bryson! Plus, we got Daddy, too! He's going to be extra happy!" Tokyo rolled her neck. That made me cry even more, because I wanted my man, the father of my children, here with me. How could he ditch me and our children like this?

After I heard their heartbeats and got some ultrasound pics, I got dressed and walked out. I was pissed off and hungry. Tokyo stayed on my heels, happy as hell the whole way to the truck. When we got in, out of nowhere she grabbed me and hugged me.

"Let's go baby shopping!" She beamed.

"How when we don't even know what they are yet?" I pouted.

"So what? We can just get everything in all colors!" She shrugged. "I know what will cheer you up. Want some crab legs and ice cream?"

"Bitch, you done read my diary?" I smiled through watery eyes.

"Only a little bit!" she laughed. "I mean, you left it on my bed in my room!"

We made our way to the Sea Food Lady restaurant and placed an order for ten clusters of crab legs and some sausage and corn. Then we left and picked up a gallon of French vanilla ice cream. I let her know that we could go shopping the upcoming weekend.

When we got home, I went in my room and lay across the bed before changing into something more comfortable. Before I knew it, I found myself calling Bryson again, with no answer yet again.

CHAPTER TWENTY-SIX

TOKYO

It was the weekend, and a bitch was feeling damned good! I danced around my room as I got dressed to go spend the day with Python. I was super happy seeing that I had Bryson's punk ass tied up in my basement and he wasn't here to distract my sister anymore or play games with her. Even if it meant that she would hurt for a while, I was cool with it. As long as he couldn't secretly hurt her anymore. She wouldn't understand anyway, even if she knew he had tried to rob us.

After putting on my all-black Baby Phat two-piece jogging suit and my all-black Jordans, I applied some makeup and then pulled my long hair into a high ponytail. Checking myself over, I didn't give a fuck what nobody said. Baby Phat was making a comeback for bitches with curves like mine.

I did a final spin, then snatched up the cell phone and called Bryson's wife again. She didn't answer, so I tried again. This time she picked up with much attitude. I just heavily breathed into the phone.

"Bitch, quit playing with me! When I catch you I'm going to fucking slit your throat!" she yelled.

"Oh, Bryson, right there, baby! Please don't stop! Mmmhmmm!" I moaned into the phone.

"Bitch, you faking! Even I know his dick ain't that good!" She hung up.

I couldn't stop the laughter that escaped my mouth as I snatched up my bag and threw the cell phone into the drawer of my nightstand. Heading down the steps, I heard India crying in her room. It didn't bother me though. I knew that she would never find that nigga. The vault was soundproof, and I had his cell phone. Believe it or not, I was helping her out. I was doing something good for my sister. Protecting her, right?

I dismissed the thought as I jumped into my truck and headed for my new boo thang's house. Out of nowhere I grew nervous. I was about to go stay the night with this man. What if he wanted to fuck? Would he make fun of me if I told him I was a virgin? All niggas did, which was how a majority of them ended up dead fucking with me. As mean as I was, I was very sensitive.

When I pulled up to Python's house, I didn't see a car in sight. I took out my cell phone and called him.

"What's up, sexy?" His deep voice flowed through the phone.

"Hey. I'm outside." I smiled. "But I don't see your whip. Are you even home? I know you didn't have me pull up and you ain't here," I started babbling.

"Girl, bring your ass in here. My brother is taking my truck to go get cleaned and make a drop-off for me."

I jumped out with the quickness and made my way up to his door. Before I could knock, he opened it and stepped aside. My pussy started throbbing hard looking at his sweaty chest and abs. I couldn't help myself as my eyes traveled from his face to his neck and farther down to the monster print in his red basketball shorts.

"My bad, I was working out real quick." He smiled as he looked down at me.

"I can see that." I couldn't take my eyes off it.

He grabbed himself, laughing, "My eyes are up here, li'l momma. You couldn't handle this if your life depended on it." He shook it and walked off.

I followed him into the kitchen, where the older housemaid lady I met a while ago cooked while listening to some old school music.

"Hello." I waved, sitting down.

"Hello, darling, would you like something to drink?" She grabbed a pitcher of orange juice.

"Sure." I took the glass and almost spit it out after the first gulp.

"Calm down, mimosas are good. Different but always good with breakfast lunch or dinner." She smiled.

This time I took my time drinking it. It actually was pretty good. Finishing the first glass, I asked for another. Before I knew it, I was smashing my food and talking the woman's head off.

"Where the hell did Python go?" I looked around.

"Probably still working out or taking a shower by now. Sometimes I think that man would die if he missed a session. You can go back there if you want. It's the last room at the end of the hall." She grabbed my plate and began to clean it. As I walked through the long, big hall, I noticed he had some really nice art pieces decorating the walls.

The closer I got to the room, the louder the music became. He was listening to "Regulate" by Warren G. Lord, watching that man's muscles flex while he bench-pressed about 350 pounds was a sight to see. I leaned against the doorframe and just watched. When I finally caught his attention, he smiled and signaled me over.

When I got close enough, he told me to remove my shoes. I did as I was told, and next thing you know he grabbed me up and started slowly lifting me up and then down over him while smiling and laughing. The nigga thought he was slick teasing me. I laughed my ass off and didn't have a doubt in the world that he would drop me. Python stood up and slowly slid me down his midsection. I looked up into his eyes, and he wasted no time leaning down and kissing me deeply in the mouth.

It had to be the drinks because I for damn sure kissed him back. When he went to pull my shirt over my head was when reality set in for me.

"Oh, shit. No. Python, I can't." I quickly pulled it back down.

"Why not?" He smiled. "What, you on your period or something? I got condoms and towels." He tried to kiss me again. This time I pushed his big ass back.

"No, I'm not on." I looked away, cursing myself.

"Aw, you wanna keep this strictly business?"

"Hell no! I just can't right now." I folded my arms, beginning to walk out.

"So then that must mean Miss Thang is a virgin!" he laughed as I whipped around. When he saw the serious straight face I was rocking, he instantly stopped. I rolled my eyes and smirked.

"Oh, damn! You fucking lying!" He rushed over to me, looking me in the face.

"Nah, that's real shit. Go ahead and throw a joke." I turned, ready to walk out again.

This time he grabbed me by the back of my neck and made me face him. He looked me long and hard in the eyes before he kissed me again, then said, "I ain't got nothing but respect for a woman who's still a virgin these days. I'm gon' fuck around and make yo' evil ass my damn wife." He smiled.

CHAPTER TWENTY-SEVEN

PYTHON

A nigga done scored a fucking virgin! A fine mother-fucking one at that! Now I knew she was evil and fine as fuck, but on my mom, a fucking virgin? She didn't know it, but she officially belonged to me.

After I showered, I hit up some of the boys to stop through so I could pay them for the week they had done hustling their asses off. That shit ain't go as planned because we ended up playing spades and shit and kicking it. Somewhere along the line, the grill got whipped out in the back and we just relaxed. Tokyo was having fun spankin' ass on the spades table. I kept my eye on her the whole time. I was trying to figure out how I was going to get her to give up them panties at the end of the night.

I knew she was feeling me and wanted the dick. Even if she didn't know shit about handling one. Once it was late at night, I kicked all them niggas out. Me and her sat around discussing everything under the sun. When I thought we would watch a movie, that's when I got the phone call.

"Yes, is this Desmond Phillips?" someone asked through the phone.

I sat up straight because no one ever really called this late let alone asking my government.

"Yes, this is he. Who's asking?"

Tokyo looked over at me and cut the TV down.

"This is Nurse Frank calling from Clark Hospital. We have you down as an emergency contact for a Jaheim Phillips?"

That shit really got my attention. I felt a lump form in the back of my throat. "Yeah, what's up?" I stood up. Tokyo kept her eyes locked on me.

"Well, we have your brother here, and he was in a terrible accident earlier today. Someone rammed his vehicle. He's alert but in much pain. But we have some forms that need to be filled—"

Before she could finish, I hung up and started putting my shoes on.

"Yo, what's wrong?" Tokyo started putting her shoes on too.

"My older brother is at the hospital. Let's go!" I could feel myself getting pissed off, only because he had taken my truck to go get cleaned and it never crossed my mind that the nigga had been gone all goddamned day. I started to assume someone had tried to set him up. I was about to fuck some shit up.

When we got to the hospital, I rushed to the receptionist's desk and gave my brother's name. When she gave me the room number, my big ass moved through those halls like a freight train. When I finally reached his room, I busted through the door and snatched the curtain back to see him getting his face cleaned and my mom sitting in the corner shook up.

"Hey, baby." She stood up and walked toward me. I quickly hugged her and then went to my brother's bedside.

"Aye, nigga, what the fuck happened?" I leaned over him.

"Yo' ass is what happened!" He tried to sit up, shooting daggers at me.

"What the fuck you talking about?" I backed up a little.

"Nigga, what, you trying to take me out or some shit? What, I have your whip too long?" He swung his arm that was in a cast toward me.

"Bro, what the fuck are you talking about?"

"Bitch-ass nigga, you rammed me! Now I done known that you want my connect, but to try to kill me for it? You a bitch! You could've handled me square up! You sent me on that run for a fucking reason! If I had a gun right now, I'd smoke yo' ass where you stand, big bitch!" he spat.

To say a nigga was lost and confused was an understatement. I ain't know what the fuck this fool was speaking about.

"Yo, Python has been at the crib with me and his boys all day," Tokyo interjected.

"Shut up, bitch! You meddling and ain't nobody ask you shit!" he shot at her.

"Bitch, fuck you! That's why yo' ugly ass about to be crippled! I'll smoke you right now and save your brother the time!" she said, hitting the cast on his leg as I pushed her behind me.

"Urrg, you funky bitch!" he growled.

"Bro, I don't know what meds they got you on, but I don't know what the fuck you talking about." I shook my head.

"I looked you dead in the face before that fucking truck flipped! I ain't fucking crazy or losing my mind! I know what the fuck I saw!" he yelled.

A nurse came rushing in. "If you all can't be quiet out of respect for the other patients, I'm going to have to ask you to leave." She looked around at all of us. When I looked at my mom, she had a look of panic on her face. Her ass knew something I didn't, and I was going to get to the bottom of it.

"Well, either way, I ain't left the crib all day. On top of that, you just plain delusional to think that I would hurt you. That's fucked up, Jay, for real."

"Yeah, whatever. Get the fuck out my room." He dismissed us, trying to turn over. My mother shook her head and grabbed her purse to head out. Tokyo followed her while I sat there a while longer trying to get my brother to talk to me. Shit ain't work, so I said fuck it and left. When I got out into the hall, Tokyo and my mom were in somewhat of a deep conversation.

"So what the fuck is he talking about?" I backed her into a wall.

"Baby, I don't think right now is the time to talk about this. Maybe tomorrow or something, please." My mom kept turning her head to avoid looking me in the eyes.

"Yeah, Python. Maybe we should wait until everyone is calm." Tokyo rubbed my arm, and I shrugged it off.

"You got me fucked up and yo' ass gonna talk. Seeing that my brother is in there laid up, bandaged up, and blaming me for the shit. Tell me what the fuck is going on before I lose my goddamned cool in here, woman." I grabbed her by the arm and led her to the exit of the hospital.

When we got out into the parking garage, my mother snatched away from me and slapped me across the face. "Boy, at the end of the day I am still your mother and you will respect me. Don't make me slap the taste out your damned mouth again! Don't you ever fucking put your hands on me!" she spat.

"Well, Mother, start talking then because none of this makes sense. I saw the look on your face when he said it was me and I denied the shit. You said we don't keep secrets from each other, so tell me what you know. Please." I sounded like a little boy.

She took a deep breath, and when she looked up at me, she had tears ready to fall. "A couple days ago while I was at work, one of the other ladies called my work cell and said you were bringing me lunch. I hadn't seen you in a while and got excited. I kept going back and forth to the door looking out. Well, at least two hours into that, I looked outside and that's when I saw you . . . I mean, him. We made eye contact, and then he made a gun gesture and drove off." Her voice cracked.

"Momma, what you trying to say?"

"Python, when I had you, I was young, okay?" She looked away. "I couldn't handle having three kids at the moment. Yaw's daddy ain't want nothing to do with yaw and I was just stressed and struggling. I didn't plan to leave that boy in the system. I just needed some time to get our lives together."

I backed up from her. "That boy? I got a brother and you gave him away?"

"Yes, you have a twin brother, baby. But why he's here now I don't know. I don't even know how he found us here. But I swear I never thought this day would come, not like this. I didn't want you to find out like this."

"If he hadn't shown up after all these years, would you have even told me? Does big bro know?"

"He may remember after I tell him, but he's never brought it up to me not once."

"Wait, I know this ain't the right time, but you the same nurse who takes care of my father. Oh, shit!" Tokyo covered her mouth. "I knew I knew yo' ass from somewhere! This is the son you were talking about?" She looked at me.

"Tokyo, not right now, ma. For real." I began to rub my face aggressively.

"Baby, I'm so sorry. I never meant for you and your brother to find out like this. I'm so sorry." My mom started the waterworks.

"It doesn't make sense though. Why would he wanna hurt Jaheim though?" I leaned against the rails.

"Python, I don't mean to meddle, but uhmm, if my mother gave me away and kept my sister, I'd be upset too. Favoritism and jealousy play a major role in all of this hand in hand. He probably got it out for you too and rammed your truck not knowing your brother was in there. How he knows what you drive is the question though." She shrugged.

"Baby, if he wrecked that car of yours on purpose trying to hurt you but instead hurt your older brother, I don't think he came to talk. He is obviously pissed off and wants to kill you. What if he kills me?" She began to panic.

I was so fucking lost and confused as I walked over and hugged my mother.

"Ain't nobody gonna hurt you, Momma. Even if we do share the same blood and you fucked one of us over. I'm going to handle this shit. You need to find a way to get ahold of him. Nobody hurts my family and doesn't pay for it." I felt my blood beginning to boil.

CHAPTER TWENTY-EIGHT

TOKYO

Five Months Later

To say India was getting big and fast was a fucking understatement! Shorty was literally eating everything in sight. That is, if she wasn't busy running back and forth to the bathroom. She was officially eight months pregnant, and I was already worn out with the shit. Almost had me feeling like I wanted to untie that funky-ass Bryson and let him out of the basement! I rolled over in my bed and grabbed his cell phone out of my nightstand. Cutting it on, I dialed his wife's number.

The automated voice picked up saying that the number was no longer in service. It was cool, because then I scrolled to the next best number: his mother's. When she picked up, she instantly started saying she rebuked me in the name of Jesus. I busted out laughing. "Girl, fuck you. Your son is a dead man, bitch!" I hung up, laughing. I know it was childish and I know you're wondering why I kept him locked up all this time. I just wanted him to live long enough to see the twins. After that, it would be lights out. My sister could and would do better. Actually, she already was! She was now seeing some mystery guy who kept her out every weekend. I didn't mind as long as she didn't cry over Bryson all day every day.

Blew my mind that every blue moon she'd still call his cell phone and leave messages. She was kind of slow for still paying the bill every month! And this fool wasn't even returning her calls. I smirked.

I got up to shower and get dressed so I could go see my man. We had made it official two months after seeing each other. It was great that we could kick it and he not pressure me into having sex with him. At first he kept trying every single time, but after a while he stopped. I just told him to fuck someone else instead. He chose not to go with that and instead wait on me. I finally gave in one night when we made it back to the city from one of our hits. Had to admit it felt good having a partner again.

When we reached the house, we made out in the driveway for all of ten minutes.

"Come on now, ma, don't get me worked up just for you to stop me when—"

I cut him off with another kiss. "I want you to do it tonight." I smiled, looking him in the eyes.

"You bullshitting?"

"If you keep me in this car any longer, I will be." I smirked.

We got out and walked into the house. I kicked off my shoes by the door and raced toward his steps with one bag in hand. I had called Cynthia before we made it back to Kentucky and told her that I was going to let him take my virginity. She told me to wear some lingerie to set the mood and that he better be gentle or she would filet his big ass. So, I picked out a nice little two-piece boy shorts lace set.

After I showered, I rubbed my body down in some vanilla-scented oil and sprayed on some vanilla-scented perfume. I pulled my hair up into a messy bun and applied some lip gloss. I was ready. Scared as hell but ready. Walking out of the room, I crept over to the stairway and looked over the railing. Python had lit some candles and poured two glasses of wine. I wanted to laugh because in all honesty I didn't think he knew what setting a mood was when he started making a pile on the floor. I proceeded to walk downstairs, clearing my throat to get his attention.

When he looked up, he instantly licked his lips and took his shirt off.

"You look damned good, baby, come here." He motioned to me.

When I was close enough, he scooped me up and kissed me hard, slipping his tongue in my mouth. He held me tighter as he walked into the kitchen. My jaw dropped when I looked at the table. There were a variety of fruits and dips laid out, candles lit, and champagne. When I got finished getting dressed, I decided to prank call Bryson's mother again, this time telling her I knew where her son was. She freaked the fuck out and then started yelling and cursing. I guess her respect for the Lord and sanity went out the window with that. Bryson had been reported missing, and after three weeks the news stopped covering it. I was always sure to turn the phone off and take the battery out before leaving it. India never went through my things, so I wasn't worried about her finding it. When I thought I was about to call the number back, India came busting into my room.

"Sissy, help me!" she panicked. "I think I'm having contractions!"

"Say what now? Call 911!" I shouted, throwing the cell into the drawer.

"No! They won't get here in time!"

"Okay, right! Uhh, grab your stuff and let's roll!" I snatched up my keys and ran downstairs to start the car.

India came wobbling out empty-handed and jumped in the truck with little to no effort.

"Where is your bags and stuff?"

"Girl, you better get this goddamn car moving and now!" she yelled, hitting the dashboard.

I got to the hospital as quick as I could, whipping into the emergency entrance. I threw it into park and leaped out. Rushing to her side, I snatched the door open and pulled her out. When we got in, it was jammed in there. I pushed past a few people waiting.

"Help me! She is in labor!" I yelled at the nurse who was on the phone.

"Okay, ma'am, calm down. What's her name?"

"India Miles!"

"Okay, and how far along is she?" The nurse hit a button on her desk and started pushing her toward some double doors in a wheelchair.

"I'm eight months, ma'am. Twins. Please hurry. This shit hurts," she panted.

Soon, some more nurses met us in the long hall. They whisked India away into a room. I walked over to the soda machine and got a Sprite. Sitting down, I waited for someone to come let me know something. After an hour, I grew nervous. Finally, a nurse walked out and called my name.

"Tokyo Miles?"

"That's me!" I stood up.

"Come right this way please. Your sister is asking for you."

When I got into the room, India had an oxygen mask on and an IV in her arm.

"Girl, what happened? Are the babies okay?" I rubbed her round belly.

Lifting the mask, she said, "False labor, and I'm dehydrated and my oxygen level was low."

"Damn, them kids ain't even born yet and they already play too much!" I laughed.

"I know, right? Anyways once this bag is finished, I get to go back to the house. Guess I won't be going out with my man tonight!" She smiled.

"Hell no, you won't, and I'm staying home too. When you gonna stop hiding this nigga and let me meet him?"

"Oh, so you mean to tell me you're going to make the famous Python wait?" She rolled her eyes.

"Yes, I am. Gotta make sure the family is good before I have fun. Now answer my question."

"I don't know. I wanna make sure this is serious first." She looked away.

"The man done only rode this whole pregnancy out with you, and I know yaw been fucking. Spending all this time together and you mean to tell me you're still unsure?" I smirked.

After three more hours, she was discharged from the ER. We decided that since we were both staying in, we would do our usual thing on Fridays minus the drinking. Walking in, I took India to her room and made her comfortable in bed.

"Now lie here for a while. I'm about to shower real quick and get this hospital smell off me. Then we can order something." I smiled.

"A'ight cool, bet."

I texted Python to let him know what was going on, and baby boy was not a happy camper at all. He did say that he understood and he admired how I always put my family first. Tossing my phone on my bed, I excitedly undressed and ran toward my bathroom. I was so happy to get to spend time with my sister!

CHAPTER TWENTY-NINE

INDIA

I rolled over on my bed and looked at the screen of my cell phone light up. I had three missed calls from Jacob and a few text messages. I ran my thumb along the screen as I looked at a picture of me and Bryson at the waterfront in front of the walking bridge. I closed my eyes and thought about the times we spent there. Sitting up, I started scrolling through my contacts trying to locate his number.

"Lord, please let him answer this time. If he doesn't, I swear I will finally let him be. I just want him to be there for the kids," I prayed to myself. I know it had been a while since I had heard from him, and the only reason I was calling him again now after all this time was because today gave me a hell of a scare. The phone rang three times on my end, and what happened next made me whip my head around.

I knew I wasn't tripping, but just in case I was, I hung up and decided to try again. It happened a second time. When I called, I heard the ringtone Bryson had saved for my number going off in the distance. I heard Bryson's phone ringing, which had to be impossible! I stood up and followed the sound of 112's "Cupid." When I reached the hall, the phone's voicemail picked up. I hit redial and waited for the phone to ring again. The sound was coming from none other than Tokyo's room! Walking closer to her door, I pushed it open. I walked over to her nightstand, and the phone stopped ringing again.

"That bitch!" I almost shrieked, opening the drawer and seeing Bryson's cell phone light up and vibrate.

"What the fuck are you doing going through my things?" Tokyo snapped as she rushed to the middle of the room.

I held the phone up. "Tokyo, what the fuck are you doing with his phone? What did you do to him? Where is he?"

"What are you talking about? What did I do to who?" She tried to play it off.

"Don't play dumb with me, bitch! Where the fuck is the father of my kids?" I yelled, walking toward her.

"Look, India, I told you that boy was sneaky and foul! Did you know he was married?"

"I don't give a fuck! Where is he? You lied to me all this time! Saying you didn't know where he was! Faking like you cared about what happened to him and how I felt. Tokyo, what did you do?"

"The nigga and his brother broke into our house trying to rob us—"

"Bitch, you lying! I don't believe you! You're a fucking liar! Bryson would never do that shit! This is so low of you! You've always hated him. And your jealous ass done did something to him because you couldn't stand the fact that I had someone for me who makes me happy and you didn't! What did you do?" I couldn't stop screaming at her. I wanted to beat her ass. The babies started kicking uncontrollably.

"Sis, you need to calm down for real. All this yelling isn't good for the twins. Besides, he has a whole wife and kids on the way with her. Sis, he was playing you. I was just helping!" she tried to reason.

"Fuck you! Don't call me your sister when you don't even act like one! You're just like your fucking mother!" I cut my tearstained eyes at her.

"Excuse me?" She twisted her neck as she cut her eyes back at me.

"Bitch, you heard me! You're disrespectful! Evil! And fucking toxic! All you do is ruin people's lives! Just like your mother!" I threw the cell phone at her, nearly hitting her face with it.

"Bitch, fuck you back! You're just like your father! Stupid as fuck and always dumb in love with someone who doesn't even fucking love your slow ass back! I do what I do so we can live the way we do! And I'm damned good at it! You got me fucked up! My evil-ass toxic ways is putting your gullible ass through college and keeping those babies seen and healthy! Look at history already repeating itself! You lucky I don't do your dumb ass like I did your dead-ass mother, may she rest in piss and shit!" She threw her hands up to her mouth, gasping at her own words.

"What the fuck is that supposed to mean, Tokyo?" I felt my legs beginning to go weak, and the tears were now coming nonstop.

"I didn't mean it. I didn't mean to say that." She covered her face.

"You killed our mother?"

"She deserved that shit and you know it! She was always hurting you and Daddy!"

"I can't believe you." I almost collapsed, but instead I sat weakly at the foot of her bed. I felt like she had just knocked all the wind out of my body.

"India, you know I don't like people hurting who I love." She walked closer to me.

I looked up at her. "But it's okay for you to hurt us? It's always okay for Tokyo to do any- and everything. I can't believe you. First you hurt me and Dad, then him again and now me again. Tokyo, I can't trust you anymore. As far as I know, one day you might end up killing me if I piss you off. Our well-being doesn't really matter to you. Feeding your anger and using everyone else's mistakes for an excuse to kill them drives you."

"No, I wouldn't! India! Don't say that. I would never hurt you no matter what!" She placed a hand on my shoulder and tried to get me to look at her.

I smacked it off. "I just can't trust you, and at this point, I could never trust you around my children. I'm moving out," I said with a low tone and walked out of her room.

CHAPTER THIRTY

TOKYO

I sat in my room crying as I watched and heard my sister packing her things and taking them out to the car. I was being punished for protecting her, for loving her too much and always trying to keep her safe. Maybe if I gave Bryson back to her, she would forgive me. *Yeah, that's it,* I thought as I stood up and rushed out into the hallway.

"India, wait," I screamed at her as she was about to leave. I rushed down the stairs and tried to run across the living room. She ignored my ass and kept walking.

"India, wait please! Just listen! I gotta tell you something!"

"Leave me the fuck alone, you evil bitch!" she yelled, walking out the door and slamming it in my face.

I collapsed on the floor, then got up and ran outside in my damn towel, clinging it to my body.

"India, please!" I screamed as she started backing out the driveway. "He's in the basement! Come back!" I shouted. She flipped me off and sped away off into the night. I lay on the sidewalk crying and losing control of myself, until one of the neighbors shouted asking if I was okay. Realizing how I must look, I slowly began to crawl toward the door, finally getting up and walking in, locking it.

I screamed and started throwing shit left and right. I lost my fucking sister. I had majorly fucked up in an innocent way. I grabbed the cordless phone and threw it into the flat screen, breaking it. Then I started smashing every snow globe on the mantle that I collected. I rushed over to the closet and snatched out a bat and started smashing the pictures on the wall of my sister and myself. I did a number on that living room until I grew tired. Falling back onto the floor into shards of broken glass, I screamed and cried as it pierced my knees and cut the sides of my legs. I lay there and thought about every-thing my sister said, which began to piss me the fuck off even more. Standing up, I walked toward the basement, smashing the big fish tank on the wall as I went.

When I got downstairs, I rushed over to the vault with the bat in hand and put the code in. Walking in, I snatched the hanging light on, scaring the hell out of a weak and distraught Bryson.

"Bitch motherfucker!" I yelled. "All because of you my life is fucking ruined. All because you couldn't treat my sister right! Trying to protect her from you! Now she fucking hates me and is gone!"

"Tokyo, just kill me and get it over with please. I don't wanna see the twins anymore," he slurred.

"You selfish sack of shit." I hocked spit onto his face. He dropped his head and began to cry.

"What do you want from meeee!" he yelled. "Hellllp! Somebody help me! Please!"

I raised the bat and came down hard on his knee. He grunted and rocked in the chair. "Shut your bitch ass up. Nobody will hear yoooouuu!" I taunted him, smiling. I walked circles around him, trying to figure out what I wanted to do. Since I was heartbroken and hurting, I was going to inflict pain on the next.

I walked back out of the vault, leaving it open as I went to get his cell phone. When I got back down there to him, he had tried to scoot his way to the middle of the floor and out the vault.

"Hellllp! Help meeee!" he screamed.

I picked up the remote and hit play on the stereo system, turning it up. Mary J's "Not Gon' Cry" blasted through the speakers.

"Ha ha haaaaa!" I laughed, picking up a half-full bottle of Hennessy and chugging some. "What a time for this shit to be playing." I shook my head and hit the phone icon on his cell phone. I waited for it to ring, then hit the video call button. I flipped the camera toward him when his mother picked up.

"Oh, my Goddddd! My baby! Where are you?" she screamed.

"Mom, help me!" he yelled to her with big-ass tears falling.

I muted the video on our end and set the phone up so she could get a good look at him. I walked back out of the vault and grabbed one of the decorative African masks off the wall. Before placing it over my face, I took another long gulp of the liquor. She screamed and yelled her ass off on the other end.

I ran into the vault and smashed the bottle into his face, causing his nose to start gushing blood. I backed up and grabbed the bat and beat his ass senseless until three songs later. I was tired as fuck but pleased looking at the handiwork in the chair that shook and coughed nonstop. At some point his mom had hung up and I had smashed the phone. I walked out and upstairs to grab some ammonia and a knife.

When I got back to him, he had thrown up on himself. "Nasty-ass fucker!" I walked up, staring him right in the eyes, and started stabbing him in his legs and arms. He was so fucked up he couldn't do anything but grunt a few times and pass out.

"Aw, nah, baby, ain't no going to sleep." I grabbed the gallon and sat on his bloody lap. I rubbed his head and kissed him on the cheek. "Since I don't have my sister anymore, nobody is going to have her, and she won't have a choice but to come back to me. After you, I'm going to handle her new man too," I slurred, then burped in his face. I took the top off the gallon and poured it on his face.

That sure enough got his attention because he screamed so loud when the liquid hit all the open wounds that he almost burst my eardrums. I laughed and emptied it on him. When I pulled out my gun about to shoot him, he lifted his disfigured face and said, "There's a special place in hell for people like you. We gon' come face-to-face again, Tokyo."

"Yeah, you're right it is. It's called VIP, nigga. Every night I close my eyes, I go there just to gamble and dance with the devil."

"Fuck you, bitch!" he spat from a bloody mouth. I blew him a kiss and then pulled the trigger.

Boom!

CHAPTER THIRTY-ONE

PYTHON

I didn't understand why this motherfucker Tokyo wasn't answering her phone. I was missing her li'l thick ass. I needed to vent because ever since that shit with my big brother, it was like my twin brother had fallen off the face of the fucking earth. Nobody knew where this nigga was, and he was constantly sending my mother threatening messages to her job and shit, which got her fired. They claimed her personal issues would most likely put the patients in danger. Lord knows I was going to kill this nigga in the worst way when I found him.

Fucked-up part was I just couldn't put a hit on the nigga's head. He looked like me. Shit wouldn't make sense. As I paced back and forth in my room, I hit the redial button on my cell. This time she picked up.

"Yes, baby?" She sounded drunk.

"What yo' fine ass doing? Get the fuck over here. I need you." I hung up on her.

There was a knock on my bedroom door, and then my mother entered.

"Hey, baby." She walked in, looking down as usual.

"What's up, you need something?"

"Well, I just came to tell you, I'm going back home. It's been five months and I am not about to keep staying here.

I miss my own bed and I cannot deal with being in here with my sister asking a thousand questions every five minutes. You know we still don't get along."

"Momma, look, we ain't going through this shit again! You will stay here until I find out where this nigga is and handle him. I can't have you out here alone risking something happening to you." I pulled a rolled blunt from behind my ear.

"And I most definitely can't handle all that damn weed smoke." She smiled.

"Try it, may help you relax." I pushed it in her direction.

My cell phone started ringing on the bed. Walking over, I noticed it was one of my boys.

"Speak."

"Aye yo, Python, I found that nigga! I think I found him. I'm following him right now. He just left a tattoo shop on Maple."

When he said that my blood began to instantly boil!

"Don't let his bitch ass out of your sight! I'm about to head out now."

Grabbing my gun, I threw on a long-sleeve black shirt to match my black sweats and Timbs.

"Bruh. This nigga done got his hair cut and everything. He dead-ass is trying to be you." He laughed into the phone.

"There will only ever be one me!" I hung up the phone and rushed out, leaving my mother standing there in my room.

By the time I met up with Buckey, he had already lost the nigga.

"Man, how the fuck you let that shit happen?" I fumed.

"The nigga had to notice me following him or something! He started weaving in and out of traffic like a motherfucker!" He hit the steering wheel.

I began to massage my temples and tried to stay calm when my phone rang in my pocket. Snatching it out, I saw it was Tokyo. I had completely forgotten that I told her ass to come over.

"Really, nigga? You gonna have me drive all the way here just for no one to be here? I got shit to do. I got a hit to leave for tonight. So, if you wanna see me, make something shake."

"What you mean, nobody is there? My mom and aunt are there. Just chill there with them until I return."

"Boy, yo' mother is not here. Your aunt said she went home to go get more clothes or some shit."

"Are you fucking serious right now!" my voice boomed through the phone. I threw the motherfucker across the roadway and leaned against the truck.

"Nigga, you need anger management." Buckey laughed.

"Bro, ain't shit funny right now. My mom's done left my crib to head to her crib. Follow me over there so I can go get her ass! She's fucking hardheaded yo."

We jumped in our whips and sped off. Tokyo started blowing my burner phone up. I just let it ring. Although I loved her, right now wasn't the time. My mother was my main concern.

When we pulled up to her home, her car was in the driveway. To say I was fucking relieved was an understatement. Her front door was sitting wide open and so was the trunk to her car. I shook my head and hopped out.

Walking past her car, I noticed the trunk was empty, so she had to be still in the house packing some things. When I walked in, my heart sank to the bottom of my stomach. Her crib was trashed, and there were traces of blood in different spots.

"Maaaaaa!" I started yelling as me and Buckey rushed through looking for her, searching different rooms.

"Maaaa!" I could feel my eyes beginning to water. When I reached her bedroom, there was a knife sticking straight up out of her bed with a note. It read:

I think it's time me and you finally meet face-to-face. Come to the address listed on the back, and come alone or I'll slit this bitch's throat!

I collapsed on the ground. I had never been faced with anything like this before. I didn't know what to do. I didn't know what to think. No man or bitch for that matter walking this earth had the balls to fuck with my family. My mother and brother were all I had. For the first time ever, I let a tear fall.

"Awww, man." Buckey shook his head as he walked in and sat down beside me. "Bruh, right now ain't the time for this. Get yo' big ass up and let's go get this nigga! I'm gon' call the crew and—"

"He wants me to come alone. Don't do that. I'm gonna handle this shit personally. Call Tokyo and let her know what's up. Don't tell her where I'm heading, just let her know I got some shit to handle and I'll see her soon." I stood up and wiped my face. Grabbing the knife, I thought about all the places I would stick this motherfucker when I got ahold of that son of a bitch! Buckey looked at the note and read it as we headed back down the steps.

Walking toward the door, Buckey stopped me and asked, "Man, what the fuck is that?"

When I looked down, I was certain it was my mother's finger. I took a deep breath and kept walking.

CHAPTER THIRTY-TWO

TOKYO

"What the fuck you mean, he said don't tell me where the fuck he's going? Yo' ass gonna be dumb enough to literally let him go by himself? You don't know if he's being set up!" I yelled at Buckey.

"Look, ma, I'm just telling you what he told me to say." He threw his hands in the air.

"Give me the fucking note!" I inched toward him.

"I don't have it."

"Well, give me the fucking address then!" I pulled my gun out.

"Bitch, is you crazy?" Buckey stood up.

I aimed my gun at him while cocking it.

"Yeah, you two crazy motherfuckers are most definitely meant to be together." He shook his head.

"Yeah, whatever, what's the address?"

Buckey told me the address and I left. I rushed home to change clothes and grab my guns and my favorite switch-blade. I strapped a small .22 to my ankle and secured my knife on my wrist, and then I pulled the sleeves to my hoodie down and patted myself down to make sure I was straight and that everything was in place.

I left and sped as fast as I could heading to the boonies outside the city. When I got to the address I assumed was correct an hour later, I noticed that there was a dirt road heading far up to a run-down house. There was literally no other home or car in sight.

I was confused, so I checked my GPS. This couldn't be right. I turned my lights off and slowly drove up the road. When I got close, I could see that the lights were on in the front of the house. I saw figures moving and got the gut feeling shit was about to hit the fan. I pulled over on the side of the dirt road. Stepping out, I made sure not to slam my damn door or make any noise for that matter. I walked alongside the trees to stay out of view in case someone was watching.

Making my way around the back of the run-down house, I hopped on top of a trash can and pulled myself up on top of a low roof to what I assumed led to the up-stairs part of the house. I took out my blade and jabbed it under the window frame to pry it open. It was dark in the room, but enough of the moonlight shined through so I could at least see my way around.

As I looked around the room, I noticed a baby crib and two sleeping babies.

"Who the fuck would have these babies in this dirty-ass house like this?" I shook my head and took my gun out as I got closer to the door. As I walked out into the hall, there were candles lit all through it. That's when I heard two male voices in the distance coming from the lower level. When I got closer to the steps to get a better view of the lower level, I saw Python tied up in a chair with a bloody face.

As soon as I placed my foot on the first step, it creaked and I froze. The guy standing in front of Python looked dead up at me and smiled. That's when I felt something with much force hit me in the back of my head.

"Fuck!" I mumbled as I tumbled down the stairs. I tried to keep my eyes open and knew my mind had to be playing tricks on me when I saw my sister India standing over me, smiling. That's when everything went black.

CHAPTER THIRTY-THREE

JACOB

"Aye, this is some real Romeo and Juliet type shit for real." I chuckled.

"I told you her ass would come for him, baby." India smiled as she patted Tokyo down.

"What the fuck, India?" she screamed as she tried to wiggle and put up a fight while I tied her hands and India proceeded to tie her feet. When India grabbed one leg, Tokyo hauled off and kicked her hard in the nose with the one that was still loose.

"You stupid bitch!" India shrieked as she held her nose.

"How could you be in on this? Why? Is this the reason you kept a nigga a secret?" Tokyo screamed at her sister as tears began to fall.

"You took someone I love and crushed my fucking soul. The whole time Bryson was missing, in the back of my mind I kind of figured you had something to do with it, because you were just a little too happy he wasn't around anymore." She cocked her head. "All you've ever done was think you're the boss of me and try to run shit like I was your fucking child! Bitch, I think it's about time I inflict some pain on you. Or do you even know what pain is?" India snatched Tokyo up and threw her onto the couch.

"You bitch-ass nigga, when I get loose from this shit, I will kill you. And I dead-ass mean I will take my time doing that shit!" Python spat in my face.

I took the gun I was holding and slapped him in the mouth.

"Bitch nigga! You won't be able to do shit when I empty this fucking clip in your skull!" I screamed with so much anger I was sure I began to foam at the mouth.

In the distance, one of the twins started crying.

"So, your dumb ass is really going to raise those babies in this fucked-up house?" Tokyo chuckled as she looked at India.

I took a few steps back so she and my brother could get a good look at me. Unbuttoning my shirt, I revealed the same exact tattoo Python had on his chest and neck.

"Me and my woman, raising our kids in a crib like this?" I let out a menacing laugh. "Nah, playboy. We will raise them in your nice, big-ass house."

"So, you really think you got what it takes to be me? I don't even know you and I can tell yo' big bitch ass would fold under pressure." Python laughed.

"Pretty much you don't do shit but sell dope and order motherfuckers around anyways." India shrugged, then pointed the gun at him and fired two shots into his shoulder. He wasn't about to die just yet.

"Python, nooooooo!" Tokyo screamed and wiggled until she fell off the couch.

"Ha! Ha! Ha! That's the pain I was looking for. You know, after all these years I never thought I would see the infamous Tokyo Miles cry over a nigga! This is a new side of you." India continued to laugh.

"Sweetheart, go check on the babies," I told her as I heard more whimpering.

CHAPTER THIRTY-FOUR

MISS NELLY

The phone rang about four times before I finally got an answer.

"Yeah, Auntie, what's up?"

"Now look, I don't know detail for detail what the hell is going on, but I do know Python done caught up to that twin of his. Something about he wanted to meet him alone. He got ya mother, too. Ya brother ain't want nobody to know or go with him."

"Who the fuck had the dumb-ass nerve to let him go by himself?" Jaheim came bursting through the door, startling the shit out of me!

"Look, I don't get in yaw's business when it comes to all this nonsense. But it's different when family is involved. Now get yo' ass the fuck in there, strap up, and get to him. Bring that boy and my damn sister back safe! I ain't call the rest of the boys. It'll draw too much attention. Besides, I'm sure that you two together can take on and shut down any damn thing. Here go the address. Go handle ya business like I taught yaw to."

I slipped him the paper with the address on it and walked away.

CHAPTER THIRTY-FIVE

JACOB

"I ain't did shit to you. Why the fuck would you be taking this shit out on me?" Python spit blood onto the rusted wooden floor.

"Shit, ask ya nothing-ass mother why she chose you over me." I lit a cigarette and sat across from him.

"Where is she?" Python gritted his teeth.

"She's straight, missing a few teeth and a finger, but she's straight." I chuckled.

"So what you wasting time for? Get all this shit over with. You're starting to fucking bore me." He let out a fake-ass yawn.

"Shut the fuck up! You don't tell me what the fuck to do!" I roared, standing up and getting in his face. When he laughed it sent me over the fucking edge. This nigga was fucking crazy for real!

Python laughed and focused on India bouncing a newborn baby. "And, bitch, I knew there was something about your weak ass that I didn't like."

India smirked and replied, "I'm just like my backstabbing-ass sister, so you better watch that one."

The look in Tokyo's eyes kind of scared me. There was nothing there. It was like looking into a black hole of complete emptiness. Even as evil as my foster mother was, the look in that woman's eyes was something totally different.

"Aye yo, ma!" I yelled out as Lynn, my foster mother, came walking out holding the other baby. "Go lay the kids down and bring that bitch out here." I waved her off. "Don't get it twisted." She cut her eyes at me. "I still run shit. No matter who the fuck you think you're about to become. And I better get my money for this shit." She switched off with the baby in one arm, while puffing on a cigarette with the other hand.

A few seconds later, she casually walked into the dimly lit room, dragging my birth mother by the hair as if she were a bag of lightweight trash. I laughed looking at the terrified look on her face. Python flexed so fucking hard and started growling at the mere sight of her. He tried to stand and lifted the chair he was tied to a good five inches off the ground. He came down hard on it, causing it to brake and collapse under his weight.

"Goddammit shit!" I tried to make my way over to him quickly, but this big-ass nigga got up so fast and charged me, knocking all the wind out of my body as he fell on top of me. I gave him blow after blow to the face, but it didn't faze him at all whatsoever. His hands were still tied behind his back, so I felt that I still had the upper hand. I flipped him over and started swinging with all my might. I felt like a weak-ass man, because he literally ate those punches and kept smiling and clenching his jaw muscles.

"You hit like a bitch!" he spat in my face.

I socked him in the nose as hard as I could and dug my finger into the bullet hole in his shoulder. He grunted, but not too much, and headbutted me in the face.

"I'm a real man. That shit don't bother me!" he said, scooting away.

When I rolled off of him, my foster mother ran up with a butcher's knife, and while she was in mid-stride, my birth mother tackled her, and they landed on the floor closer to Tokyo.

CHAPTER THIRTY-SIX

TOKYO

There was so much going through my head. What really hurt me the most was that my sister was in on all of this. I couldn't believe this bitch! All over a nigga? A nigga who was no good for her at that? At this point, all I had left was my father and Python. Fuck India! She was now another enemy and dead to me.

Lynn and Sherryl both fell to the ground right next to my angry ass lying on the couch. I kicked Lynn in the face, making her roll over. Sherryl lay there panting, starting to panic as she stared at the knife sticking out of her stomach.

"Oh, my God, oh, my God." Her hands shook as she reached for it and snatched it out while letting out a bloodcurdling scream. She rolled over to me and tried to stand but fell on top of me. She pushed me over and began to cut the rope around my wrist off. As soon as I felt my hands free, I sprinted toward the stairs where I saw my sister go with the baby.

"Go fuck that bitch up!" she yelled after me and then fell to the ground.

By the time I was making my way to the top, India kicked me with so much force in the chest I was sure whatever little bit of heart I had left flew straight the fuck out of me. I grabbed the railing and clutched my chest, catching myself.

"You traitor-ass bitch!" I let out weakly.

"Fuck you!" She raised her foot again, but this time I let the railing go and grabbed her leg and yanked her, which caused us both to fall down the steps. Lynn was still dazed, and Sherryl was trying to prop herself up against the couch. I ran over and kicked Python's twin in the face with much force.

"Fuck off my man, bitch-ass wannabe!" I lunged for the knife on the ground so I could try to cut Python loose, but his brother grabbed me by the hair and slammed my face into a table.

India jumped up and raced over to me, and she pounced on me, grabbing me by the hair, and banged my head into the ground. I didn't know how much more of this shit I could handle.

Leaning in closer, and still gripping my hair very tightly, she whispered in my ear, "As much as I hate you for what you did to me, I'll always be your sister, and I'll always love you. But just because I would never betray you does not mean I'd never get my lick back!"

She loosened the grip on my hair. I was confused as I stared at her while she stood over me. I was so stuck I couldn't move, because those bright green eyes were as dark as night by now.

"Baby, what are you doing?" Jacob yelled at her. "Kill that bitch!" he panted.

I glanced over at Jacob, then at Python, then back up at India.

"India, no, please," I begged as I jumped up. "Please! I'm so sorry for everything. India, please don't!" I ran right in the line of Python and the gun she pulled from behind her. Boom! Boom! Boom! Boom!

It felt like the side of my head fucking exploded. I heard ringing in my ears. The pain I felt rip through my body was way worse than the pain I felt the night I got shot at the club. Python held me. I couldn't look him in the eyes. I didn't want him to see the pain in my eyes, the hurt. I kept my eyes locked on India with every word. "Python." I began to cry. "I'm not ready to die. I don't want to. I'm not ready."

"No, no, no!" India screamed. "It was supposed to be you! Not her! Noooooo! What the fuck? Tokyo, why would you do that!" I heard her screaming.

"Baby, look at me please." Python shook me. I felt my body going weak as I tried with everything in me to keep my arms around him.

"Baby, please, not like this." He held me tight, finally scooping me up in his arms.

As everything started to fade in and out, I thought about my life and everything that I had ever done. Had karma finally caught up to me? Who was going to take care of my father? When the fuck did my sister even give birth to my niece and nephew? Was I wrong for playing the cards I was dealt? I started having flashbacks of my childhood and all the good times me and my sister and father had. When everything did finally go black, the first faces that popped into my view were my mother's and Bryson's. I remembered the last thing he said to me before I killed him: "We will meet face-to-face again."

CHAPTER THIRTY-SEVEN

PYTHON

My heart hurt as I held the first woman I had ever fallen in love with as she bled out. I glanced at my mother as she lay there crying, bleeding out her damn self. Then I looked at India as she lay on the floor in the corner, crying her eyes out. I stared at a brother I never knew trying to grasp everything that just happened. I had never been put in a position where I had absolutely no control over the situation and no way to figure things out.

I rocked my baby and for the first time ever I began to pray, "Lord, I know you don't care for or listen to people like me. But if you are as forgiving as my mother says you are, please don't take this woman away from me. Lord, please, if anything, I'd rather you take me please. Don't take my baby away from me. Please, dear God, please." I began to cry.

Out of nowhere the front door busted open and Buckey and Jaheim came rushing in.

"What the fuck?" Buckey grabbed his head as he looked around at all the chaos and blood.

"Momma!" Jaheim screamed, rushing over to her.

"I'm fine," she coughed. "Get that girl to a hospital." She pushed him away. Jaheim stood up and walked over to me and then looked down at Tokyo. I didn't know what to say as I looked up at my big brother with tears drenching my face. He checked for a pulse.

"Bro, we need to get her out of here quick! She still has a pulse. Get up and let's go!" He snatched Tokyo out of my arms and rushed out the door. I grabbed my mother and led her out. When we got them outside there were ambulances already pulling in front. In the distance I could see cop cars heading this way. Me and my brother got Tokyo and my mom in the back of the trucks.

Buckey came out. "Aye, I'll stay here and handle everything else because the police and shit are most definitely on their way." He pointed.

"How you gonna handle this shit? Ain't no clearing this up."

"Nigga, I'm yo' number one since day one. I have had a plan. Now get the fuck out of here!" He turned around, heading back in the house.

CHAPTER THIRTY-EIGHT

BUCKEY

I walked back in the house and shook my head. India got up off the floor and was trying to help Jacob up. I pulled my gun out. "Nah, sit yaws' tight asses right there." I aimed at them.

"I have to go check on my sister." She sobbed and stumbled in my direction.

"You betrayed your sister. Not to mention, the way she's looking she may die before she even makes it to the hospital." I smirked.

I could hear the sirens out in the front of the raggedy-ass run-down house, and I was going to make sure they stayed there until the police and detectives rushed in. As I sat down on a bloodstained sofa, I heard a baby whimper upstairs and some commotion.

"Who the fuck else is in here with yaw?" I stood up.

"Nobody." She gave me a look of panic.

"Bitch! Is you dumb? You heard that baby just like I did!"

"Be my guest, motherfucker, and go see who it is," Jacob, Python's twin brother, suggested.

"Ha! And risk letting you and her get away? I think the fuck not!"

A few minutes later, a lady came rushing down the stairs with a baby in each arm and darted toward the back. I started to take a shot at her but couldn't risk hitting one of those babies.

"No!" India screamed. "Bring me back my babies, you bitch!"

When she tried to run after the woman, I shot at her, causing the bullet to graze her leg. "No, ma'am, I need your ass right here. You know, Python was right about you. As much as you and her look alike, you could never be Tokyo or have the heart that she has."

I puffed my blunt until I heard the tires of the cop cars screeching in the front. I stood up and went to open the door. When I reached the knob, I heard quick, heavy footsteps. I whisked around to see Jacob hauling ass in the same direction.

"Baby, don't leave me! You can't leave me here like this!" India sobbed, scooting in that direction and holding her leg. The police came rushing in and so did my mother.

"Sir! Drop the weapon!" one officer said, pointing his gun at me.

"No, no. He's fine. He called ahead of time to let us know where to come to."

"And I'm a cop, dumbass," I said as I flashed my badge. "Python ran out the back, ma." I pointed.

The police ran back there quick, and soon we heard them yelling, "Freeze."

"Tokyo Miles, my name is Detective Washington, and you are being placed under arrest for the murder of your uncle Marvin Miles, the murder of his body-guard Johnathan Hinkle, and the murder of Brittany Wadlington." She snatched her up and slapped the cuffs on her.

"What the fuck are you talking about? I didn't murder anyone!" she started screaming as she jerked and yanked but couldn't get free.

"Ma'am, if you keep trying to resist, I will pepper spray you, and I'm sure you don't want that. I guess your ass ain't as tough as you seemed at first with these cuffs on you." Detective Washington shoved her toward the door.

"Fuck you, bitch! Let me go! You stupid bitch! I didn't do it!" she screamed and kicked her way out the door and to the police car.

When they had India and Jacob in the back of the squad cars, my mother walked over to me.

"Son." She shook her head while she placed a hand on my shoulder. "I didn't think you would actually have it in you to turn your own friend in." She rubbed my shoulder.

"I don't know about all that, but I will say the apple doesn't fall too far from the tree when it comes to a dirty cop raising one." I shrugged her off and walked over to the squad car where India continued to scream and cry.

I leaned down toward the patrol car and got as close as possible. Then I whispered, "This is the least you could do seeing that you just killed your sister. I hope you rot in there, bitch."

"But I didn't mean to. I would never hurt Tokyo!"

"You mean you would never hurt India?" I spat in her face and slammed the door shut.

As I was headed back to my own car, my mother was right on my heels. "What the fuck is that supposed to mean?" She snatched me around to face her. "Are you trying to say—"

"I'll never turn my nigga in after all he's done for us and even you! But in that car you do have his twin brother nobody ever knew existed. You got India in the back of that car too over there. Seeing the fact that I have wayyyy too much dirt on you, I suggest you take 'Tokyo and

Python'"—I pointed to the cars—"on down to the police station and get the ball rolling." I smirked then opened the door to my whip.

"You sneaky son of a bitch." She glared at me.

"Loyalty means everything. Oh, I forgot, you don't know shit about that." I pulled off.

CHAPTER THIRTY-NINE

TOKYO

"Ms. Miles, can you hear me? Try to keep your eyes open!" a slim mixed-looking woman said while cutting the blood-soaked shirt off of me.

Beeeeeeeeeeeep.

"Turn the defibrillator on now! She's flatlining!"

The slim lady pushed and pumped on my chest and blew into my mouth performing CPR but still got nothing.

The beefy EMS guy cut the bra off of me and began prepping for the IV. "It's at three hundred, ready!"

The lady yelled, "Cleeear!"

My body jerked, the machine beeped a few times, and then it stopped again.

"Have you gotten the IV started yet?" she asked as she rubbed the defibrillators together again.

"Yes, I'm injecting the adenosine now!"

"Come on!" The lady rubbed and squeezed my hand. "Come on, baby! You've got this!"

"It's at four hundred! Ready!"

"Cleeeeaar!"

My body jerked again. The machine beeped twice then stopped.

"Go for six hundred! Let me know when it's ready!"

A few quick moments passed, and the beefy guy said, "Go!"

"Cleeear!" My body jerked hard this time, lifting me off the bed. It felt like God Himself had snatched me up by the chest and slammed me into the gurney. I inhaled hard and deep and then dropped back onto the gurney. My eyes shot open as I began to look around for a familiar face. I felt myself starting to panic when I slightly realized I was in the ambulance and didn't see Python. I began to shake badly and jerk while my eyes rolled to the back of my head.

"Dammit! No! Come on! You gotta work with us! Fight! Come on! Dammit!" She pounded on my chest.

CHAPTER FORTY

LYNN

I sat in the truck taking long drags off my cigarette as I watched the ambulance drive off, sirens blasting and lights flashing. I sat off in the cut and watched everything. Those pig motherfuckers snatched Jacob's dumb ass up like a hawk. They had that dumb bitch India in one squad car and him in another. I looked in the back seat at the two sleeping government checks I had just inherited. As soon as I turned my head, the boy started to whimper.

"Shut the fuck up! Damn!" I yelled, looking back. Big fucking mistake on my end because that startled the other one and then she began to cry.

"Aw, hell to the fucking nah!" I started the truck up and backed up farther away from the house and deeper into the woods. I jumped out, walked around, and grabbed one car seat, then grabbed the other and sat them side by side behind the trees. I went back to the truck and grabbed the two baby bottles out of the passenger seat. I propped the bottles up in the crying brats' mouths and finally it was quiet.

I turned around just in time to see the squad car with India in it, pulling off.

"Grandma will be back for you two little guaranteed incomes in a few!" I smiled, throwing the blankets over them and jumping into the truck. I took a long gulp of my whiskey and revved the truck up. I pulled around the house and had a perfect beeline for the squad car that Jacob was in.

"Even if it is for the money, I ain't taking care of them damn things by my goddamn self!"

As the squad car slowly took off starting to head down the dirt road, I put the pedal to the metal and charged it full speed, lights out. The closer I got, the more my heart pounded.

"Aaahhhhhh!" I screamed as I rammed the small vehicle, causing it to instantly flip over and slide alongside the road, finally rolling and flipping into a ditch.

"Holy fucking shit! Oh, shit! Oh, fuck!" I laughed at myself as I hit the brakes and gripped the steering wheel. I stared in the direction where the car flipped off the side of the road. Finally, I got out and slowly crept over to take a look.

"Hhhhhelp me please." The officer reached out for me. He was pinned under the car and began choking on his blood while still reaching a hand out. I walked over to him and kicked him in the face, then grabbed his keys and flashlight. I began to frantically search the dark woods for Jacob. After a good fifteen minutes I spotted him face down next to a leaning tree.

"Get yo' bitch ass up. I may not have been shit to yo' ass, but I for damn sure taught yo' ass how to get the fuck back up!" I tried helping him up. Leaning him against the tree, I uncuffed him.

"Momma, we gotta get India," he said in between breaths.

"Boy, fuck her right now. We need to get you out of here."

I tried with everything in me to lift that big-ass boy, but he damn near broke me in half.

"It's broken," Jacob whined, referring to his torn, bloody leg.

"Well, hop on the other one, dumbass! I'll fix you up when we get home!"

When we got to the truck I put Jacob in the front. Climbing in myself, I put the whip in reverse and went to go get the twins. When I spotted them, I rolled my eyes, because one of them was hollering so damn loud.

"Yaws' mammie got yaw spoiled already and it ain't even been that long since yaw asses been born!" I snatched up both car seats and placed them in the back. Finally I got back in the truck, took a drink, and then peeled out. The sirens in the distance didn't bother me none.

CHAPTER FORTY-ONE

PYTHON

I paced back and forth in my living room with my mind racing about Tokyo's condition.

"Hey look, are you gonna come sit still so I can stitch up those holes in ya damn shoulder?" Doc asked as he watched my every move.

"I need to know if she's okay!" I almost yelled out in frustration.

As if on cue, my brother Jaheim came rushing through the door. "Mom is straight. She'll have stay for a few days, though no organs were hit. As far as Tokyo," he said, looking me in the eyes, "I don't know."

"What the fuck you mean you don't know?"

"You act like you more concerned about her ass than your own mother!" He got defensive.

"Man, don't fucking play that bullshit with me right now!" I shouted.

"They said they didn't have a Tokyo or an India Miles there! I had the bitch checked three times!"

"If you sit your ass down and let me fix you up, then I'll make a call for you and see where they have her." Doc smirked, holding a needle.

I sat down, and a couple minutes later Doc was on the phone.

"Oh, okay. Well, could you do me a favor and keep her listed as Jane Doe?" he said as he gave me a thumbs-up.

"Thank you, Lord," I said to myself.

Doc hung up the call. "Okay, so she's at St. Anthony's Hospital listed as Jane Doe. You cannot go and get her tonight or tomorrow, Python. There are two cops guarding her door. She's in really bad shape."

"How much for your wife to come take care of her?" I eyeballed him.

"Did you not just hear what the fuck I said?"

"How much?"

"I don't know! That's something you would have to ask her! Python, there is no way that girl will make it from that hospital to here and survive," he tried to reason with me.

"Well, I guess you don't know Tokyo like I do. I'm giving it three days, and then I'm going to get her." I walked off, leaving Doc and my brother alone.

"He's hardheaded. He doesn't listen." Doc shook his head.

"It's just blowing my mind that he's actually in love." Jahiem shrugged.

"In love? Python?" Doc busted out laughing, unable to control himself.

"You got a problem with me loving someone?" I walked back into the room dressed in all black.

"Where the fuck you going?" Jahiem asked as he watched me strap my guns on.

"To meet up with Buckey. You rolling or nah?"

"You need guns to meet up with Buckey?"

"Yep, because it's blowing my mind that he told us we could go and he would handle everything. It's also quite strange that he knows that my twin brother never made it to the police station. Plus, how did he know where we were tonight?"

"Well, Aunt Nelly told him and me."

I quickly looked up at him. "Well, that doesn't explain everything else." I walked toward the door.

"Well, let me get my shit too." Jaheim walked over to the safe that was on the side of the entertainment system.

"You guys mind if I tag along? I ain't had some fun in a long while." He smiled as we all burst into laughter.

CHAPTER FORTY-TWO

INDIA

"Ms. Miles, we can do this the easy way or the hard way. I'm only going to ask you one more time! What was your motive behind your uncle's death?"

"I didn't kill him!" I screamed for the thousandth time.

"Stop fucking lying!" Detective Washington slapped me hard across the face.

"I'm not." I began to cry. I was weak, and she was breaking me slowly but surely. My mouth was dry, I looked a mess, and the bitch wouldn't let me call my fucking lawyer or my father.

"You look kind of thirsty. Would you like some water?" the chubby detective asked as she filled up a Styrofoam cup. As bad as I wanted to taste that water, they could also kiss my ass.

"Fuck you, pig!" I snarled. The detective threw the cup of water on me.

"Hey now! Back away from my client!" Mrs. Peters, my and Tokyo's lawyer, entered the room.

"Oh, well, I bet you think you're hot shit because the number one lawyer in Kentucky is here." Detective Washington rolled her eyes.

"She is! Now give her some water and do as I said before I have you charged with psychological coercion!"

Detective Washington sucked her teeth and did as she was told. After I guzzled the water, I threw the cup at her. "I wanna speak to my lawyer alone."

"You heard her. Exit the room." Mrs. Peters cocked her head.

After a few moments, the detective left us alone, and Mrs. Peters turned toward me. "Tokyo, tell me what happened from beginning to end."

"Well, for starters I'm India." My voice cracked.

"Excuse me?"

"I'm serious. Tokyo is, well, I don't know."

"Sweetheart, I can't help you until you start making some sense."

"I'm not Tokyo. I shot Tokyo. But not on purpose! I don't know if she's alive. It's all complicated." I dropped my head.

"Well, I've got time." She took out her recorder, a notepad, and a pen. "Tell me how everything happened from beginning to end. We'll get this shit figured out."

I hesitated for a moment. Was I doing the right thing? Was this going to make me a snitch? I thought about what Python's friend said, and then I thought about my twins and started telling my lawyer everything from how Tokyo made Bryson disappear to the hits she had done and all. I wanted my babies and they needed me. I even told her about Jacob and his foster mother.

"This is all some sick, fucked-up, twisted, confusing shit!" Mrs. Peters sat back in her chair.

"Is there any way you can try to prove that I'm not Tokyo?"

She thought for a long, hard minute. "Wait, you said you gave birth to twins?"

"Yes."

"Well, there you go. All we have to do is get DNA from you and them, proving you're their mother."

"I don't get it."

"Tokyo is still a virgin, right?"

"I believe so."

"Well, that means she ain't gave birth to a child. There are records of your pregnancy with those twins and their birth."

"Well, not really. I mean, there are records of my pregnancy, but not their birth."

"What?"

"I had them at the house. They haven't even been to the hospital yet."

"That is a small bump. Tell me where the twins are, and we can prove who you are and get you the hell out of here."

"Jacob's foster mother took them."

"Well, where does she live?"

After I told Mrs. Peters everything she needed to know, she stood up to leave. No sooner than she got out of the room, Detective Washington entered the room.

"Let's roll, buttercup."

I got up slowly, trying to fight back the tears. As she walked me down the long hallway to my temporary cell, she whispered in my ear, "No matter what that lawyer does, it won't work. I'll make sure you go down for all those murders."

I whipped around and stared her in the eyes before hawking spit in her face. She wiped it off and chuckled. Next thing I knew, she headbutted me in the nose. I stumbled back, falling into the bars of an empty cell. Detective Washington grabbed me by the collar and hair and walked me toward the last cell in the hall. When it opened, she shoved me in and entered herself. She beat me until I could no longer scream.

When she finished, I was a bloody mess. Even with the pain that I felt, I still managed to say, "Bitch, when I get out, your ass is mines." She shut the cell and smirked before walking off.

CHAPTER FORTY-THREE

PYTHON

When I pulled up to Bryson's, I sat in the driveway for a minute. Because of tonight's events my mind was still cloudy. I watched his shadowed figure from the whip. "Bro, you good?" Jaheim laid a hand on my shoulder. "I don't know." "Well, let me tell you like this. Buckey is yo' right hand, and it's been that way since you guys were little. He ain't never done nothing to make you question his loyalty up until tonight, and even then he made sure you were straight. Don't go in there with that crazy shit. Hear him out."

I looked my brother in the eyes through the rearview mirror. "A'ight, I got you. Let's go."

Me, Jaheim, and Doc headed toward the door. When we reached the steps, Buckey opened the door.

"Aye, what's up?" He embraced me while nervously watching Doc and Jaheim. When we got in and sat down, I stared a hole into Buckey with a blank expression. He scratched his head and looked around at all three of us.

"You got me kind of nervous right now, Python." He chuckled.

"Tell me how you know everything you know." I continued to eyeball him.

"What you saying?"

"Buckey, we been cool for years. You know I don't like a motherfucker playing mind games with me."

Jaheim and Doc looked back and forth between me and him as we exchanged words. Next thing I knew, Buckey took out a badge and tossed it on the table, folding his arms. If that fool had been a snake, he would've bitten me in the ass.

"A fucking cop?" Jaheim's eyes got big.

"Detective. There's a difference."

"Nigga, when the fuck did you plan on telling me that you were a fucking pig?"

"For one, watch your fucking mouth, and for two, had you come to my ceremony, you would've known that. Or did you forget that I ever even invited you? You missed everything."

"Nigga, I told you I had a lick to do that week out of the country!"

"Well, then guess what? It's your fault you ain't know! I don't see what difference it makes! I'm still your best friend and right hand! I been keeping yo' ass safe and off them fuckers' radar ever since I was able to log into their system! And trust me when I say they were on to your ass! Especially my mother!"

"Fuck you mean?"

"Nigga, if it weren't for me, your ass would've been got buckled! I'm the one clearing they leads and evidence on you every time you slip up!"

Doc sat there looking dumbfounded and so did Jaheim while we argued. I don't know why, but after a while we all busted out laughing.

"So, you a dirty cop?" I shook my head.

"Nah, I do my job. I just look out for my best friend while doing so." He shrugged, then sat down. "And seeing that you ain't got nobody else doing it, you dead-ass kind of need me, Python."

"Well, now that that's over and we don't have to torture and kill his ass, can we figure out what's next?"

"I'm still going to get Tokyo. Let's focus on that. Doc, don't say shit. You know we can make it happen."

"I'm sure we could, but I think you need to have everything set up at your crib first before doing it. There's no way she'll make it more than a couple hours off those machines."

"Well, get it together. You know I have the money. In the meantime, I'm going to see her."

CHAPTER FORTY-FOUR

JACOB

I was mad as hell that Lynn took those fucking babies and brought them home with us. Seemed like they were crying every five minutes all day every day. If she wasn't trying to soothe one, then I was. It made it no better that she picked up a damn bottle of liquor instead of the baby bottle and almost stuck it in the baby's mouth.

"Hey! What are you doing?" I rushed over to her as the bottle touched the baby's lips.

"Boy, shit!" She took a swig. "I'm fucking tired! I didn't mean to! Take these damn things in there with you for a little while. I need some sleep!" She placed the baby back in his car seat and plopped on the couch, closing her eyes. I just shook my head and grabbed both car seats up and their diaper bag. They were running low on milk, and I needed to go get them some.

I took them downstairs in the lower part of the apartment building to Mrs. Betty to see if she could watch them while I went to go do so. She was more than happy to, saying that was the most company she had in years. I rushed out and drove to the farthest grocery store. I got out of the car and limped my way in.

Walking up to the young boy on the register, I put on a fake smile. "Hey, guy, where is your baby formula?"

He looked me up and down, then pointed straight ahead. "Aisle seven, the baby aisle." He watched me as I made my way to it. When I got right there, I was confused as fuck. There were so many different kinds. I read over all the labels and decided on Similac. Grabbing eight containers and placing them in my basket, I rushed back to the front. When I walked up to the young guy again, he jumped hard as hell. I didn't know why, but for some reason he looked really nervous. He rang them all up, occasionally looking at me.

"Will you be paying this with cash or voucher?" He stumbled over his words.

"How much? You ain't tell me a price."

"Uhm, that's going to be $126.25, sir." He looked at me, then the formula, and dropped his head. That's when I noticed the wanted poster behind his head. It was a picture of my twin though. Now I knew why the little shit was so fucking nervous. I was even more pissed off that I didn't have enough for that high-ass formula.

"Hey, I'm going to go back out to my car really quick and get my card. Keep these right here for me, is that cool?" I put on a cheesy smile.

"Sure, that's perfectly fine."

I walked out calmly. Once I made it past the doors I spotted a security guard. When I got to my car, I pulled out my gym bag and emptied everything onto the back seat. Then I pulled out my winter mask and put it on. I went to the front and grabbed my gun and cocked it, putting it into my waist band. But when I walked back up to the doors, I grew nervous as hell.

There weren't that many people in there, so I knew I could make this quick without hurting anyone. As soon as I got close to the counter, the young guy instantly knew what was up.

"Oh, shit." He instantly got ready to cry.

"Look, make this shit fast. Put all those cans into the bag along with the money in the register." I flashed my gun on my hip. The lady on the side of me began to back up slowly. He did as he was told, and that's when I heard someone yell, "Freeze!" just as the boy emptied the register. I grabbed the bag and spun around and started firing shots, taking the security guard down with three others. People started running and screaming and ducking for cover.

My big ass ran as fast I could out of there as I shouted, "Fuck! Fuck! Fuck!" the whole time. When I got in the car, I peeled the hell out and almost wrecked into a small SUV. Swerving around it, I sped past the stop sign and right into traffic. I did at least eighty the whole way back to the projects. When I got there, I parked around back, snatched the bag out, and ran around to the front.

Rushing into the building, I knocked down a young guy throwing a basketball against the wall.

"Damn, watch out, big bitch!" he spat, looking up at me. I didn't have time to reply to his little smart ass as I made my way to Mrs. Betty's door. After three knocks she answered.

"You gotta be quiet. Them babies is sleeping in my room. The girl is fussy. She got a rash. Are you babysitting for somebody?" She looked at me suspiciously as I held the gym bag.

"No, ma'am, they are mine." I blushed.

"Say what now? Yo' momma ain't told me nothing about them cuties in there, and that bitch tells me everything." She smiled while patting me on the back.

"Yeah, we just wanted to make sure they were mines first."

"Makes sense to me. Well, anyhoo, I fried some flour and put it in her diaper to soothe her little butt. It's an old-school remedy. I got some more I put into a plastic baggie so you can take it with you."

"Thank you so much." I kissed her on the cheek. "You ain't as fucked up as my mother makes you out to be." I walked into her room, getting the twins.

"Mmm hmm, that no-good wench. And tell her ass she still owe me fifteen dollars for washing them damn clothes for her drunk ass." She folded her arms.

I reached into the gym bag and pulled out a $20 bill, handing it to her. She took it and quickly stuffed it into her bra. I tried my best to balance the duffle bag, diaper bag, and the twins as I made my way up to our floor. When I got in, Lynn was nowhere in sight.

"Thank goodness," I said as I walked back to my room. I set them down gently on the bed, took off the hoodie I had on, and placed both bags on the floor. I went into the duffle bag. I pulled out a can of formula and went into the kitchen to make them a bottle before they woke up. When I walked into the room, I scooped them up one by one and laid them on my bed, placing a blanket over them.

This shit wasn't as hard as Lynn made it seem. I crept out of the room and went to take a shower. By the time I got finished, I heard the door unlocking. I rushed out, wrapping a towel around my body so I could get in there and tell Lynn they were sleeping. She stumbled her way into the door with her arms full of bags smiling from ear to ear.

"Shhh!" I signaled her. She sucked her teeth and started dropping the bags.

"Don't tell me to shush!" she said in a whisper.

"They sleeping, so you wake them up, you get them!" I said sternly and low.

"Aw, damn! But look!" She started cheesing again. She started grabbing bags and emptying them onto the floor. Baby bottles, onesies, pacifiers, sleepers, booties, and all fell onto the floor.

"What's all this?" I looked around.

"Well, they need things and they ain't had no damn bath! Did you go get some formula? If not, I got a few of them cans, too." She emptied another bag.

"Where did you get all this, and like how?" I picked up a pack of bibs that was obviously for the boy.

"Boy, you know how I get down. I took your brother's credit card. I was swiping away for these babies." She laughed. A few moments later, some slim, skinny guy came barging in the door with more bags and carrying a big-ass box that contained a baby tub.

"Who the fuck are you?" I looked him up and down.

"Mind yo' damn business." Lynn stood up and walked toward him. "Thanks, Albert!" She snatched a bag off his arm that I was sure had nothing but liquor in it.

"It ain't nothing, doll baby." He set everything down and headed toward the door. He turned around when he stepped out. "You still gonna go on that date with me?" He put on a crooked, toothless smile.

"I'll think about it!" She slammed the door in his face. Big mistake, because one of the twins started to whimper.

"Gaaaaat damn!" I shouted as I made my way back to my room.

CHAPTER FORTY-FIVE

PYTHON

I paced back and forth through the living room, trying to figure how the fuck somebody swiped $3,000 off my fucking card. There were people bringing in and setting up everything I would need in order to keep Tokyo here and safe. Doc's wife was here telling them what to do and where to put things and setting up all the meds she would need for her. She noticed the look on my face and walked over.

"You okay?" She placed a hand on my shoulder.

"Yeah, I'm smooth. How much longer is this shit going to take?" I asked out of frustration.

"Damn!" she laughed. "You're really anxious to get her here, huh? Go fix you a drink or something. In a few hours, she will be right here in the comfort of your home for us to keep an eye on her."

"Yeah, but that shit seems like it's going to take forever. I should've gone with them to get her." I cursed myself.

"Well, that would've screwed shit up seeing that your face is on the news for a lot of fucked-up shit that done went down in this past week."

"But it wasn't me. That's just like somebody been using my fucking credit card. I had to cancel that shit today."

"I got someone who can look into that for you and find out who." She rocked back and forth on her heels.

"Yeah?"

"My and Doc's oldest son. The apple didn't fall too far from the tree. He's one hell of a tech genius and a damned good hacker. Give me a few and I'll call him for you." She looked at one of the guys setting up a machine. "What the hell are you doing? Don't set that up right there! It'll be too damn far from the bed!" She walked off fussing.

I went to the minibar and fixed a big-ass glass of whiskey straight. Guzzling as much as I could handle at once, I grabbed my vibrating cell phone out of my pocket. It was the people Doc sent to go get Tokyo.

"Speak," I answered.

"We're an hour away. Is everything ready?" a chick asked on the other end.

"Yeah, just about."

"See you in a few." She hung up.

"Yo, hurry the fuck up. They are about to be here in an hour!" I yelled as I headed for my basement. When I got down there, I went straight to my safe. Once I stepped inside, I filled up a bag with money. Doc and his wife could do the honors of paying their crew. When I got back upstairs, I finished my drink and sat on the couch with his wife as her crew began filing out.

"Everything is finished. That's the money?" She pointed at the bag.

"Yeah." I handed it over. "Five hundred twenty thousand dollars."

Doc came strolling in and she gave the bag to him. "It's payday, gentlemen!" he yelled. The men he had there followed him to another part of the living room as he began to hand out money.

"You really love this girl?" she asked as she looked at me out of the corner of her eyes.

"Yeah, and I ain't never loved no woman except my mother. All these hoes want nowadays is dick and money.

Tokyo is about her own bread. She done ran a few hits with me and I ain't even have to teach her shit. She crazy like me, love her family, and she loyal. You know loyalty plays a big part with me. Especially with the shit that I do."

"Understandable."

We sat around talking until I heard a knock at the door. When I opened it, they wheeled Tokyo in on a bed.

"Man, why the fuck would yaw bring her in on a damn bed to the front door! I said the fucking back door!" I was mad as hell as I looked around outside to make sure nobody saw.

"Well, she's here now. Pay up, playa." The short chick in scrubs put her hand out. I wanted to choke the shit out of that little short bitch. I pulled a stack of money out of my back pocket and handed it to her as the males with her sat Tokyo in the bed and covered her up. They left and I walked over to her. She was sleeping. Doc's wife began to hook her up to all the machines. I just sat back and watched. Looking her over, this seemed like this was the most peace that girl had ever had in her life.

"Okay, now that that's finished, let her rest. I made sure that they gave her enough morphine before hitting the road to keep her asleep. She may or may not wake up in a few hours, but that's okay. At least she is breathing on her own, which is odd. Nobody gets back to doing that with those types of gunshots."

"I wanna see." I pointed.

"See what?"

"The gunshot wounds." I looked at her.

She pulled the cover back and lifted the gown, exposing Tokyo's naked body underneath. There were three scars, two not far from each other on her chest and one under her right breast.

"I thought they said she was shot four times," I said.

"She was. The other shot was in the side of her head. Now that's where an issue may or may not lie. She could suffer some type of memory loss to be honest." She began to take the head wrap off.

"I don't wanna see that shit." I backed up.

"It's not as bad as you think. They did, however, have to shave the side of her head in order to fix it and put the plate in and all that mess. The scar is long but not too big. I'm sure her hair will grow back quick."

"I'm sure she gonna be pissed the fuck off when she see it." I laughed a nervous one.

"Well, I'm going to change her IV and then I'll be on my way. I'll be back in a few hours, gonna head home and pack a few bags. She'll be fine." She rubbed Tokyo's arm. "She's a beautiful girl, and I don't see what she saw in your big ass." She laughed.

"Shiiittt, I'm a handsome-ass guy." I rubbed my beard and walked her to the door. When she pulled off, I fixed another drink, turned the TV on, and occasionally glanced over at the sleeping, beautiful demon in my living room. A few times I had to mute the TV because I thought I heard her moan or make a sound. I would be lying if I said I didn't jump hard as fuck when her hand moved up to her head and then went back down to her side. I got up and walked over to her.

"Tokyo?" I leaned over her. Got no response. "Tokyo, can you hear me?" I rubbed her arm and still got nothing. I sighed and went back over to the couch. After a while I dozed off watching ESPN. When I woke up around three in the morning, Doc's wife was sitting in a chair next to Tokyo reading a book, and my Aunt Nelly was in the kitchen cooking something. I stretched, then went in there.

"You hungry, boy?" she asked as she quickly eyeballed me while she worked her way around the kitchen.

"Yes, ma'am."

She set a plate down in front of me, with fried chicken and rice. She then poured me a glass of orange juice. She fixed herself and Doc's wife a plate, then sat down at the table. We ate in silence. It was an awkward one.

"You got something you wanna say, Aunt Nelly?" I bit a piece of my chicken.

"I wanna know why you thought it would be a good idea to go there by ya damn self when all this happened. Thank God I ain't listen to your ass and I told your brother and Buckey. I also wanna know why you thought it would be a good idea to bring that girl here with the condition she in." She glanced up at me.

"I had to. There's a lot that happened, and eventually when she woke up, they would've arrested her, I'm sure."

"Because of you or her own doings?"

"Both."

"Okay."

I finished my meal and was about to walk out of the kitchen when she asked, "You sure you doing the right thing, boy?"

"Yes, ma'am."

"Well, then I guess that's all that matters."

Doc's wife ended up having their son come over the next morning. I didn't know if he looked more like her or him. He was excited as hell to meet me.

"Man, this shit is sweet!" He beamed as he looked around. His mother walked up and slapped him in the back of the head.

"Don't be cursing around me, junior."

"Sorry." He rubbed his head. "So anyway, I put your info in and tracked where your card had been used at. Somebody spent a lot at Babies"R"Us and at a liquor store called JR's Liquor. I have the footage of her." He sat down and opened his laptop, pressing a few keys. When it showed the footage, I instantly became furious as fuck! It was that bitch-ass brother's foster mammie of his using my shit. It also struck me that the bitch still had those babies. What other reason would she have to be buying all that baby shit?"And in this clip from the liquor store. It's the same woman." He zoomed in on her face.

"Send me a pic of that bitch to my phone."

"Cool, you know her?"

"Hell yeah, little guy. You don't know how much shit you just helped me with and ended for me." I rubbed my hands together.

"I told you, he's a good one." His mother smiled, rubbing his head.

"Ma! Geez! Don't do that!" He tried to finger comb his blond hair back down.

I jumped on the phone and called my brother and Buckey. When they got there, Buckey set his computer down.

"I need you to find out who adopted my brother. And where they live at now. He still has the same last name."

"That won't be hard. Give me a few minutes."

"What's up?" Jaheim asked.

"I'm going to end that fucker and that bitch who raised him." I bit my bottom lip. "Plus, she has those twins."

"How you know she got those babies?"

"She's the one who's been swiping my fucking card buying all types of baby shit. It only makes sense, right?"

"Yeah, you right." He sat down. "But why would you be going to get the twin babies?" He looked at me suspiciously.

"Because with India behind bars, Tokyo is going to want them with her. I know that for a fact. Might as well kill two birds with one stone, right?"

CHAPTER FORTY-SIX

JACOB

When I went back to Mrs. Betty's apartment to get the twins after me and Lynn got back, she told me there was a cop who knocked on our door and was asking the younger cats in the building if they had seen me around anywhere. That shit made me nervous as hell.

"You sure they were looking for me?" I asked, picking up the twins.

"Yeah, they had a picture of you and Lynn."

"Where is she anyway?"

"She went upstairs already. She drunk as hell." I shook my head. "Hey, Mrs. Betty, thanks for everything." I turned to her, giving her an apologetic look.

"You wanna tell me why this is going on?"

"I honestly don't know. When I find out, you'll be the first to know since I can only talk to you about things anyway."

"I know that's right. That damn momma of yours don't stay sober enough for a decent conversation."

I walked out, headed for our apartment. I was going to tell Lynn to pack what she could so we could hit the road. After the shit we had done, we had stayed there far too long anyway. Which was dumb as fuck on our part with all the cop shows and what not that we watched on her thirty-two-inch TV.

When I reached the door, I heard a little commotion on the inside. I sat the twins down and pressed my ear against the door.

"Bitch, tell me where he at with those babies!" I heard someone say.

"I don't know where the fuck he is, nigga! Get the fuck out!"

"Bitch, you going with me then!" I heard something crash then heard a loud thump! When I heard footsteps coming toward the door, I picked up the twins and hauled ass. Skipping a step or two, I held them high in the air to keep a good balance and to keep from hitting their car seats against the railing or walls. When I reached the third floor, I heard gunshots ring out. Bullets flew past my head, bouncing off the concrete walls.

"Oh, shit!" I fell against the wall.

"Don't run, bitch nigga! Give me those babies!"

I looked up at a furious Python. "Fuck you!" I regained my balance and continued down the stairs. When I got outside, busting through the main door, the same kid I had knocked down a few days ago ran up to me smiling with two other boys in tow.

"Hey, mister, you need some help?" I handed him one car seat and handed the other one the diaper bag.

"Follow me!" I ordered.

"Hey, I can carry the other one! My mom lets me all the time!" the chunky one shouted. I glanced over my shoulder as we darted around the back of the building.

"Hold this." I handed him the other car seat as I turned around to unlock the truck. Lynn never returned. "Put them in the back!" I ordered, but when I turned around the boys were running off with the babies.

I began to run after them until Python's big ass came running around the building firing shots at me. I quickly turned around and jumped into the truck, speeding off. I banged the steering wheel as I sped out of the back parking lot. I vowed to kick those kids' asses when I saw them again. I drove until I was sure nobody was following me. Driving up to a run-down motel, I parked and counted the money in my pocket. I was glad I still had the money I got from that stick-up move I pulled at the grocery store even though eight hundred bucks wasn't much. I got out, checked my surroundings, and walked in the main entrance.

There was a bald, older guy watching a tiny television. I stood there and waited for him to take his eyes off the TV, which he never did.

"You gonna stand there looking silly or you want something, boy?" he asked as he continued watching the gray and white screen.

"Uh, yeah, can I get a room please?"

"For a couple hours, a couple days, what?"

"Just a couple of hours I guess." I pulled out the money and he finally looked up.

"Well," he said, looking around me to see if there was anyone else there, "we don't allow that whoring and pimping shit here. So if a complaint comes in, I'll be asking you to leave. No refunds either."

"That's cool." I handed him the money and took my room key. When I got in, it stunk of mildew and weed, and there was an empty rice container on the table by the bed with a half-empty pop bottle.

"Damn, they don't even clean these fucking rooms." I sat down on the bed about to think about my next move, when I heard something coming from the bathroom. I jumped up and patted my waist for my gun, then realized I had left it in the truck. I grabbed the lamp off the nightstand and wrapped the cord around my hand and arm. Whoever was in there was about to get a migraine straight from hell, maybe even a fucking concussion. I snatched the door open, and a woman fell out screaming.

"Holy fucking shit!" I yelled as I lifted the lamp, then lowered it.

"Oh, fuck! I am so sorry! Please don't tell my boss!" she pleaded as she picked up the blunt she dropped.

"I ain't gonna tell. What the fuck are you doing smoking on the job though?" I unwrapped the lamp cord and set it back down.

"Mind your business." She got up, dusting herself off.

"Uh, you in my room. I'm not the one at work." I pointed at her nametag.

"Well, I guess you're right about that." She took another drag, then looked at me. "You smoke?" She held it out in my direction.

"Nah, not really."

"Well, not really don't mean no, so here."

I took it from her and took the longest pull that my big-ass lungs could handle. I instantly started choking when I exhaled.

"Yeeeah, buddy, that's that good shit." She laughed, taking it back from me. "You from around here?"

"No," I answered, still trying to get some air in my lungs. "Why you ask?"

"'Cause I ain't never seen a guy as fine or as big as you around here." She looked me up and down, smiling seductively. I looked around the room then back at her. She wasn't ugly, and I could tell she had a nice body under that maid's dress. It had been a while since I had some ass, and if she was about to offer, I sure as fuck wasn't about to turn it down.

She walked over to me and sat down on the bed and passed the blunt back. "You got a condom?"

"What? No."

"I do." She reached in her bra and pulled one out. My fucking jaw dropped. Soon the weed kicked in and she left to go steal a bottle of liquor from the front desk. When she returned, she was already drinking from it with no problem. I took a few swigs of it, then took my clothes off, throwing them on the chair. She didn't bother undressing. She just climbed on top of me and put the condom on my dick after she sucked it until it got hard.

It felt so damn good when she slid down on me. I gripped her waist and rocked her back and forth on me, feeling my dick get even harder. She stood on her feet and started bouncing up and down until she worked up a climax. I was so fucking high and tipsy I didn't care that she got off me. She slid the condom off and kept sucking my dick until I came all in her mouth. I had never had a female do that shit before, and I had to say, she sucked dick a lot better than India ever did.

Soon after, she got me back hard and climbed back on top of me without another condom. I didn't even care. You only live once, right? We went another two rounds before I passed out in the bed with her in my arms.

When I woke up, the clock on the wall said it was well past four in the morning. I sat up quick, looking around the dark room. The girl who was in there with me was no longer in sight. I noticed my pants were on the floor. Jumping up, I ran over and picked them up, searching the pockets. That little bitch had taken my money and the credit card I had in my pocket.

I didn't give a fuck about the card, that was Python's, but she had taken the only money I had left! I was pissed the fuck off as I put my clothes back on. When I was done, I snatched the keys to the truck and ran toward the front office.

I burst through the door and startled the old man this time.

"What the hell is wrong with you?" He jumped back, grabbing his chest.

"Where is the girl who was cleaning rooms! She stole my shit while I was asleep!" I roared.

"Say what now? How you know it was her if your ass was asleep?" He smiled.

"Look, old timer! Don't fucking play with me! That was my last! I need that money! Now where is she?" I banged my fist on the counter.

"Hey now, just calm down," he chuckled. "She quit when she came back from your room. Might I add, she was in your room with you for a long while. I ain't no damn dummy. You fucked her and she fucked ya ass back when you passed out." He laughed hard and loud. That pissed me off even more.

"You think shit is funny?" I sucked my teeth. "I got something funny for your ass." I walked out, headed for the truck. I got my gun out, cocked it, and walked back in. He was still laughing, bouncing around his raggedy-ass chair.

"Give me all the fucking money you got in that god-damn register, nigga!" I pointed the gun at him.

"Holy goddamn fucking shit!" His eyes grew big.

"You heard me! Give it up! Since me getting robbed was funny, let's see if you think it's funny, my nigga!"

"Calm down!"

"I'm not gonna ask again." I took the safety off. This time, fear washed over him as he opened the register. He handed me two twenties and a ten. I looked at it, then at him, and smirked.

"What?" he asked with his hands up. "That's all I got, what you gave me to stay here."

I stepped back and fired two shots into his head, sending him flying back against the wall. Blood shot everywhere. I quickly scanned and searched through the office looking for anything of value. I came across a small wooden box that was attached to the bottom of the counter. Snatching it off, I opened it, revealing four big knots of money.

"You lying sack of shit!" I spat on his lifeless body and kicked him before taking the chain around his neck and the gold Rolex he had on his wrist.

CHAPTER FORTY-SEVEN

PYTHON

I never thought I would see the day that I would be catering to a baby. Hell, even when me and Tokyo talked about it, she would brush that shit off. I didn't see what all the hype was about when people said dealing with babies was hard. Let alone two at the same time. My aunt Nelly was a big help and so was Doc's wife. Even though I told her she didn't have to help, seeing I had her there to take care of Tokyo. But they were both so excited to have newborns in the house it didn't make any sense.

My mom was there too, but she didn't really wanna touch them because she felt it wasn't right after everything that happened. I didn't see the issue with anything because, at the end of the day, they were Tokyo's niece and nephew. I kind of liked them being there. It gave me something else to keep my mind on besides Tokyo. It had been two weeks since they were there. We hadn't seen or heard anything about Jacob. It was even hard for Buckey and Doc's son to track him down and they were working together.

After laying the twins down in their cribs, I went to take a shower. When I got out, my mom was coming out of the guest bedroom.

"She's been moving her hands and feet more. I think she's going to wake up soon, baby." She leaned against the wall.

"That's good."

"You seem a little distracted."

"I am. This shit is just going to keep going on until I kill that nigga. I gotta kill him."

"What about India?"

"She's locked up. They about to charge her with everything Tokyo did."

"And you think that's right?"

"You reap what you sow, you know that?"

"Man, what is it that you want from me?" I turned toward her in frustration.

"Why did you have to choose this lifestyle?"

"I didn't, it chose me. Hell, Jaheim introduced me to this shit. It seemed like a good idea at the time. Did I think I would get this far and high up in it? No. But I did and ain't no turning back."

"So you gonna sell drugs, kill people, and just do what the fuck you wanna do for the rest of your life?"

"Pretty much. Anything else?"

"Nope, I am going to head over to Carlos Miles's house though." She smacked her lips. I couldn't do anything but shake my head and smile. Anything to keep her from carrying on the conversation she tried to start. The whole thing about me changing my life around. I was a street nigga and that's how it was going to end for me.

I threw on some sweatpants and T-shirt and my house shoes and went back downstairs. I didn't see Doc's wife anywhere around so I figured she would be in the room with the twins. I glanced over in Tokyo's direction and almost shit myself when I saw her sitting up, giving me the look of death.

"Bitch-ass nigga, if I could walk, I would kill you! Why am I here?" she screamed, looking around. I guess the pain she was in humbled her ass, because she grabbed her side and winced.

"Tokyo, baby, it's me, Python." I slowly walked over toward her. It was dimly lit on her side, so I turned the lights on completely.

"What the fuck?" she yelled, covering her eyes.

"Oh, shit, my bad, baby." I laughed.

"Stop calling me baby, nigga! And turn that shit back off!" she demanded.

I shook my head and left them on. "Just give your eyes some time to adjust to the light." I folded my arms. Her monitors started beeping uncontrollably.

Susan came rushing in. "Hey, sweetie, take it easy." She walked to Tokyo's side.

"Where am I at?"

"Well, do you remember Python? Or anything about what happened?"

"I don't know, everything is kind of . . . I just don't know." She lay back in the bed.

"Well, just stay calm, gorgeous."

"Why is this bandage on my head?" She started tugging at it.

"Let me help you with that. I'm going to tell you now, you won't be happy about this, but your hair will grow back, okay?"

"The fuck you mean my hair will grow back?" She put her hand to the side of her head as soon as the bandage came off. "What the fuck?" She jumped up from the bed and fell to the floor.

"Tokyo!" Susan grabbed her before she could fully impact.

Once she was back in bed, I brought her a handheld mirror. She snatched it from me and looked at her head as she began to cry.

"What the fuck?" she whimpered as she ran her hand along the staples on the side of her head. The scar wasn't that big, but that shit was definitely noticeable. I stood there and waited for her to stop.

"You were shot in the head." I looked at the floor. "And in the chest and shit."

She glanced at me. "What you mean?"

"Tokyo, you dead-ass don't remember who I am?"

"I know who you are, but why am I here?"

"Because I thought it would be better for you to wake up here than to wake up in the hospital handcuffed to a bed. Then have them take you to jail."

"Jail for what?"

After I explained everything to her, she actually let me hold her while she cried. Eventually, Susan gave her some more pain meds and she soon fell back to sleep.

CHAPTER FORTY-EIGHT

TOKYO

I didn't know if I wanted to believe him. Everything was funny about what happened. I didn't believe my sister shot me. I didn't remember her having the babies. I didn't remember anything but Python fighting and gunshots. I just couldn't make sense of anything. I sat in bed watching some movie called *Zombieland: Double Tap* while eating my breakfast. The nurse, who I assumed Python hired, sat next to me. Every time I reached for something, she was getting it for me. I rolled my eyes when I reached for my throw-up bag and she jumped up onto her feet.

"Look, Susan, calm down, okay? I got it." I threw up in the bag. She had told me not to eat too heavily because, with the meds, it would make me sick. After I was done, she still wiped my face and mouth with a hot rag. I shook my head and smiled.

"Sorry, this is literally my job. I actually take care of people."

"Well, thank you anyways. I'm sorry, this whole thing just has me so fucked up."

"Well, I will say this, if it'll help out any, I saw your hair beforehand and the look you're rocking with your head half shaved is actually pretty fucking dope on you." She shrugged.

"You really think so?" I rubbed the side of my head again.

"Yeah, I love it. Get it shaped up and get some curls thrown in and you'll be killing shit more than you were before."

"Okay." I smiled. "I can rock with that."

"Another thing, you should believe Python. I've known him for years and he is seriously telling the truth. He has a detective friend working on everything for you two. Some chick got arrested named India and she is taking the wrap for some stuff you did supposedly."

"India is my twin sister." I looked away.

"Well, now it all really makes sense. Wait a minute! Those beautiful babies up the hall are her babies?" she almost squealed.

"Yeah, hey, can you bring them in here so I can see them please?"

"Sure thing." She walked off. Soon she returned carrying two car seats.

I was in shock and awe at how handsome and beautiful they were. They looked just like India and Bryson. I felt a queasy feeling in the pit of my stomach. When I picked up the girl, who had the same color eyes as her mother, I let a few tears fall. I felt like a piece of shit. If everything Python said was true, then I had royally fucked over my sister.

After me and Susan fed them both and burped them, she changed their diapers and took them to lie back down. Python entered the house a few moments later.

"Hope you don't mind, but I went to your house and grabbed you a few of your jogging suits, shoes, and all that."

"She doesn't need any shoes. She does not need to be walking around right now." Susan sat down.

"She's gonna have to. We need to go somewhere right now and quick." He looked worried.

"Fuck that, tell me what the problem is." I glared at him.

"Your father is in the hospital. He had a heart attack, Tokyo." He dropped his head.

When those words left his lips, I made my way out of the bed and slowly got dressed in one of the jogging suits he handed me. Susan and Miss Nelly stayed at the house with the twins. When we got to the hospital, Python asked for a wheelchair for me. The nurses gave him one, and we went to my father's room. Before we made it to the door, I felt a cold feeling rush over me. I had come into contact too many times to know when death was nearby. My heart sank when I saw a chaplain walk out of the room.

I looked to the ceiling as tears threatened to fall. Python placed a hand on my shoulder as he wheeled me into the room. The shades were drawn and there was gospel music playing lowly in the background. When I got close enough to my father's side, I grabbed his hand. It was cold. I tried to squeeze it to see if he would squeeze it back, but he didn't. I noticed the machines weren't plugged up or even on.

"Dad!" I yelled, crying on his hand. "I am so sorry, Dad! I'm so sorry! Please forgive me!" I couldn't control myself. All the while I had all this shit going on, I hadn't spent much time with my father. I had barely even called him.

"I should've been there more. You were always there for me and India. I fucked up so bad this time. I fucked up really bad. I'm so sorry. You didn't even get to see the babies." I screamed so loud. I felt like my whole heart had been shattered into a thousand pieces and set on fire. I didn't think I would have to go through this alone without my sister. She was locked up and didn't know what was happening. It really sucked because neither of us got to say goodbye. He was already gone.

I stood up out of the wheelchair and lay in the bed with him. I cried until I had no more tears left to cry. I now didn't have my father or my sister here with me. I pulled my father's arm over me just to feel some type of comfort one more time. After a while a nurse came in with papers for me to sign to release my father's body to the funeral home.

A few hours later, they came to get him. I didn't want to let them take him away. I just wasn't ready. I cried even more when they asked us to leave the room. I sat outside the door and watched as they cleaned him up and then placed him into a body bag. I shook my head and told Python to take me back to the house. When I got there, all I could do was sit next to the twins' crib and rub their tiny arms and hands.

"We all we got left now, and I swear with everything in me, I'll always be there for the both of you every single day and I'll always protect you guys." I began to cry. After I said a silent prayer over my niece and nephew, I rolled myself back to my bed.

"Hey, Tokyo, I know now isn't the right time, but I have the twins' birth certificates right here. I hope it wasn't a problem, but me and Python named them both because no one else had."

I looked at the birth certificates. Python and I were listed as the parents. Ryan and Rya'Lynn Miles were their names. I had to admit, they had a ring to them. I slightly smiled, said, "Thank you," and rolled over to go to sleep.

CHAPTER FORTY-NINE

PYTHON

I shook my head as I adjusted my tie. Today was Tokyo's father's funeral and I was ready to get it over with. Everything had been so hectic up until now. I was ready to get Tokyo and the twins away for a while. She needed some relaxation away from everyone and everything. It was even more awkward when she came into my room last night and asked me to make love to her. She had started regaining her memory and it was a damn good thing to me.

I walked out of the room and into the twins' room where she and my mother had just finished getting the twins dressed. I stood watching from afar admiring the good job she had done. They looked like little lawyers or something in their black-and-white suits. I smiled as she and my mom held them up, smiling.

We left and headed straight for the church. When we got inside, there were a ton of people there. Everyone turned around and looked at Tokyo. She strutted her stuff, head held high as she carried one of the twins. She walked and sat right up front, and my mother and I did the same. Everyone walked up to view his body and gave their condolences as they passed, some hugging her and some just rubbing her hand or shoulder.

My mother stood up and walked up to the podium. She read a letter that Tokyo's father had written to her before he died.

"'Dear Tokyo.'" She sniffled. "'Before anything, I want you to know that I love you and India dearly. If this is being read to you right now, then you know the good Lord has called me home. Don't cry for me, because I lived my life and was blessed enough to see you and India grow up. Don't ever feel like you didn't do your best, because whether you see it or not, you did.'" She smiled. "'I am so proud of you girls, and I pray that India completes college. That nurse's badge would look really good on her. Look at my girl, a nurse. I'm so happy and proud writing this. I love you girls. And I will always be a step behind you in whatever you do. You two have to remember to take care of each other and love each other no matter what. Never let anyone or life come between you, because in the end all you girls have is each other. I love you and take care.'"

People clapped and some shouted, "Amen," as my mom walked back to her seat. It was finally almost over, and everything was going smoothly until they were about to close the casket.

"Wait a moment," a voice called out.

We all turned to look, and a lot of people gasped as India was escorted down the aisle buckled at the ankles and wrists. Tokyo instantly threw up looking at her and started crying. India leaned over and kissed her father, placing a rose on his chest. She turned to face Tokyo and me. They just looked at each other before India burst into tears. Tokyo stood up and hugged her sister.

"I am so sorry," she whispered in Tokyo's ear. "Please take care of my babies until all this blows over. Please." She sobbed some more. The guard walked up and pulled her away. I watched as they escorted her back out.

Glancing in the back, I noticed some detectives in the back. Buckey's mom stood out like a sore thumb, smiling. When everyone stood up to leave the church, I grabbed Tokyo by the arm, and we all left through a different door. When we got in the truck, I sped off for the airport. I had been in this situation one too many times not to know what was about to happen. India's ass had figured out a way to get Tokyo buckled. Not on my watch though.

"Python! We have to go to the gravesite! Where are you going?" she panicked.

"Baby, I'm sorry and I'll make it up to you." I looked in the rearview. "But we on the run now."

CHAPTER FIFTY

JACOB

I walked into the bank searching for a particular teller. When I spotted the fake blonde, I casually made my way over to her window. She looked up at me, then at the clock. I waited a few moments for her to give the signal.

"Tabitha, I'm headed out for lunch. Want anything back?" A chubby black guy who was obviously security smiled at her.

"No, I'm good, Mr. Griggs. What time is Allen coming in?"

"He's a few minutes behind. Should be here within the next five minutes. I'm sure you all will be okay for a few minutes while I go get something to tame this hungry beast!" He patted his big, round belly.

"You know I keep some Mace on me anyways." She smiled.

I started to grow impatient as he walked out the door. Me and Tabitha made eye contact, and then she tapped her fingers.

"Hello, sir, how may I assist you today?" She smiled nervously.

I pulled out my gun. "Give me all the fucking money you have back there and make the shit quick!" I gritted my teeth.

"Oh, my God!" she shouted and threw her hands up.

"Don't fuck with me, bitch! Do it now!"

People dropped to the floor, and some let out a few screams. I spun around. "Don't nobody move and won't nobody get fucked up in this bitch!" I aimed at different people attempting to make their way toward the door.

Tabitha rushed off and was back in a flash with two duffle bags and a backpack.

"Please don't shoot me!" she begged with fake tears falling.

I snatched the bags and ran out the door as quick as I came. As soon as I reached my car, the alarms inside the bank went off. The chubby security guard who had been there earlier was crossing the street.

"Hey! Stop right there!" he yelled as he reached for his gun, dropping everything else in his hands.

I dropped the duffle bags next to the car and fired two shots at him, causing him to dive on the ground. When he did, I snatched the car door open and threw the money inside. I hit a parked car as I backed up and then peeled out, occasionally ducking my head at the shots the officer was firing.

Every few minutes while I was driving, I checked my rearview. That was the easiest shit I had ever done in my life! I thought it would've been more complicated, but with an unhappy ratchet bitch working in a place like that—who was hypnotized by dick—anything was possible, I guess. I drove another hour headed back to the motel where me and my foster mother, Lynn, were staying.

When I pulled into the lot, it was almost empty. I grabbed the bags and got out. Walking into the room, I noticed Lynn packing her bags back up. She jumped at the sight of me.

"Going somewhere?" I smirked.

"Well, shit, I ain't think yo' dumb ass was gonna pull it off or make it back." A loose cigarette dangled from her lips. "Anyways, that old-ass maid been snooping around here too much for my liking." She continued to pack.

"And?"

"And she had a newspaper in her cart with yo' damn picture on it. So I took care of her ass. Now get ya shit and let's head to the airport."

"Where we gonna go?"

"Back to Alabama! Now hurry up before they come looking for her ass."

"I gotta get Tabitha first, Ma, and where is the maid at?" I asked, walking toward the bathroom. I had to piss like a racehorse. When I opened the door, the maid was in the tub with a barely recognizable face. I threw up at the sight and smell of all the blood.

"What the fuck!" I tried to catch my breath.

"Bring yo' weak ass on. You can cry in the fucking car!" she almost shouted. I did as I was told and followed her out of the room.

CHAPTER FIFTY-ONE

PYTHON

"Baby, stop crying please." I tried my best to soothe baby Rya. The twins were officially a year old, and they always needed so much attention. Well, wanted it anyways. I always had the girl, and the boy always wanted to be up under Tokyo. Rya'Lynn was the fussy one, and Ryan was the laid back one. They were just like Tokyo and India—although they looked alike, they were as different as night and day.

As I bounced her up and down, I tried to fill her sippy cup with orange juice. I wasn't good at this, but I had actually learned pretty quickly. The cup slipped out of my hand as I tried to screw the top on it.

"Man, fuck!" I bit my lip.

Tokyo came walking in the kitchen, laughing, and grabbed a rag and started to clean up the mess. I must have scared baby Rya because she gave me a look of shock, and then her lips frowned. She started crying and reached for Tokyo. When she grabbed her, I plopped down in the kitchen chair and prepared to make her another cup of OJ.

"Where is Ryan?" I screwed the top on.

"He's already down for his noon nap. That boy could sleep through a terrorist attack, I'm telling you." She began to rock the baby.

"Yeah, I wish she would sleep through one. She has been way more of a fuss these last couple of days. You think she sick or something?"

"Did you two forget she's teething?" My mother walked into the kitchen, cradling bags of food.

"Dammit, I actually did."

"Me too, Ma." Tokyo hugged her.

"Hand me that baby, and yaw put the groceries up. Nana is going to have her asleep in no time once our story comes on." She smiled and gently tickled her.

We did as we were told, and then Tokyo pulled out a bottle of water. "Python, I need to talk to you about something." She eyeballed me.

"Then talk, baby." I put the last item up and gave her my full attention.

She nodded her head and walked toward the back patio. I followed behind her and welcomed the warm breeze that hit my face. We had gotten a nice-sized house on the beachfront, and at least three times a day, I would kick it back here and just watch the scenery. It wasn't like I could do shit else.

"I know you said I said I never wanted to get married, but . . ." She hesitated. "I don't want to be your forever girlfriend. Even Bonnie and Clyde were married, and we ain't no different from them." She leaned on the railing while watching the waves.

"I told you, baby, when Buckey sends our new identity papers and all that in, I will most definitely make you my wife. I promise. But in the meantime, because there's levels to this shit"—I reached in my pocket and pulled out the ring I had my mother pick out for her—"I need to know if you really want to be my wife." I got down on one knee.

"Really, nigga?" Tokyo whipped around to face me, and her jaw would've hit the ground if it weren't attached.

"Yeah, really." I smiled.

"Yes! Yes! Yes! Yes! Yes!" She jumped up and down while clapping.

"Well, then let me put this on your ring finger, woman."

After I did, she kissed me long and hard.

"What is going on out here?" My mother came out the sliding doors.

"Look!" Tokyo screeched.

"Oh, my word!" My mother clutched her chest and started laughing.

"Aw, hell nah! You knew, didn't you?" She threw her hands on her hips, shaking her head.

"You better believe it, little Miss Thang." They hugged.

"Also, Tokyo, we have something to do tonight."

"I bet yaw do." My mother smirked.

"Nothing like that, Ma," I laughed. "That's coming too though. We got a job to do at the beach party."

Tokyo winced at the thought of that.

"I don't know if I'm ready, Python. That's not what I do anymore. Can I even say that?" She ran her hand over her scar on the side of her head.

"Trust me, baby, the old Tokyo would've beat me out the door to get that finished and get that dust."

She still didn't remember much about who she used to be and a lot of things I had to remind her of. The whole "hitta" thing, though, she didn't want to believe that she used to do that. I was determined to get back the woman who I'd fallen in love with. Buckey had said that maybe she needed to do something familiar to bring her memory back fully and get back to her old self. So, I figured if she pulled a trigger or killed someone, maybe it would jog her memory.

CHAPTER FIFTY-TWO

TOKYO

I couldn't stop looking at my ring to save my life! I was more than pumped. My man had finally given me a ring, and soon I was going to be rocking his last name, whatever that was going to end up being. I walked into the twins' room to do a quick check on them. I was ready to take a nice, hot shower and then chill around until it was time for us to go to the beach bash tonight.

When I walked into our room, I cut on some Jill Scott and let her powerful voice move through me as I found something to slip on. I swayed my hips and snapped my fingers to her song "Golden." When I cut the shower on, Python crept into the room and shut the door.

"Your ass isn't slick." I smiled, seductively walking over to him.

"I'm slick enough. I got your fine ass." He kissed me deeply.

"You want some? Then get undressed and follow me." I went back to the bathroom.

"Shit! You don't have to tell me twice!" He quickly undressed.

I stepped in and let the water soak my naked body. I ran my hands over the scars on my chest. I soon felt Python's hands sliding around my waist. He began to kiss and suck on my neck. I reached up behind me and caressed his head, enjoying the touch of his lips on my skin.

He began to rub on my clit as he kissed each one of my scars on my body. I ground my pussy right on his fingers and began to build up a climax. When he grabbed one of my titties with the other hand and massaged it, I felt myself about to cream all on his fingers.

"Mmh, baby, right there." My head fell back as my legs began to shake. I started bucking on his fingers and squeezing my own breasts.

"That's right, cum for daddy. Chase that nut and get that shit, Tokyo!"

As I felt my juices flow, he slowly began to bend me over. The water instantly fucked my hair up. When I was finished, he positioned himself firmly behind me and slid his thick dick in.

"Mmmmh," I moaned and worked my pussy the rest of the way on to him. He slapped my ass and grabbed a handful of my hair. After a few more strokes, our rhythms began to match. He fucked me long and hard in the shower until I finally had to tap out. If he kept that shit up, I was bound to fall and bust my ass from the orgasms I was having back-to-back. When we got out of the shower, I heard nobody other than baby Rya start crying.

"Damn, glad we finished when we did." I laughed, making my way toward the bedroom door.

"I got it!" his mom called out, walking past the door and down the hallway toward the twins' room.

Python laughed and signaled for me to come back to him. He was laid back on the bed, with his dick thrown over his right leg.

"Boy, not again." I smiled, climbing next to him.

"Nah, baby, we gonna take us a nap before we decide to go handle that issue later."

I rolled my eyes and lay on his chest. I knew who he said I was and used to be. I just couldn't believe the shit. Every time he mentioned what I used to do and how I used to act, he would get this sparkle in his eyes. Then, it would fade as soon as it came when he was done. He was missing a part of me that I had no idea how to get back to. I did not feel the rage he said I used to. I didn't feel the need to take someone's life for a quick buck. I just wanted to live peacefully and off everyone's radar like we were doing now. But with us starting over, we were beginning to run low on money. He said we were, anyways, but I felt like $23 million was enough for us to be comfortable and raise the kids comfortably until we were old and gray.

When we woke up, we got dressed and headed downstairs. The sun was beginning to set, and Sherryl had the twins in their highchairs, feeding them. I walked into the kitchen and spun, making my skirt flare.

"Well, don't you look nice." She smiled at me as I tried to imitate a hula dancer.

"Thanks. How are Mommy's twins doing now?" I tickled them both.

"Don't you get them all worked up knowing you two are about to leave." She pointed behind me as Python walked into the kitchen.

"Your ass looks even phatter in that skirt. Let me touch it." He grinned.

"Da da da!" Ryan said, clapping his chubby, messy hands together. We all looked at him.

"Oh, shit!" Python's face lit up. "My little man."

"What type of shit is that? Say 'momma' first. I always have you." I pouted.

"Maa maaaa!" Rya'Lynn cooed and began sucking the sauce from her spaghetti off her hand.

"Yes!" I did a little jig and rubbed her chubby cheeks. We spent a few more minutes trying to record them saying momma and dada, and then we finally left.

CHAPTER FIFTY-THREE

INDIA

I was nervous as fuck as I sat in the courtroom with my lawyer, rubbing my leg. The judge looked at the papers, then at me, and back at the papers.

"Mrs. Peters, on what grounds do you feel the need to dismiss the charges filed against Ms. Miles?" He looked up at her.

"Well, Your Honor," she chuckled, "on the grounds that the detective who was conducting this investigation didn't even have the decency to show up again, for whatever reason. Also, her evidence was half-assed to begin with, and the DNA that she claimed she had in the beginning could've belonged to my client's twin sister or whoever else. After all, it was a strip club. That could've been anyone's hair on that towel for all we know. They never sent that evidence in."

"Mrs. Peters, let me say this, that will be the last time you use foul language in my courtroom or I will hold you in contempt of court. As far as the evidence goes and the presence of Detective Washington, you are absolutely right. So," he said, "because of that, all charges will be dropped, and that makes you, India Miles, a free woman."

"Yes!" Mrs. Peters silently pumped her fist.

"Well, if you have nothing else further to say, that settles it. Tokyo Miles, consider yourself lucky." He banged his gavel.

I stood up and found it hard to breathe. I was so thankful, I really was. But for some reason, I felt like crying because I was sad. I missed my babies. Hadn't seen them, talked to them, or anything besides a couple of random pictures that were mailed to me from someone unknown. I knew exactly who had them, though, by the way they were dressed in nothing but designer everything: Tokyo.

"So now that you are free, what do you have planned?" Mrs. Peters asked me as we walked out of the courtroom.

"No matter what, the first thing I'm doing is going to get my babies back."

"Do you know where they are?" She stopped me.

"Not really, but I know who has them."

"Need my help?"

"Nope, I'm going to handle this all on my own." I walked out into the sunlight and loved the breath of fresh air I was able to inhale.

"No more nasty-ass food or a cell for me." I placed my hands on my hips and looked around. The fuck was I gonna do right now at this moment? I needed to find Tokyo and Python. If I found them, then I would find my babies. That's when Jacob crossed my mind.

I recited his number in my head. "Hey, Mrs. Peters, can I use your cell phone please?"

"Sure." She dug in her pocket and pulled it out. I prayed like hell that he would answer or even help me for that matter. He picked up on the third ring.

"Who is this?" he asked.

"It's me, India, Jacob. Oh my gosh, it's so good to hear your voice! Can you please help me?" I almost panicked at the sound of his voice.

"Oh, shit! What the fuck? Where you at?"

"Standing in front of the courthouse actually. They let me go free." I smiled.

"Uhhh, I can be to you later tonight! It's gonna take me a couple of hours to get back to Kentucky."

"That's fine. I don't know where to tell you to come get me. It's not like I have a place to go."

"You can stay with me until your family comes to get you if you would like to," Mrs. Peters chimed in.

"Well, I guess just call this number back once you get here. Where are you anyways?"

"Alabama, and okay. See you then." He disconnected the call.

"Thanks." I handed the cell phone back to her.

"No problem. Now let's go get you something comfortable to wear and some good ole soul food." She chuckled and grabbed my hand.

CHAPTER FIFTY-FOUR

PYTHON

"Like dead-ass, ma! What the fuck were you thinking?" I yelled at Tokyo in frustration.

"I said I was sorry, Python, damn!"

"A fucking sorry wouldn't have kept a fucking bullet from penetrating my goddamn skull! You don't fucking freeze up when some shit like that happens! The Tokyo I know would've smoked his ass and dipped out like nothing ever happened!"

"Well, I ain't that fucking Tokyo you used to have, and I'll be glad when you get that through your goddamn head, motherfucker!" she yelled back, then walked out of the room, slamming the door behind her.

I sat down on the bed and regretted even arguing with her. She was right, but at the same time, anyone would've pulled the trigger when somebody had a gun pointed at them or their loved one.

"Well, you can't say she didn't tell you she wasn't ready." My mother leaned against the doorframe to our master bedroom.

"Ma, not right now, please." I shook my head.

"No, you need to learn to listen to her more than you do. Baby, you can't bring that back out of her. She's gonna have to do that herself. I'm sure, eventually, she will. She lost a part of herself when she was shot in the head.

Sometimes, it can take people years to even get back as much as she has now. Maybe it's a good thing that she isn't that way anymore. Stop forcing her and quit looking at the negative. Love who you have now, baby." She patted my shoulder and left.

I heard her, but I wasn't trying to hear that shit. I could've been dead right now because of that bullshit freeze-up move of hers. I still felt like shit though. I got up and went to go look for Tokyo. When I got downstairs, my mother pointed to the patio. I slowly inched my way out. She was sitting with a bottle of wine, crying.

"Baby, I'm sorry." I looked past her and out at the ocean. She continued to cry and shake her head.

"I don't know what to do. I don't know what you want from me. I don't know. I just don't know anymore." She dropped her head and cried. I wanted to punch and kick myself right now. I didn't like seeing my shorty cry.

"Tokyo, I said I'm sorry. Baby, please don't cry. It was my fault anyways for trying to get you to do something that you weren't ready for." I sat next to her.

"No, what if you would've been killed? I fucked up." She looked away.

"Well, it didn't happen. So, let's get past that. Besides, you know it's gonna take a lot to get a big nigga like me down," I flexed.

She chuckled a little bit and exhaled. "Python, I want you to be happy too. If it weren't for me fucking up, we wouldn't even be here. I need you to help me get back to the person you said I once was." She finally looked me in the eyes.

"I can't. You have to do it yourself. When you ready and when the time is right, that mean-ass Tokyo will rear her ugly-ass head." I laughed.

"Aw, fuck you!" She hit my leg.

"Well, to make you a little more happy, Buckey sent our new identities in."

"Really?" She beamed.

"Yes, so now I think you and Moms better start planning that wedding."

"Shit, it ain't like we can invite people." She shrugged.

"You been keeping in touch with Cynthia and her daughter. Then I got Buckey, Doc, and his wife and moms, and we got the twins and our neighbors."

"Looks like you've already taken care of the invitation list."

"Something like that. We just gotta get Cynthia and them here."

"That shouldn't be hard. I'll give her a call."

CHAPTER FIFTY-FIVE

JACOB

The whole ride back to Kentucky, I was nervous as hell. Lynn kept saying it was a setup, and Tabitha just didn't give a fuck about what reason I was going to get India. I thought shorty was either dead or never getting out. It made me start thinking about the night that everything went down and how I'd left her there. I mean, I did take the twins and all, so that had to count for something, right? Even if I did let my brother's crazy ass steal them back. I started to think of how they were doing. They were the only thing positive in my life when I had them. Before I left, I told Tabitha that she needed to be gone before I got back, since she didn't want to leave with me and get a free ride back. She pitched a bitch and so did my mother.

When I got to the gas station on Broadway, I parked and dialed the number India had called me from.

"Hello?"

"Uh yeah, India called me from this number this morning. I was wondering if she was around?"

"Yes, she is, may I ask who's calling?"

"You can tell her that it's Jacob." I bit my lip. I didn't know if this lady knew I was on the run or what.

"Oh, okay, she was waiting for you to call. She's in the shower. She asked me to give you my address just in case you called while she was away."

When she gave me the address, I put it into the GPS and checked the distance.

"Damn, thirty minutes from here?" I checked again and started the car back up.

It led me to some nice-ass apartments out Middletown, on the other side of the city. Those motherfuckers looked expensive as hell. I got out and walked up to apartment 3C. After I rang the doorbell a couple of times, I heard someone yell that they were coming.

A slim chocolate sista opened the door. I sized her up, not because there was a problem. Only because if you looked up the words to the song "Slim-Thick with Yo' Cute Ass," her pic would probably pop up. She was more than fine.

"Come on in, Jacob." With her words trailing off, she had a confused look on her face.

"Thank you," I said nervously.

"You look like—"

"Yes, he does, because that's his twin brother," India interrupted, walking up and giving me a hug. She smelled so damn good and looked even better than her lawyer. I guess the time in the big house had done her some good because she was even thicker now. Just more toned, as if she needed it.

"Oh, shit really?" The lady damn near licked her lips.

"Oh, my word! You're the one! He's the one!" she stuttered, trying to get her words out.

"Awww, hell!" was all I could think to say. This bitch was probably about to call the cops on me.

"Don't be worried, baby, this is my lawyer. She knows about everything that happened. She is damned good, too, and got me off."

She blushed when India said that. "I had to play a little dirty, but my clients pay me good money to make sure they are free as soon as possible. And I have never lost a case yet," she boasted.

"So, what's up?" I walked over and sat down.

"I need your help, Jacob. I need to know where my babies are."

"I can't tell you that."

"What you mean?"

"I can't tell you because I don't know. He stole them from me and left town after the funeral. I mean, didn't you see them at your father's funeral with them?"

"How would you know they were at the funeral?"

"I was there too. I was gonna make my move on both they sneaky, conniving asses right there! But then I saw the detectives walk in, from the night that, uhhh, they did all that stuff." I cleared my throat, noticing that the lawyer was watching everything that came out of my mouth.

"You were there? I didn't see you."

"That was the point. When I saw the detectives come in, I figured fuck it. Let them handle their asses. But then you came in. When I saw you hug Tokyo, and the detectives were making their way to you, I hurried up and got my ass out of there."

"And you didn't think to follow them?"

"Hell no! Those fucking cops were deep as hell out there! I jumped in my truck and peeled out."

"I need to find my sister. I know that she is taking care of them, really good care of them, but those are my babies! They deserve to be with me!"

"But how are we going to find them is the question." Mrs. Peters sat back in deep thought.

"Wait." India stood up and started pacing. "The night that everything happened, that one detective said he was Python's close friend and that he knew Tokyo, too."

"Yeah, so?"

"Yeah, but even I'm not that slow-minded. I know my sister like the back of my hand! She's keeping in touch with someone, and I can bet he is too. The dude's name was Bucket. No, Buckey, and that lady who was there is his mother!"

"Hold on, you're referring to Detective Washington's son? Her son's name is Clifton, not Buckey." Mrs. Peters laughed.

"Buckey is his street name, Mrs. Peters. Either way, I'm going to get in touch with him and see if he can help me out."

"Now you know damn well he's not going to just up and tell you where they are," she replied.

"No, he won't. But what's wrong with asking a few questions and snooping around just to see if he has any clue about their location or anything?"

"Nothing at all, with his crooked cop ass. I have his number in the system. Let's give him a call, shall we?" Mrs. Peters waved her cell phone around.

She did a little typing on her computer and then called a number on her cell phone. She placed it on speaker once it began to ring.

"This is Detective C. Washington, who's calling?"

"Hey, Clifton, this is Mrs. Peters, India and Tokyo's attorney. I was wondering if you had heard from her? Her sister is out, and I got everything dropped on her end, too. Is there any way you can relay that to her? She was supposed to call me weeks ago."

"Nope. Why would I know anything about where she is?"

"Well, you are the best friend of her boyfriend, aren't you?"

"No, I am not. After that night, me and him haven't spoken since. Is there anything else I can help you with? I'm kind of busy right now."

"Also, Tokyo has the babies, and India wants them back. I just need you to relay the message for me, that's all. Can you at least do that? That's all. Just try to relay the message?"

"Well, tell her crazy ass to take her to court, but I'll see what I can do." He hung up on her.

"I don't believe him. He's lying!" I stood up.

"Me either. He didn't deny that she has my babies. His ass knows something." India smirked.

"Well, I have to work tomorrow, so, India, if you're going with me, then you need to come on."

"Well, damn." She stood up.

After she said a lot of thank-you's and told Mrs. Peters goodbye, I started the car and sat there for a moment, thinking. She needed my help, and I owed her. I was going to get her babies back by any means. I knew that if Tokyo had those kids, then her ass had Python, too. She wasn't doing that shit on her own with two babies.

"So, what you thinkin' about? And where the hell you work?" India got in, putting on her seat belt.

"We gonna go pay that nigga Buckey a little visit. I ain't got no job. Always remember to cover your ass."

"Okay, but how? We don't know where he is."

I tossed my cell phone into her lap as I pulled out of the parking lot. "When she was on the phone with him, I took a picture of the screen of her computer. Name, number, address, everything was right there."

"You sneaky shit." India grinned.

"I'm gonna make his ass talk. I'm going to beat the fucking shit out of him until he tells where they are. Watch!"

CHAPTER FIFTY-SIX

BUCKEY

I sat next to my mother's bed, trying to piece shit together. Something wasn't right and just didn't add up. She had been shot in the face by someone while she was out getting gas after work the day before she was supposed to go to court to testify and get India put behind bars for good. I didn't know how, but I had the gut feeling that she most definitely had something to do with this. I just couldn't prove it.

I sat there every day for the past week for hours, just thinking of everything. My mother wasn't the best detective and was grimy to a lot of fuckers. Not to the extent that someone would try to kill her ass though. Not to mention, the phone call I'd received from India's lawyer asking about Tokyo. I was no fucking fool. I knew what they wanted. I wasn't about to give my boy or my sister-in-law up to anyone.

Once *Wheel of Fortune* went off, and my mother's nurse returned from her break, I got up, kissed her on the forehead, said a quick prayer, and left. She was in a coma, and there wasn't any telling if she would wake up or pass. She was still in the woods.

I pulled up to my home and went in just to grab a bottle and start drinking. Sometimes, I hated my mother for what she did to people, but I wasn't much different.

When was my time going to come? I plopped down on the couch and stared at the ceiling. Out of nowhere, my phone started to ring.

"Talk."

"Like seriously, Buckey? I haven't seen or heard from you in a week almost! What the hell is really going on?"

"Look, I told you I had a family emergency. Now what is it?"

"Damn, motherfucker! I just wanted to know that your ass was okay! Don't fucking get jazzy with me, okay? Don't even go there!" Jasmine, my Puerto Rican shorty, started going off. I had to laugh. She was right. Shorty was always down for me and always cared. Sometimes a little too much.

"Baby, look, if you miss me, then just say it."

"No, don't try that shit with me! You have me fucked up on thirteen different levels right now!"

"Man, shut the fuck up and get your fine ass over here and make me feel better, girl."

"Motherfucker, I'm grown! Not a little girl. But I'm on my way." She hung up.

I got up and did some quick straightening up. Not that I needed to because she would've done it for me, but she would've complained the whole time while doing so. After that, I took a long, hot shower. As soon as I got out, my doorbell was ringing.

I wrapped a towel around my body and walked into the living room. As soon as I opened the door, Jasmine went in for the kill, kissing me and licking my neck and chest. We worked our way back to my couch where she snatched my towel off and pushed me down.

"Ay, *papi*." She gave me a naughty, freaky smile.

"You like what you see, baby?"

"I love it every time I see it!"

"Then stop playing and get that shit." I made my dick jump.

She started slowly sucking my dick with no hands while massaging my balls. I reached under and made her titties pop out of the tight-fitting yellow shirt she had on. Once my dick got as hard as it could, she stopped and tied her hair up. Spitting on the head and then stroking me up and down with a firm grip, she looked into my eyes and licked her luscious-ass lips before swallowing me whole. I loved when she would do that and tickle my balls while my dick was in her throat. After about thirty minutes of that, I came all over her face and titties while holding a fistful of her hair.

My fucking heart was pounding damn near out of my chest! She always drained me in one session. Talk about a much-needed stress reliever. Jasmine stood up and headed for my bathroom.

"I'm going to clean myself up, *papi,* and then you're going to fuck me crazy like you always do. You not getting off that easy, baby." She threw her soft, round ass from side to side while walking off.

"Damn, for real?" I laughed to myself. I got up and checked my cell phone to see that I had a missed call from Python. I hit the call back button.

"What's up, ghee? How's that beach life treating your ass in Puerto Rico?" I lay back.

"Shit's all good. Thanks for everything you helped me with, yo."

"You good. We brothers for life. You know I got you. Plus, man, India's and them lawyer called me asking where Tokyo was and saying some shit about India got out and wants her babies back. Plus, she got everything dropped against Tokyo."

"The fuck? What you say?"

"That I ain't know where the fuck yaw was. The fuck you thought?" I laughed, lighting a cigarette. Jasmine came prancing out of the bathroom and then froze up like she'd seen a ghost. I stood up and turned around, following her gaze, just to see Python's twin brother, Jacob, standing there.

"Nigga, what the fuck is yo' ass doing in my house?" I yelled, looking around for my gun.

"I thought you said you didn't know where they are, nigga!" He pointed the gun at me.

"Aye yo, Buckey! What the fuck is going on!" Python yelled through the phone.

"This bitch-ass brother of yours is in my fucking house!"

"Hand me the phone and watch that 'nigga' word. I don't give a fuck how cool you and Python is, don't use that shit around me."

I looked at Jasmine, who had a look of evil all over her face. "Baby, don't do nothing stupid okay?" I handed him the phone, putting my hands up.

"That bitch ain't that stupid." India walked in, holding another gun.

"You have got to be kidding me! Bitch, didn't you just get out?" I yelled.

CHAPTER FIFTY-SEVEN

JACOB

This had to be one dumb motherfucker for real. Me and India had been scoping him out for a couple days. We followed him around from work to the hospital to home, then repeated the same shit. The opportunity for me to make my move presented itself when I saw that bitch and him making out in the doorway. His dumb ass didn't even fully close the fucking door. I kind of enjoyed watching the dick sucking myself.

"What's up, twin? When you trying to meet up and hand those babies over?"

"Bitch-ass nigga, you just don't give up, do you? When I get a hold of yo' ass, this time I will fuckin kill yo' ass slow! You can bet that shit!"

"Yeah, whatever. You motherfuckers got two days to make it here with them babies, or I'm going to body this nigga and his bitch." I ran the gun over her titties. She slapped me hard in the face.

"Do it then, bitch motherfucker you!" she spat.

India walked over and slapped her with the butt of her gun. Shorty stumbled back and fell over the coffee table.

"As a matter of fact, two would be too complicated. You want this nigga to live? Give those babies back, ASAP!"

"Don't give that motherfucker a damned thing, Python!" Buckey yelled.

I sucked my teeth and said fuck it and shot his ass, blowing his ear off in the process. He fell to the ground like a sack of potatoes. His girlfriend started screaming and saying some crazy shit in Spanish. India kicked his girl in the stomach, causing her to roll over in pain, and then shot her three times in the back.

"Nigga, if he's dead, that's your ass! You motherfuckers will never see these kids ever again! Yaw won't even live to make it past Christmas," Python growled through the phone.

"I wouldn't be so sure about that. Now, I'm about to find your mammie and her sister and get their asses. When you make it back with the twins, call me on his phone. It's not like he's going to be the one using it anyways." I laughed, hanging up.

"Let's get the fuck outta here, baby, now!" India grabbed my hand.

Running out to the car, I saw neighbors start to turn on their lights and come outside. Once we were in, I sped out. I had no idea where we were going to go. I was tired of sleeping in hotel rooms and shit. I thought about just driving all the way back to Alabama and having him meet us there instead. Yeah, that's what I was going to do. Have his ass play my game, on my turf.

"Where we going?" India asked, pulling her hair out of the tight ponytail it was in.

"To Alabama."

"For what?"

"Because he's going to play on my turf this time. How the fuck he gonna have help or anything if nobody knows him or where he is?" I smiled at my master plan.

"Babe, you dead-ass don't know Python. He's a big-time drug lord! He knows everyone everywhere! That's not smart at all if that's all you thought of. Your ass is dumb." She laughed.

I slapped her hard and fast in the face. "Now, laugh at that shit. Don't you ever fucking call me dumb again! Since yo' ass so smart, why you call me for help? You come up with a plan then, but don't you ever call me stupid again." I pointed at her.

"Sorry." She held her nose and looked out the window.

That shit made me feel good as hell. I looked out my side and smiled a little on the inside. Is that what having some type of control felt like? Let me have tried that shit with Lynn and her ass would've had my head sitting right on a shelf for decoration. I shook my head at that thought and continued to drive.

CHAPTER FIFTY-EIGHT

INDIA

"'You come up with a plan!'" I silently mocked Jacob in the bathroom while cleaning the blood from my nose. "'Don't you ever call me dumb again!' Dumb-ass nigga ain't even tough!" I threw the bloody tissue in the toilet and flushed it.

"So, you come up with anything?" he called out.

I walked out and sat on the bed of the small motel room. I racked my brain for ideas as I stirred my now-warm shrimp fried rice. I no longer gave a fuck about what issue Jacob had with Python. I just wanted my babies back and to move on in life. Knowing my sister, things weren't about to be that easy.

"Not really. I need more time to think."

"Ha, but you called me dumb? Come on, college girl, hurry up." He smiled.

"Don't do that. At least I went to college! You got me fucked up!"

"Then do it on your own!" He got upset again.

"You act like I can't! You need me just as much as I need yo' ass! You can't even get close to Python without me! I have a reason and you really don't!" I rolled my eyes, shutting him straight up. "Yeah, that's what I thought!"

"Whatever. So, what's the plan?"

"Like you said to begin with, we need bait, so find you all's mother and aunt. This time, we will not hurt them! We don't need to give them a reason to be like fuck it or hurt my babies for revenge."

"He wouldn't do that, would he?" Jacob looked at me, this time with sincere concern.

"I honestly can't say. Python most definitely can get very evil and nasty in the blink of an eye. From what me and my sister have talked about before all this, that man has no limits."

"But he wouldn't hurt babies?"

"I don't know, and I'm not going to risk it. We find them, take them, and hide them, call Python, and tell him where to meet us. I don't know if it should be somewhere public though."

"Somewhere public would be good."

"But do you honestly think he would give a damn? He wants your ass dead just as much as you want him dead. He won't give a damn where he kills you as long as he does."

"Well, let's find out where my mom is staying, and she'll lead us to my aunt."

"Fuck it! Call his ass back! We the ones making demands and in control here!"

Jacob pulled out Buckey's cell phone and dialed Python.

"What, nigga?" he answered immediately.

Jacob held the phone away from his mouth. "What you want me to say to him?" he asked.

I snatched the phone from him. "Python, tell me where your mother and aunt are now."

"I knew Jacob's ass wasn't the brains behind this shit."

"Do as I said."

"And just why the hell should I do that? Yaw already killed Buckey. That was yaws' only way to get me to cooperate."

"That may be true for you, but not so much when it comes to Tokyo." I smirked.

"You a weak-ass bitch, you know that?"

"Yeah, well, that ain't the first time you've said that to me, sir. I'm more than sure my sister will fly her ass back to Kentucky to save Cynthia and her daughter. So, it's either Cynthia and hers or your mom and hers. I don't think we should bring more people into this, sir."

"Bitch, fuck you. They ain't no relation to me."

"Damn, I thought you loved my sister." I laughed, hanging up.

"Why you do that?" Jacob stood up.

"Wait on it." I smiled, knowing Python would call back.

Ten minutes later, the cell phone rang.

"Yes, darling?" I sang into the phone.

"Where you want us to meet you? And when?"

"The old school building on Lynn View Road and Hykes. Bring my babies and don't be on no bullshit. In three days. That's more than enough time. Also, I need some money, half a mill. A trade for a trade. Real simple and easy, and we can all live happily ever after. Well, me and mine can anyways. When yaw touch down, give me a call." I hung up.

"Damn, that shit was sexy as fuck!" Jacob smiled excitedly.

"It was, wasn't it?"

He got up and took his shirt off, exposing his ripped upper body. My pussy instantly started throbbing. I was still mad at him, but I hadn't had a man touch me in a year! And at this moment, my body craved to feel his and his hands all over mine. I quickly undressed and lay on the bed with my legs spread far apart.

"Do whatever the fuck you want, just make me feel damned good, baby." I gave a wicked grin.

CHAPTER FIFTY-NINE

TOKYO

"Hell, no! These are my babies! No!" I screamed in disbelief.

"Tokyo, but they aren't! Aren't you ready to get this shit over with?"

"Yes! But not that way! You the boss! Killa! Do what you gotta do! But she ain't getting my babies! Fuck her and him and whoever else when it comes to them! I'll die before I let her have them! They don't even fucking know her! And how could you just be willing to give them up so easily?"

"Tokyo, don't you dare fucking say it like that! I love them too! But if she were to take yo' ass to court, who the hell do you think would win?"

"Me! That's what the fuck money and lawyers are for! Her ass just got out! My name is clear now! And so is yours, right! Fuck it! Handle it in court! I don't care who gets hurt when it comes to them. They are mine, and I love them, and she can just go straight to hell!"

"So, even when it comes to me?" Python asked.

"You ain't in this. She ain't after you. Your brother is. She is not capable of taking care of them. This bitch had them in an abandoned house with some damn weirdo and his crazy-ass mammie, trying to kill everyone and shit! Like all her damn brain cells went out the window for that lame-ass, ugly piece of shit brother of yours!"

"You dead-ass just called me ugly?"

"No, I didn't!"

Python placed his hands on his sides and stared at me long and hard.

"I called him ugly." I cracked a smile. "You always find a way to change the convo." I shook my head.

He walked over to me and sat me down. "Baby, look, I'm going to give you a day to think about this. Giving them back to their mother is the right thing to do. If they mean that much to you, then fix things with your sister, and you will still be a part of their life."

"But it's not the same." I looked away.

"She won't rest until she has them back, and even you know that."

"Then I guess I'll have to lay her ass to rest then."

"You aren't going to do that."

"You don't know what I'll do for them and their well-being. I suggest we start packing to head back to Kentucky. I don't understand why you didn't say something when they first called. We could have warned Cynthia and her daughter before they even got to them." I rolled my eyes and went to go take a shower. I needed to relax, ASAP.

When I got out, Python was already asleep in the bed. I wrapped my robe around myself and went to the balcony. I listened to the sound of the waves and watched them rise and fall and pull back just to do it again and again. I didn't know if I was wrong for the way I felt about those babies, but I honestly didn't care. Who would have ever thought I could love them the way that I did? Like I had actually given birth to them myself. Python just didn't understand. If he thought I was going to give them up that easily, then he and India had another think coming.

The next morning when I got up, Python was nowhere next to me. I got up, brushed my teeth and washed my face, and went downstairs. His mother was in the kitchen already eating. She looked like she had been crying.

"What's the matter, Ma?" I walked over to her.

"He told me what you two were arguing about last night." She sniffled, scooting her eggs around on the plate.

"Oh, that? It'll be okay. I'm going to handle it, okay?"

"How, Tokyo?" She looked up at me. "He done already left!" She smacked the plate off the table.

"What the fuck you mean he already left?" I jumped back in shock and ran back up the stairs to the twins' room. "Ryan! Rya!" I screamed. getting closer to their rooms. When I busted in, they were nowhere in sight.

"Nooooo! Goddamn you! No!" I screamed as big tears began to fall. I dropped to the floor and felt like all the air had been knocked from my lungs. I instantly felt sick and threw up right in my own lap.

Sherryl came in and snatched a towel out of their bathroom and started wiping me off.

"Get up, baby." She tried to pull me off the ground.

"How could he do something like that? How could he do me like that?" I sobbed. She didn't have an answer for me. After a few moments, I finally gathered myself and got up off the floor. Walking into our master bedroom, I undid my robe and stood in the mirror. I felt confused as fuck. My neck felt hot, and my hands burned like they were literally on fire.

"Godddd!" I screamed at the top of my lungs and banged my fist into the mirror, shattering it instantly. I pounded that mirror over and over again, until there was blood and glass everywhere. "You son of a bitch!" I kicked and screamed in the bathroom while throwing things and breaking them, then punching holes in the wall. I didn't know what had come over me, but I felt betrayed and pissed the fuck off beyond belief.

When there was nothing left to destroy, I washed my hands off in the sink. After drying them, I poured peroxide all over them in the sink. The pain I felt from the cuts felt so damn good. I didn't know if I had lost my mind or if I had lost feeling in them. Drying my hands off, I walked out of the bathroom and went to get dressed. Walking into the walk-in closet, I got even more pissed noticing the clothes missing from Python's side.

I snatched down a black and gray jogging suit and threw it on. Grabbing my all-black Forces, I sat on the edge of the bed and put them on. I felt a rush out of nowhere and had to rub the sides of my head to keep myself calm. Taking a deep breath, I stood up and walked over to the closet again, this time getting my Glock off the shelf. I loaded it and got two extra clips. I grabbed my bag and put two more jogging suits inside.

Walking over to the dresser, I threw my perfume inside and some gloves along with some money. When I looked up into the mirror, I didn't recognize the woman looking back at me, but I felt like she had been there all along.

"These motherfuckers should have left well enough alone," I said to no one in particular and licked the side of my gun, smiling.

When I got downstairs, Sherryl was cleaning up the mess she had made earlier.

"Tokyo, where are you going? Are you okay, baby?"

"Never felt better," I said, walking out the door.

CHAPTER SIXTY

PYTHON

I felt like a piece of shit the whole plane ride back to the States. I knew Tokyo was probably losing her fucking mind right now and mad as hell. I had everyone's best interest at heart though. The twins deserved to be with India and that was just as simple as it got. It wasn't like they would be able to tell the difference anyways. Besides, I wanted to start my own family with Tokyo.

When we got to the airport, I got off and sat down for a moment. I needed to gather my thoughts. The twins were still asleep in their car seats.

"Phyllips?" I heard someone call out.

I looked up and saw my driver standing with a sign that read my last name. I grabbed the twins and headed in his direction.

"I'm Phyllips." I handed him a car seat. He almost looked terrified while looking up at me. I smirked and walked off. Getting outside, I instantly noticed the all-black 2020 Ram 1500 limited edition truck I had ordered. "That's what the fuck I'm talking about." I grinned.

"Uh, sir, I don't know if there's enough room on the inside—" he began.

"There's not." I pulled out some cash and handed it to him. "Get lost. You never saw me, and I never made it. I don't care." I snatched the keys and began strapping the twins inside.

"Got it." He stuffed the cash into his pocket and walked over to a taxi.

I pulled out, checked the rearview, and cut the radio on. I left it on a station that was playing an old No Limit song.

"Make'm say unnnh, na na na!" I bopped my head as I made my way to the Marriott hotel where me and the twins would be staying for the time being. When I finally got there, they were just waking up. I rushed to get the room key and go up to our suite.

"Da-da!" Ryan smiled, reaching for me while I changed his sister's diaper. That shit broke my heart when I looked over at him.

"Hold on, little man, I got you next." I buttoned her pants and sat her at the top of the bed with her teething ring. While changing him, I thought about if I really wanted to hand him over and not be able to see him again. When I was done, I called Buckey's phone.

"Speak, nigga," Jacob answered. It sounded like he was getting his dick sucked from what I heard in the background.

"Tell that bitch to come up for air. Me and the kids are here."

"What?" I heard India excitedly say in the back.

"Damn, you ain't waste no time getting ya ass back here! What about the money, you got that, too?"

"Man, either yaw want these babies or yaw don't!" I growled.

"All I know is yo' ass better have the money, or shit gonna get real personal for us all. See you at ten thirty tomorrow night," he retorted.

I bit my lip, ready to lash out at the nigga, but I kept my cool instead. I was going to handle his ass in the worst way. Nobody threatened me or made demands on my behalf. I was and always had been my own boss. I moved on my own time.

CHAPTER SIXTY-ONE

INDIA

"Yes! My babies are here! I can just imagine how cuddly and cute they are in person! Thank you so much, Jacob! Thank you!" I jumped up and down, clapping my hands.

"Yeah, yeah, yeah. I guess we work better as a team." He threw a chicken bone at Cynthia.

"You motherfuckers are just rotten!" She shook her head while sitting in a corner tied up.

"So what? Sometimes you just gotta do what you gotta do. If your whorish ass weren't so eager to make a quick loose dollar, you wouldn't even be here right now. Who the fuck meets up with a stranger for a couple hundred?" I sat down on the bed.

"What's ya point? I'm a go-getter, something your lame ass wouldn't know anything about seeing that Tokyo is always taking care of your ass. I don't understand how the fuck your ass is related to Tokyo! She would never sell out and betray someone like your ass did. I hope she kills both you motherfuckers when she catches up to you." Cynthia smiled.

"She won't catch up to shit or kill shit!" I spat in her face.

"Yeah, right, let's be for real. Even you know the devil always has the last laugh, and her ass will most definitely come for you, him, and those babies. She loves them too much! And they love her."

I don't know why, but when she mentioned the love part, I got pissed the fuck off and slapped her across the face.

"Those are my babies! They don't know any better! They will never have a bond with her! They will never love her more than they love me! I'm their mother!"

"A mother wouldn't have put them in this type of situation. A mother would have given birth the proper way in a hospital to make sure that they were okay. A mother wouldn't have let some probable child molester take them and care for them!"

"Who this bitch calling a child molester?" Jacob darted his eyes from me to her.

"Yo' good-for-nothing, slow ass."

"I've had enough of her rambling. Where's the tape? I'm not about to let her ruin my damn mood!" I stood up and started looking around the room.

The next morning when I woke up, I stretched a little and prepped myself for whatever could happen or go wrong. Jacob had left to go get us all something to eat. I dead-ass didn't have an appetite though. I just wanted to feel and hold my babies finally. Python had called and confirmed that he had the money and was ready to meet up when we were. I was glad he was complying with everything. I wanted this all to be over. Not long after, Jacob came walking through the motel room door.

"After we eat, we need to go ahead and head there. If he is the way you claim, he may try to set some shit up or something and catch us slipping blind."

"That's cool." I grabbed my breakfast waffles and began eating. "You load the guns up?" I asked with my mouth full.

"I thought you said you would?"

"You're right, I'll do it once we get there."

We untied Cynthia and let her use the bathroom and eat. She hadn't said shit else the whole time. I was kind of upset because we were only able to snag her ass and not her daughter too. She obviously had more class and whatnot than her mother.

Once the sun had started to go down, we packed up everything and made our way to the schoolhouse. That shit looked mad creepy, like something out of a Freddy Kruger movie. We parked around back where the gym was located. Some years ago, during a storm, the school was struck by lightning. The building was so old, they felt no need to repair it, and it had just been rotting ever since.

We waited and waited and still saw no signs of Python. I began to get worried and was growing impatient as time went on.

"What the fuck! Call him! See what's taking him so long to fucking get here!" I pounded my fist on the dashboard.

"Okay, hold tight." Jacob dialed the number, and Python picked up on the third ring.

"What's up?" He smacked into the phone.

"Oh, I bet you think you're real cute! Where the fuck are you with my damn babies!" I yelled.

"Aw, my bad. I think we should meet up tomorrow instead. I took them to see my aunt, and baby Rya still isn't feeling too well."

"The fuck you mean? What did you do to her?" I almost panicked.

"I didn't do anything. I love her. She's teething."

"Python, quit playing and bring my babies to me, please?" My eyes began to water.

"I will tomorrow. Just stay calm. I got the money and all. Make sure you keep Cynthia safe, though, or the deal is off." He hung up on us.

Me and Jacob just stared at each other.

CHAPTER SIXTY-TWO

TOKYO

I sat across from Python, watching him as he fed the twins. He had no idea I was there, and that's how I was going to keep it until I confronted his ass. When I had gotten back to Kentucky, I checked into the Marriott hotel. As I was getting on one elevator, I spotted Python getting off another with the twins. My blood began to instantly boil. He had tried to pull a fast one on me, and I wasn't having it.

A smile crept across my face as I watched baby Ryan smear apple sauce all over his face. As I almost laughed out loud, he made eye contact with me and reached in my direction. I didn't budge or try to cover my face when Python turned around to look. I just smirked and sipped my orange juice as if everything were fine.

Python dropped his head and shook it. I just kept on drinking and then finally stood up to leave and go to my room. Before I could make it out of the lobby/café area, Python stood up.

"Tokyo! Don't fucking turn yo' back on me! Get yo' ass over here!" his voice boomed.

I turned around and walked in his direction with the look of the devil on my face.

"What is it?" I folded my arms.

"What you doing here?"

"Don't ask me no fucked-up, dumb-ass question like you don't already know. You hand them over to her and we are done, and I mean that shit. You can bet that! Even then, she still won't get them because I will off all you motherfuckers!" I got a little heated all over again.

"You gon' off who?" He towered over me.

"I'll kill your ass too for them and over them!"

He placed them both back in their car seats and told me to follow him. I could tell what I said had just pissed him off, but I didn't care. I was the one who deserved to be upset. When we got up to the suite he had booked, I kicked my heels off and sat down. He put the twins in the bedroom part and closed the door after turning on some *Paw Patrol* for them.

"Now would you like to say that shit again, Tokyo? You gon' do what?" He inched toward me.

"I said exactly what the fuck you heard me say the first time."

"You ain't gon' kill shit. Your ass is too fucking scared and traumatized to even pull a trigger. Or did you forget about that freeze-up move of yours?" He snickered. That instantly pissed me off. I stood up and pulled my gun out and fired off a shot, making him jump back quick.

"Keep fucking testing me, my nigga! You got the right, bitch!" I yelled.

"Bitch, is you crazy! If you ever do that shit again around my kids, I'll—"

"Bitch? You'll what? Hit me? I ain't like the young bitches you used to dealing with, my nigga! I wish upon a million stars and a thousand fucking pennies thrown into a wishing well that you would ever put your fucking hands on me in a violent manner!" I threw the gun down on the couch and started swinging on his big ass like crazy. He grabbed me by my wrist after he got tired of those blows connecting and threw me on the couch.

"That's what the fuck I'm talking about! My baby is back!" He grinned hard as hell.

"Fuck you!" I rolled my eyes. He slowly backed up, taking in all that sat in front of him. Turning around, he went to go check on the twins.

"They are asleep. Now time to put Momma down for a nap." He ripped his shirt off and walked over toward me. I could practically see his dick beginning to grow through his pants that he had on, and the shit had me hot and bothered. Every time I looked at this man's body, it drove me crazy. As soon as we got started and my juices got to flowing—pussy ready to grip and drip all over him—we heard a knock at the door.

Python yelled out, "Who is it!"

"Hotel security."

"Damn." He looked around, then got up to go to the door.

"Hello, sir, the other party that you share the floor with called down, saying they believed there was a domestic situation taking place. I'm just making sure that everything is okay. Something about a gunshot going off?" He mentioned as he tried to peek around the big giant before him.

"Everything is fine, sir." I walked up behind him, rubbing his massive six pack. "We were just having a little adult fun." I smiled.

"Oh, okay." He eyeballed me and licked his lips. Python removed my hands and stepped closer to him, getting in his face.

"You see something you like?" He clenched his teeth.

"Oh, shit, no, sir. Sorry. You all have a good night." He almost tripped over his own feet turning around to run down the hall.

"Baby, you mean as fuck!" I laughed.

"Nah, did you see that shit? He a bold motherfucker to be doing that shit like I'm invisible or some shit!"

"You most definitely are not that, baby." I licked his stomach, then his chest.

"Shit."

"Mhmm." I kissed each one of his pecks and started sucking on him. Python picked me up and carried me over to the sofa where we started grinding against each other. By the time his tongue was running over my breast, I was already creaming my panties.

"You ready?" He undid his zipper and let his pants fall to the ground with his large monster springing out to greet me.

"Hell yeah!"

As soon as he climbed on top of me, he told me, "Tokyo, I want us to start our own family. I want us to have our own babies."

I kissed him. He was right, and I wanted my own with him, but that wasn't going to happen. At least by round two, we were fucking like animals but quietly so we wouldn't disturb the twins. The shit felt so good and so right, I'd forgotten where we were and that they were there. Once we both were ready to climax for the second time, Python's phone rang.

"Man, fuck!" he panted, long stroking me from the back.

"No, baby, they can wait. Don't stop." I threw my ass back on him.

"Baby, hold on." He looked in the direction of his cell phone jumping around.

"Python, don't you dare stop, and I'm about to cum, baby. Please don't." I arched my back and reached up under me, caressing and squeezing his balls. Then, I tightened and loosened my walls around his dick. He started pumping faster and harder, and I kept doing what I was doing so he wouldn't pull out. Once his strokes became too powerful and I felt him about to bust, I couldn't help the screams and moans that left my mouth.

"Gat damn, Tokyo!" He slapped me hard on the ass just the way I liked it, knowing it would bruise. Then, he gripped my waist, digging his nails into me and breaking skin. He held me tight and close, releasing all of his nut inside me like I told him to. When he was finished, we both collapsed on the floor out of breath and laughing.

"Now, you can go get your phone." I smiled.

"Damn, I don't wanna move." I watched his chest rise and fall. Then, one of the twins started crying.

"Well, we don't have a choice now." I slid my dress over my head and went to go see which one of my angels demanded attention this time.

CHAPTER SIXTY-THREE

PYTHON

When I glanced at the phone, I saw I had two missed calls from Buckey's phone and some random number. I called them back as Tokyo came creeping back out of the room with Rya'Lynn in her arms.

"What's up?" I sat down on the couch while she bounced her around, soothing her as always.

"My nigga, you real bold for a motherfucker on a time limit. You act like this bitch's life don't matter or something!" he yelled.

"Bring me my babies, bitch!" India screamed in the background.

As soon as Tokyo heard her voice, her eyes changed colors and she marched over and snatched the phone out of my hand, putting it on speaker.

"Bitch, you better watch your mouth talking to mine, and I ain't even five motherfucking seconds off of you! You think I forgot about what you did to me!" she yelled back. The phone grew quiet.

Then, we both heard Cynthia yell out for Tokyo and say, "Aw, it's on now, bitch! Tokyo, help me!"

"Shut up!" Jacob yelled at her.

"Cynthia! Oh, my God." Tokyo sat down, holding the phone and the baby. "Are you okay?"

"Fuck all that! Meet us tonight and bring the babies and the money! You know where! Show up a minute late or early and I'm going to shoot this bitch in her fucking face!" Jacob hung up.

"Python, they got Cynthia!" Tokyo was on the verge of panicking.

"I know, baby. Trust me, we will get her back, okay? We need to think first though on what's the best way to go about it."

"By killing both those motherfuckers! I'm sick of going through this shit! The only way to fix everything is to end both of them, or this shit will never stop."

"Baby, that's still your sister and the mother of those babies. You can't do that, can you?"

"The bitch didn't care when she shot me, almost killing me! She has a heart, and I don't! She tolerates bullshit, and I don't! That's the difference between me and her."

"I just know yaw better than that. At some point, you loved that girl to no fucking end. I know it's still there. We just gotta figure out a way to get them to turn against each other or something. Jacob, on the other hand, I don't know that nigga and don't care for him, especially with what he did to my mother."

Looking at my cell phone, I decided to call back the random number that showed up on the screen. Nobody had my cell number in the States except Buckey and Tristan, who I had looking after my traps while I was away.

"Hello, this is U of L Hospital. How may I direct your call?"

"Someone called me from this number a little while ago."

"Oh, I'm sorry about that, sir. Is there anyone you know of who would do that?"

I grew nervous as I asked, "Do you all have anyone in there by the name of Clifton Washington?"

I heard her do a little typing, and then she finally confirmed that he was in fact there.

"Let him know I'm on my way there, now." I got up and ran to the shower, jumping in and washing quickly like there was a fire lit under my ass.

"So, what do I do?" Tokyo stood, watching me move around the room.

"Get the twins ready and head that way to the old, burned down schoolhouse. Not until I call and tell you to though, Tokyo. I want everyone that I care for to make it out and away from this shit in one piece and okay."

"Cool. Guess I'll order up some room service while I wait."

"Good, the twins love their applesauce and chicken strips. Barbecue for—"

"Barbecue for Rya and ketchup for Ryan. I know, I got this." She smiled.

"That's my girl. You know, for shit that's about to pop off you sure are calm." I stood up, walking toward her.

"Tokyo don't fold under pressure. I welcome death and everything associated with it with open arms, baby." She kissed me, and I kissed the twins on the head and left.

CHAPTER SIXTY-FOUR

BUCKEY

To say God or someone of that nature had saved my ass and looked out for me would've been an understatement. Or the fact that that dumb son of a bitch, Jacob, had no aim was what really did it. When he pulled the trigger, the bullet grazed the side of my head, taking a piece of my ear off with it. I hit the ground cold and knocked out.

When I came to, my neighbor, Susan, was kneeling over me on the phone with 911.

"Are you okay? Where's Jasmine?" I tried to roll over, but she pushed me back in the same spot.

"They said for you not to move, Mr. Washington, and I think your girlfriend is dead. Oh, my God!" She shook her hands, trying to calm down.

"I'm okay, stay calm, sweetie," I grunted. "Where is your mother? Where is Cynthia?" Cynthia and Susan were mother and daughter and had been my neighbors for the last seven years. Cynthia always had a crush on me and always looked out for me, sending cooked meals and whatnot every other day. I could've been with her if she weren't a stripper at the age of 50.

"The ambulance is on the way, so just stay still, Mr. Washington. I can hear them in the distance." She looked at the door as I blacked out.

When I woke up in the hospital, I called Python, remembering his number by heart. I got no answer. A while later, a nurse came into my room and told me that he'd called back and was on his way. I lay there thinking about my mother on the fifth floor in ICU. I needed to see her. When I got up to use the bathroom, I heard someone entering my room. I assumed it was Python but was a little shook when I came out to see Susan.

"Hey, thanks for doing that for me. Are you okay?" I got back on to the bed.

"Yes and no. My mom hasn't come home in two days, and I'm worried. She never pulls moves like that. And if she were to, she would at least answer my calls or return a text. Something isn't right." She sat down, fidgeting with her fingers.

"Okay, where was the last place you know she was?" I winced at the sharp pain I felt when I talked.

"She was at work, you know, the strip club."

"Have you tried calling there to see if anyone has seen her?"

"Yes, but the girls said she left with some tall, big guy. Said he sells drugs. I know my mother like the back of my hand, and my mother ain't on nobody's drugs, Mr. Washington."

"Please, I'm not that old. Call me Buckey. Did any of the girls know him personally or anything?"

"They said his name was Python or something. I have a picture of him that one of the girls sent to my phone a few hours ago. My mother is leaving with him in the picture." She handed her phone over after she was done scrolling.

I was shocked but not so much when I saw Jacob in the picture. Those damn iPhones would get anyone caught up as clear as that picture was for them to be in motion.

When Python walked through my hospital room door, Susan jumped up. "Hey, you, where is my mother? Have you heard from her?"

"Susan, sweetie, calm down, he's not who you think." I sat up.

"He's the one in the picture though!"

"Wait, what? What picture?" Python looked back and forth between the both of us.

"Apparently, Jacob has Cynthia." I shook my head.

"Yeah, I know, and I have to get her back before Tokyo does something stupid to get us all fucked around."

"Wait, you know where she is? Take me to her! Is she with Tokyo?"

"No, she's with India. She's been taken. But I promise you, if you keep quiet and let us handle this. I will bring your mother back to you."

After me and Python talked, I threw on a T-shirt and left with him. I wanted my fucking lick back. I didn't care who felt what type of way, but I was going to kill India just like she did my baby, Jasmine.

CHAPTER SIXTY-FIVE

INDIA

"Oh, my God." I sat with my hands clamped together. After hearing my sister's voice and the threat in her tone, I was beyond terrified. No one knew her like I did. If she promised an ass whooping or a bullet to your dome, shorty was most definitely going to do just that. I kept pacing back and forth until Jacob got irritated and told me to sit down.

"Look, I got your back. I won't let her hurt you. You really that scared of her?"

"You don't know her like that." I shook my head.

"So, I see we about to go heads-up again, twin against twin." He sat back, smirking.

Little did he know, I wasn't about to go up against shit! I just wanted my kids. Whatever happened after that was on him. I glanced over at the bag with our guns and belongings in it.

"Looking like you about to piss yourself. You was tough not long ago. Told you Tokyo was going to get your ass." Cynthia laughed.

"For a bitch who going to die, you sure got a lot of mouth!" Jacob glanced in her direction.

"Who's going to die? You heard what the fuck Python said: no me, no deal."

"You think I give a fuck? I want him. All that other shit is what it is."

When I heard him say that, that let me know everything that was about to go down was most definitely the right thing for me to do. I kept my thoughts and words to myself. I had a trick for his ass since it was just about him getting revenge on his brother.

When we got the phone call from Python to meet him and that he was on his way to the school, I grew nervous all over again and threw up. After cleaning myself up and changing shoes, we threw Cynthia in the truck and pulled off. I kept checking my gun, making sure it was loaded, and shaking my leg. Jacob reached over and squeezed it.

"Please calm down. If you go into this nervous, everything will go wrong." He kept his eyes on the road.

When we pulled up, there was no one in sight. No cars or anything.

"What the fuck? Where the hell is he?" I threw my hands on my hips, glancing around in every direction. Then, I spotted a light being flashed in the school building.

"Something ain't right about that shit. Call that nigga." Jacob handed me the phone.

When I called and heard the ringing come from behind us, I jumped around and fired off a shot. Python busted out laughing.

"Well, well, well." He walked up with a duffle bag. "Where the fuck is Cynthia?"

"Where are my babies, Python?"

"Give me Cynthia, and I'll hand you this bag and take you to them. Tokyo is inside with them now."

"I don't believe you, and I don't trust you." Jacob stood in front of me.

"Well, then, go in and see for yourself."

We grabbed Cynthia out of the car and began walking toward the building all together. As soon as we entered the building, I heard one of my babies whimper and then say, "Momma." I rushed down the dark hallway toward the sound. When I got to the end, there was a set of double doors that led into a cafeteria. When I pushed them open, I grew nervous and sick as I spotted Tokyo standing by two car seats, rocking them.

It was almost as if I could see horns sticking out of her head as she watched me stand there.

"Tokyo," I stammered, "I'm so sorry for the way everything went."

"No, you aren't. Don't apologize for things you meant to do," she said as everyone else walked in behind me.

"Can I please have them?" My eyes watered.

She glanced behind me and looked at Cynthia. "You good, boo?"

"Hell nah, but I guess good enough," Cynthia replied.

"A'ight, enough of this shit. Hand them kids over and yaw can take this bitch." Jacob held her by the arm.

CHAPTER SIXTY-SIX

TOKYO

I wanted to spit dead in this bitch's face as I watched her before me. Even more, I wanted to put a bullet in both of them. They didn't know that the twins weren't even in the car seats that were on both sides of me. I had recorded one of them and had it playing under a damn blanket. "Come here and see them. After all, you are the mom." I sat down. Nobody said a word as she crossed the cafeteria. It seemed like everything was moving in slow motion. I saw a dark figure creeping up behind them all and began to smile. When she got close enough and out of ear's reach of everyone else, I simply told her, "Say anything, and I swear this shit will go sideways. Act like everything is cool."

She froze up as she looked and saw the empty car seats. Buckey pushed Cynthia to the ground as Python turned and swung on Jacob, knocking him to the ground. I pulled my gun out quick and pointed it at my sister.

"Don't you dare, bitch!" I stood up.

"Tokyo, please! I just want my babies. I said I was sorry for everything. I'm not on no funny shit or anything!" She began to cry. I grew disgusted as I looked at the pathetic bitch. I couldn't believe we shared the same DNA.

"Fuck you! You shot me and left me for dead all over some dick!"

"Tokyo, you killed my kids' father!"

"Yeah, after you left me!" I looked past her as Python and Buckey beat the holy shit out of Jacob. "I tried to tell you he was tied up in the basement! What hurt me even more is that you didn't even believe me when I told you that he broke into our house with his peoples!"

"Tokyo, because you're fucking crazy!" she screamed at me. I don't know what came over me, but I lunged for her, and we both hit the ground hard, fighting.

"Get off of me!" she screamed, punching me in the side of my head.

"Fuck you, bitch! I hate you!" I grabbed her by the hair and began banging her head on the ground repeatedly until it dazed her. When I stood up, I looked around for my gun. I was ready to get this shit over with as soon as possible. I had nothing else to discuss with her ass.

I stood over her and pointed my gun at her. I couldn't shake the fact that if I didn't kill her, she would come for the twins again. Python and Buckey stood up and pulled their guns out, aiming at Jacob.

"Not so fast, bitch niggas!" Some blond bitch rushed in and started firing shots. Everyone took cover.

"Who the fuck is that!" Python yelled, ducking behind a broken table.

"I don't know!" I stood up and aimed at her, firing two shots. One missed and the other hit her in the arm.

"You funky bitch!" She tossed the gun to the other hand and fired back. "Nobody fucks with my man!"

"Who the fuck are you!" I yelled out.

"Thank God!" Jacob yelled, rolling over and trying to get to the doors of the cafeteria. Python shot him in the leg, making him hit the ground again. That motherfucker wouldn't give up though as he inched his way on the ground toward the doors.

"Tokyo, no!" Python yelled out as I aimed at India. "Tokyo, please!" India cried out, trying to scoot away. As I was about to shoot her, the new bitch in the room fired another shot, making me jump behind a table. "You know what I can't stand about bitches like you?" I yelled at her. "Yaw ain't got no fucking aim!" I snatched my empty clip out and shoved another full one in. It was music to my ears when I heard her gun start clicking. I jumped up and ran in her direction. She jumped hard as hell when I jumped over the table and gave her the look of death.

"Aw, fuck." She tossed the gun and rolled her eyes. "Get it over with, bitch!" she spat as I put a big-ass hole in between her eyes.

CHAPTER SIXTY-SEVEN

JACOB

I'd tried my best to find a room to hide in. When I heard the gunshot go off, I had already known that one of them had killed Tabitha. My fucking leg was on fire as I looked down at the blood pouring out. I took my shirt off and ripped it, tying it around my leg to slow the blood flow. When I heard footsteps rushing in my direction, I pulled my gun out. I watched someone rush past who I assumed had to be Buckey. I didn't know how the fuck that nigga was even here. I could've sworn I'd shot his ass in the head.

I waited because I knew Python couldn't be far behind him. When I saw the bigger figure rush past, I ran out the door with my gun drawn.

"Stop right there, you big bitch!" I pointed it at his head. He slowly turned around with his hands up.

"So, you ready to end this? Pull the fucking trigger," he flexed.

"Yeah, you try it, nigga." I heard Tokyo coming up behind me. When I glanced at her, she had a gun to India's head. "I'll blow her shit clean off!"

I looked at the fear in India's eyes. I owed her for everything going wrong and them even getting the kids in the first place. I wasn't about to let Tokyo kill her.

"Tokyo if you shoot her, I will shoot him."

"Well, then pull the trigger, Jacob, this is your moment. You've wanted this shit so much," India said, looking past me at Python.

"I don't want them to hurt you." My eyes began to water as I looked and saw Buckey coming back up the hall. I just knew we weren't about to make it out of this. So, I figured if we were going to die, he was at least going to go with us.

"Kill him, Jacob." India gritted her teeth.

"Fuck it!" I said as I pulled the trigger, and nothing happened but a click. I pulled the trigger over and over to constantly hear it clicking. "What the fuck, India?" I glanced at her.

"I didn't load your gun, Jacob. You should've never put your hands on me. You got a little too high up there with this whole thing, and I'm just ready for this to be over honestly." She dropped her head.

"Why the fuck would you do this? I'm the one who helped you even find them and get this far."

"Don't talk to me like I'm just some dumb ass. I only needed you because I knew Python wanted your ass still."

"Well, thank you for the kind gesture, ma'am." Python raised his gun and aimed at me.

"Damn, that's fucked up. You just keep on changing up on everyone trying to help your ass out." Tokyo laughed. I couldn't do shit but shake my head as Buckey raised his gun and aimed at me too.

"Hold on, Python, this nigga killed my baby Jasmine." Buckey fired three shots into my chest, sending me flying back and slumped against the wall. I tried to stand back up because I wasn't about to go out like some bitch.

Python raised his gun and aimed at me. "I told your ass you wouldn't make it to see Christmas fucking with me. I don't understand why you ain't just try to reconnect with us and make shit right."

I guess I should've left well enough alone and tried to go about this shit the right way, but my feelings and my pain got the best of me. I looked up at the ceiling as my body began to go weak from all the blood loss.

Boom!

CHAPTER SIXTY-EIGHT

TOKYO

"Well, damn, that's the end of that." I smacked my lips.

"Tokyo, can we talk please?" India faced me.

"There is nothing to talk about. I'm going to let your ass live. But you can never come around me or the twins ever. Ain't that what you told me? Because you can't be trusted!"

"What the hell, those are my babies! Not yours! How many times do I have to apologize?"

"A fucking sorry won't remove these scars from my body or my head! Do you want to see if you can survive this shit like the fuck I did?"

"Yaw can argue some other time. We need to leave before the police or some shit show up. Tokyo, whether you like it or not, she is still your sister and the mother of those babies, and she is going with us. Me and my brother couldn't fix what was broken with us, but you two can." Python tucked his gun away and began to walk off.

"You dead-ass going to just let shit die and go like that?" I asked in shock.

"Yes, as you should. The real problem is right there, dead and gone!" He pointed to Jacob's lifeless body.

I shook my head while looking at my sister with anger and followed my man. When we got outside, we could all see lights in the far distance. We all jumped in the car and left. We were all quiet the whole ride back to the hotel. I wanted so bad to put a damn bullet in my sister so her ass could feel what the fuck I had felt and gone through.

"Girl, I should knock the fucking shit outta you now!" Cynthia broke the silence as we stepped out of the car.

"Yeah, whatever, I did what I had to do to get my babies back."

"And how did that work out for your ass, dummy?" She walked past India, shoving her hard.

"I should've let him kill your ass," she mumbled, but I heard her.

"Cut that shit out!" Python barked.

As we walked in the hotel, the clerk stared at us as we entered the elevator.

"You know that bitch about to send security up to our room." I rolled my eyes.

"So, I'll handle it." Python stepped off the elevator first then the rest of us followed.

When we walked into the room, Susan was playing on the floor with the twins.

"Mom!" She jumped up and ran toward Cynthia, hugging her long and hard.

"I told you I would bring her back to you." Python smiled.

I walked over and sat down with the twins, kissing both on their heads.

"Ma! Ma!" Baby Ryan clapped his hands, smiling.

"I wanna try something." Python pulled his phone out and began recording. "India, go sit over there with Tokyo and the kids."

She did as she was told and sat across from me and them. The twins looked back and forth between the both of us. I guess he figured they wouldn't know who was who, but they proved him wrong when they started crying and crawled over to me.

"Exactly." I smiled as I saw the hurt wash over her face.

"Well, that fucking sucked." Python put the phone back into his pocket.

"So now what, we all supposed to live happily ever after?" I looked up.

"Yeah, me and you need to be making our way back to Puerto Rico. We have a wedding to plan, ma'am, or did you forget?"

When he mentioned that, everyone gasped.

"Wait, what?" Cynthia walked in from talking to her daughter.

"Yes, ma'am!" I stood up and walked over to show her my rock my baby had sitting on my finger.

"I mean, damn though! Yaw can do it here now that everything is over!" Susan chimed in.

"Well, baby, she is kind of right." I laughed while looking at Python.

"Whatever you want." He came and kissed me gently.

When I turned around, I could see the envy in India's eyes. I almost felt bad for her. Both of the men she'd fallen in love with were dead and gone, and all she really had was herself. Call me petty, but I didn't know when I would get over what the fuck she had done to me. Maybe one day I would, and we could pick back up where we left off.

Buckey, Cynthia, and Susan gathered themselves together and ended up leaving. Me, Python, and India sat around talking about the things that happened. He was trying his best to have us make up, but I wasn't a fool. I loved him even more for trying, but there was just no hashing things out that quick for me, especially after what she did. When I got sleepy, me and Python went into the room to shower and lie down.

When we got out, I walked back out of the room to check on the twins. India was reading a book to them that

I assumed she took out of her bag. They were actually quiet as she did.

Python walked up behind me. "Baby, do you really wanna keep them away from her?" he asked.

"She can't have them, Python. She doesn't know what they like or anything. When and if she can prove herself worthy of being their mother, then maybe yes. Until then, nope." I turned around and went to lie on the bed.

"Tokyo, why do you want them so bad?" He sat down.

"Because I just do, and I love them."

"But we can have our own. That's what I want."

"I know, but I doubt that's going to happen." My eyes began to water.

"Tell me what you're talking about." His voice was stern.

I shook my head because I had never mentioned that there was a possibility that I would never be able to have children. I had never spoken on it, the real reason why I hated my mother. I looked up at Python and told him exactly why I was the way I was. My mother was one of them mothers who really didn't let anything get in the way of her high. Me included.

One night, when I had gone looking for her by myself and found her, she was too high and heavy to move or for me to carry. So, I figured I would stay with her until she sobered up enough to walk. That was the worst thing I could've done on my part. Because that was the same night that my mother sat slumped in a corner on a pissy mattress while two of the young guys she used to cop from raped me.

That shit fucked me up and that was when I knew she really didn't give a fuck about me, or my sister, or my father. To make matters worse, when I told her what happened, she responded with, "Your ass will be okay. You better not mention this shit to your dad because you know I'll lie, and he will believe me over you." And with that, she took me to the hospital and claimed I was a hot-tailed little girl and that she had caught me fucking two guys and needed me to be checked out.

I never spoke on it to my father, and I never told India. She sensed something was wrong with me though because, after that, she claimed I was never the same again. Would anyone be if that happened to them though? That was when all love and respect and care went out the window for my mother. Me killing her was me getting my lick back.

After telling Python everything, he said he understood and held me that night as I cried and tried my best to let all that hurt go. I was upset that I told him though because now I wondered if he would still want to be with me, knowing that I may not be able to have children.

The next morning, I woke up to Python yelling,

"Tokyo, get the fuck up!" He busted back into the room.

"What the fuck is going on!" I threw my robe on and ran out.

"She took the fucking twins!"

"I knew it! I fucking knew it! I told your ass we couldn't trust her! You should've let me put a fucking bullet in her ass!" I yelled back at him. I looked around at everything, and all she had taken was the diaper bag. The money and everything else was still there.

CHAPTER SIXTY-NINE

INDIA

As I walked up the hallway, I heard a lot of commotion coming from the room. As soon as I opened the door, Tokyo jumped up and ran toward me.

"What the fuck, India!" she yelled as she had tears in her eyes.

"What the fuck, what? The hell is wrong with her?" I asked as Python walked out, rubbing his face and taking a deep breath.

"She thought . . . we thought . . ." he stuttered.

"What? That I took my own babies and left?" I smirked.

"Yes! That's exactly what I thought!" Tokyo faced me with her hands on her hips.

"Well, even if I did, they are mine is what you keep seeming to forget." I unstrapped them both in the stroller. Tokyo bit her lip and walked away in frustration.

I shook my head as I let them out and stood them up. They both took a few steps, then stopped and fell at the same time.

"What the fuck? Oh, shit!" Python got excited. "Baby, they walking!" He squatted down and stood my son up. "Come on, li'l man, I been waiting for this here!" He smiled as he walked toward him. Tokyo's whole mood changed as she watched and walked over to do the same.

"What did you all name them?" I watched as they interacted with my babies.

"Ryan and Rya'Lynn." She looked up at me.

"Those are beautiful names." I stood back just watching them. They really did look like a happy family. My heart began to ache because she didn't know that our lawyer was on her way to the hotel with the sheriff so I could in fact take my babies with me.

I knew that all hell was about to break loose in that room. I got nervous and impatient waiting on them. As soon as I was about to use the burner phone I had to text her, there was a loud knock on the door. We all looked back at it.

"You wanna get that?" Python continued to stand Ryan up.

I took a deep breath and asked, "Who is it?"

"The sheriff. Could you please open the door?"

Tokyo and Python both looked at each other, then at me.

"The fuck is the sheriff doing here?" Python asked.

When I opened the door and our lawyer walked in along with the sheriff and a few police officers, Tokyo sucked her teeth and stood straight up.

"The fuck you doing here?" she asked.

"Tokyo, we are here to remove those beautiful twins from your custody. India is their legal and rightful mother. They deserve to be with her. Let's make this as peaceful as possible." Mrs. Peters stood firmly in front of the police officers. The sheriff went into his folder and pulled out a piece of paper.

"This here though, is a protection order warranting that you and you"—he handed her and Python a piece of paper—"stay at least five hundred feet away from India Miles and her children at all times. If you do not abide by—"

"Yeah, whatever! We know how the fuck it goes." Python snatched it and balled it up.

"You are one fucked-up bitch." Tokyo gritted her teeth, giving me the look of death.

"I'm sorry, but this is the only way I know how to handle this."

"Just like a snitching-ass bitch. And just to think I gave your ass the benefit of the doubt." He shook his head.

"It's cool. You'd better believe we are taking this shit to court," Tokyo said.

"Are you sure you want to do that? I mean, I don't think you want to. This could go all wrong."

"On your end too, with your crooked ass." She smirked at Mrs. Peters.

"Grab the twins and their belongings and let's go, India." Mrs. Peters walked out the door, leaving me and the police right there.

I slowly walked past them and grabbed the twins' bags. I glanced at the duffle bag filled with money.

"Don't you even fucking think about it." Python picked it up.

"You want them, you get your own money to take care of them." Tokyo began to cry. "But I swear to your ass, you will see me in court! Soon at that! You know you can't take care of them!"

"I'm their mother, and I'll do whatever it takes to take care of them. You know that. I am sorry it had to be this way though." I put both the twins in the stroller and walked out. When I got downstairs, a text came through on Buckey's phone, saying, This shit isn't over. You just started it all over again.

"Yes, it is," I said to myself and threw the cell phone back in my bag before getting in the car with Mrs. Peters and pulling off.

"Everything will be okay. I will get you all the help that you need in order to take good care of them and to prove yourself in court if need be. First things first, you all can stay with me for the time being until we get you a job and an apartment." She leaned over and kissed me on the mouth.

"We still have the house, so we can stay there for now. I'll search for something in the meantime."

"Are you sure you would want to do that? I mean, we both know Tokyo and, I guess, Python too. You don't think she will come there looking for you?"

"Ehh, you might be right. I promise you, I will only stay with you for one week or two at the most. I have a little bit of money stashed away that I need to go get right quick. It's at our old house, and I know Tokyo's money is still there too."

"Damn, I'm glad women know to always put shit away for a rainy day." She laughed, stopping at a red light. "Plus, where is Jacob?"

"Uhmm . . ." I hesitated. "Me and him got into an argument, and he left to go back to Alabama," I lied.

"Well, damn that was fast!"

"Yeah, I know, right?" I turned around and looked at the twins, who were gazing out the windows at everything zooming by.

CHAPTER SEVENTY

BUCKEY

It had been one week since me and Python had killed Jacob. I had started drinking even more knowing that I no longer had Jasmine. It was hard as hell trying to explain to her parents what had happened to her. There was no search for Jacob, her killer, because I'd told them exactly where he was and lied about how everything went down, making sure not to mention Python and Tokyo's part in it. As usual, me and my team swept that all under the rug and let it be. I was sitting in my mother's room, watching TV when her nurse came in.

"Well, she is doing a whole lot better. We should be expecting her to wake up any day now." She removed the bandage from her face and began to clean around the wound.

"Good because I need to know who did this to her. I won't be able to rest until I do."

As the nurse kept cleaning, my mother began to whine. I instantly stood up and rushed over to her side.

"Mom!" I gently touched her arm, and the nurse backed up.

"Mmm, what in the goddamn fuck?" Her eyes shot open, and she tried to sit up.

"Calm down, Mrs. Washington." The nurse laid her back down and rubbed her shoulder. "Do you know where you are?"

"No, no, what happened? What's going on?" She looked around, trying to get a grip on everything.

"You are at the University of Louisville hospital. Your son is right here. He's been here almost every day." She smiled.

I squeezed her arm a little and smiled when she calmed down at the sight of me.

"My mouth is dry. I need something, some water or something please."

"Okay, I'll be right back with that. You make sure you stay calm and stay in bed, and I'll let your doctor know that you're awake." And with that, she left the room.

"Mom, do you remember anything that happened?"

"Hell yes, I do! That rotten bitch, Peters, shot my ass! Is it bad?" She touched the side of her face.

"Yeah, it kind of is. Wait, what the hell you mean Peters?"

"The fucking lawyer! Well, she didn't actually do it, but she was there! I know I saw her in a parked car that night at the gas station. She didn't get out or anything. I went to pay for my gas, and when I came back out, I remember I was pumping it when I glanced in her direction, and she winked at me, then pulled off. Next thing you know, I heard a loud bang, and everything just went lights out!"

The machines started going off, indicating that her heart rate was increasing.

"I knew that damn India had something to do with this." I bit my bottom lip, feeling my neck get hot.

"What do you mean?"

"It only makes sense, Mom. You were supposed to get India put away for good for all that shit that was going on then you get shot in the face before court? She is India's lawyer, and that shit makes perfect sense!" I pulled out my new cell phone, ready to call Python.

"Who are you calling?" she asked, sitting up more.

"The person I know she's with at the moment—Python!" I dialed his number and was even more pissed off when he told me what that bitch had done and that she was already gone.

"Well, now what? Because I saw her there doesn't mean that you can just go and pick her up. Even you know that's not enough."

"I can't arrest her ass, but I can surely question her and see if she knows anything or if she slips up."

"She's a lawyer, a sneaky snake of a lawyer at that. Her job is to lie. She won't slip up. This is her type of thing."

"How do you know that?"

"Because I've helped her a few times set some things up. I just can't believe the bitch had the balls to try to do me the same way." My mother lay back and began watching TV. The nurse came in and helped her sit back up to drink her water. Once she gave her a shot of morphine and my mother began to doze off, I left to go start on my mission.

First, I had to stop home. When I walked in, I avoided looking at the spot where the blood from me and Jasmine once was. Cynthia and Susan had spent hours scrubbing that and straightening things up for me. I walked into my kitchen and grabbed a half-full bottle of E&J and took a long swig. I had to gather my thoughts as I contemplated what my next move would be. I didn't want to just show up to her house asking her questions, but at this moment, I had no choice.

I grabbed my badge and gun and walked out of the house. When I did, I noticed Cynthia sitting on her porch with her music going. I waved to her and jumped into my car and peeled out. I knew exactly where Peters lived and did damn near ninety getting there. When I walked up the stairs to her door, I could hear babies crying on the other side. I knocked three times and stepped back. After a few more knocks, she opened the door.

"And to what do I owe this surprise, sir?" She smiled.

"I need to talk to you now. Either I can come in or you can step out." I looked past her to see India bouncing one of the babies. She stepped out and closed the door behind her. As soon as she did, I backed her up against the wall and put my gun to her face.

"My mother is awake, bitch. Now tell me what the fuck you had done to her and why."

"I don't know what the fuck you're talking about." She clenched her jaw.

"Don't fuck with me because you know I can and will murder your ass right here."

"Is that alcohol I smell on your breath? Are you drunk while wearing your badge?" She giggled.

I slapped her with the butt of my gun, causing blood to seep from her nose. Her eyes grew wide with fear as I put my hand around her throat.

"Okay, since you wanna play games, we'll do that. Your ass is about to walk back into that apartment and tell India that you have to go downtown with me to discuss an issue for an upcoming case. Don't do anything stupid or try to signal her because I will murk both you sneaky bitches. The only reason I'm not about to take her with us is because she has those kids in there with her. Do as I said and make it quick." I released her and handed her a folded napkin I had stuffed in my pocket.

She snatched it and wiped her nose while looking at me like I was crazy.

"You won't get away with this shit. I promise you won't. I'll make sure you lose your badge and all, you crazy motherfucker!"

"Yeah, I'm sure. Now, get to it." I shoved her into the door. I stood in the doorway and watched her. India gave me a smirk and continued to bounce baby Ryan.

"Is everything okay?" she asked.

"Everything is fine. She needs to hurry up though," I spoke up for Peters.

"Well, all right then. I'm about to lay the twins down for bed, it's really late. You want me to wait up for you?"

"Please do." Peters grabbed her purse and walked past me and out the door.

"You think your ass is real cute saying that shit, huh?" I opened the car door for her.

I was about to drive her ass straight to Python's house where his aunt still was for the past year, keeping everything straight. When I pulled up, the lights were on in the living room area. I saw the rental truck and some other car that looked like one parked on the side. I got out and went and opened the door for Peters.

Walking up to the door, I tapped twice and walked in. Python, Tokyo, and his aunt were sitting in the living room talking. Everyone looked up, and then Tokyo ran over and swung on Mrs. Peters, knocking her in the eye.

"You bitch! After all the money I've paid you and all the clientele I got your ass, you switch up on me for India!" she barked at her.

"And this shit is exactly why! I hope with whatever yaw do, you all know that you won't get away with it! India knows that I left with him, and she's waiting up on me."

"Go ahead and do your thing, dawg." Python stood up and pointed to the basement. I was about to torture this bitch until she told me what I needed to know and who she had shoot my mother. That's who I really wanted. She most definitely wasn't going back home to India. I didn't give a fuck what she said. I was going to kill her ass tonight. If I had to, I would go back and kill India too. She out of all people deserved that shit the most with all the hell she was raising.

I did everything I could to break that woman in that basement. She held out on me until I started cutting her toes off one by one. Then she finally told me who she had to shoot my mother.

"Tristan did it! I paid him twenty thousand to do it for me. He always does my dirty work for a nice penny," she sobbed.

"Tristan who? Python's Tristan?"

"Yeah, Mr. Dumbass! We all connected in some type of way! He has always worked for me. Me and your mother worked together to put a lot of people away and to get a lot of them out. Now because the shoe was on the other foot, you motherfuckers wanna come for me! Yaw know how this shit goes!" She spat blood and two teeth out on the ground.

"What the fuck though? You switched up on my mother for India?"

"Because I have worked for Tokyo and India for a long time. The money is good as fuck and more than anyone has ever paid me. They were paying me just to keep me around for 'just in case' reasons. What do you know? India ended up needing me. I would do anything for her, I love her."

"The fuck? Is you bitches fucking or something?" I laughed a little.

"We have had each other more than a couple of times. Nobody treats me the way she does, and nobody can love her the way that I can."

"You one weird-ass bitch. Well, anyways thanks for the info, but you fucked up in a major way this time. Slippers count, don't they?" I stood back and emptied the clip into her, turning her midsection into a lot of mush.

I walked upstairs and sat down with Python. "Man, you ain't gonna believe what the fuck this bitch told me." I sat back and sipped the drink Tokyo brought to me.

"What's up?"

"Nigga, Tristan been working for her and my mother, doing hits for them for years."

"Not my Tristan!" Python shook his head.

"Yeah, nigga, the one you got watching the trap spots. We gonna have to handle that shit. Ain't nobody gonna hurt my mother and get away with that bullshit." I downed the rest of it and rubbed my head.

"What type of snake-ass shit is that?" Tokyo walked back over and sat down.

"Right, plus she said that she been working as yaw lawyer for years and that her and India is fucking. They been with each other for years and shit, fucking around, and that she loves her."

"Say what now!" Tokyo stood up.

"Yeah, that's what she said before I killed her ass."

"That bitch talk too much. She and India deserved each other. But it makes sense on why she was ride or die for her type shit."

"Yeah well, she completed the riding and dying. Now what we gonna do?" I asked.

"I don't know what's first, but at least we ain't gotta worry about her ass representing India in court."

"You right, which means you also don't have to worry about her bringing up no bullshit either. That'll be smooth sailing for yaw asses to get them babies back."

"I was thinking about just killing her ass and making it look like a suicide or overdose." Tokyo sucked her teeth.

We sat around talking about getting Tristan and India. We came up with a plan to get her to come around, and Tristan wouldn't have been shit. I was sure that after all this was over, we could all live the way we wanted with no drama.

CHAPTER SEVENTY-ONE

INDIA

"I don't understand how the fuck they did this shit! Stop crying, please!" I yelled in frustration at baby Rya'Lynn. She had been crying nonstop, not to mention she was running a fever. Then, I remembered she was teething. I searched the diaper bag for some teething gel and found nothing. I looked over at Mrs. Peters's car keys and wallet. I opened it up and took out thirty dollars, knowing she wouldn't mind. I snatched up the keys and the babies and left.

When I got to the CVS, I searched up and down the aisles, trying to decide which one would be best for her. I also decided to grab some teething rings. I opened it right there and gave it to her. She began to bite on it immediately. I pushed the stroller to the front and placed the money on the counter.

"Sorry, I already opened the teething ring." I smiled.

"I understand, but you do know that you're supposed to boil those first? I mean, that's only sanitary, sweetie." The older woman looked at me, then the twins.

"Bitch, I ain't even ask you all that! Plus, add on a pack of cigarettes while your meddling ass is at it." I gave her ass attitude because she had given me one. After she handed me my change, I snatched my bag and pushed the twins out of the store. Strapping them into the car seats, I grew nervous about Peters not being home yet. Everything had me nervous and looking over my shoulder, mainly thinking and wondering when my sister was going to pop out on me.

I pulled into a McDonald's drive-through and ordered two double cheeseburgers and two orders of chicken nuggets, remembering that Python mentioned they loved them. I didn't know what type of sauce they liked and figured it didn't matter because they were babies. I soon found out that they didn't like ranch as they both rejected that shit when I tried to feed them.

When I finally got them down for a nap, I lit a cigarette and began looking into getting back into college. I had a point to prove to my sister. She was about that thug life shit, and I was about the good ole American dream, you know, the big house with the white picket fence. She had managed to fuck that up for me twice, but a third time was a no-go. Me and Mrs. Peters would raise my babies together and away from everyone of that nature and live happily ever after.

I sat on the computer for hours, occasionally wondering where she was until the house phone rang. I glanced over then at the room where the twins were, hoping and praying that the ringing didn't disturb them. When it stopped, I continued doing what I was doing until it rang again. This time I snatched it off the hook and whispered, "Who's calling?"

"It's me, Tokyo. I think that we should talk about all this. I really don't have the time for court and whatnot seeing the fact that I have to get back to Puerto Rico to plan my wedding!"

"How did you get this number? Don't even answer that because I can imagine."

"So, you going to talk to me or not, India? I mean, after all, we are sisters, and I really do want the twins and you to attend my wedding."

"I don't know. I'll have to think about it."

"You can meet me somewhere public. Please? I really wanna see the twins."

"Tokyo, quit talking to me like I don't know you. As soon as you get the chance, your ass is going to do something to me."

"But why would I do that? I'm serious, and for once, I want and need you to believe me."

"Like I said, I'll think about it. In the meantime, what type of sauce do the twins like with their chicken nuggets?"

"Barbecue for Rya and ketchup for Ryan."

"Thanks, I'll be in touch."

"No, wait a minute!" she yelled before I hung up on her.

I lay back on the couch, then thought about finding an apartment. Although me and Peters were messing around and she cared for me, until things got serious, me and my children needed our own space. More like I just wanted my own just in case. I lit a cigarette and began my search.

Sometime later on that night, I heard one of the twins crying. I jumped up and checked my cell phone. It was nine at night, and I had fucking dozed off. I ran into the room to see Ryan hanging off the edge of the bed, hollering his ass off. I scooped him up just before he let go.

"Goddammit, boy!" I sat on the side and kissed him on the head. The back of his shirt and pants were wet. "Fuck!" I stripped him of his clothes and put him in a clean diaper, and then I changed baby Rya. I pulled out some pajamas for them and began running them some bathwater after I cut on *The Princess and the Frog* to watch. As I was getting them out of the tub, there was a knock at the door. I continued to get them ready, taking my time.

Once I had them settled on the floor, I went to look out the peephole. I saw Buckey with a few other officers. I snatched the door open.

"Yes?"

"Are you Ms. Miles?" One officer stepped forward.

"Yes, I am, why?"

"Well, we were told that you were a close friend of Attorney Peters, and she has no other family or relatives that we know of."

Buckey stood silently behind them and said nothing. I was nervous because I could tell by the way that they looked that something wasn't right, and I knew all too well that Buckey had something to do with this all. I stepped aside to let them in.

"Tell me what's the matter. Is she okay?" I folded my arms.

"Well, no, in fact, uhh, we received a call this morning of a body tossed in a park in the far west end area. After everything that we had to do and investigating, I'm sorry to inform you, ma'am, but it was Mrs. Peters."

"I fucking knew it!" My eyes began water. "So you all don't know who did it? I mean, now what?"

"Speaking of that," Buckey finally spoke, "there was a note left next to her body saying, 'Your little girlfriend is next!'" He kept eye contact with me.

"So, what is that supposed to mean?"

"Can you tell us if you two had the same enemy in common or any enemies at all?"

"Not that I know of." I wiped away at the tears. Maybe I was just bad luck, and it wasn't meant for me to love anyone. It seemed like everyone I fell in love with got tied up in my bullshit and got killed.

"Well, is there anything you can tell us, like who she last saw or had spoken with?"

I glanced up at Buckey, then looked at the floor. "No, sir, I can't. If you don't mind, I need to get back to my children, please."

"Well, if you can think of anything, please don't hesitate to give me a call." He handed me a card and walked off. Buckey stood there until they were no longer in view.

"You know what's up. She did what she did to my mother because of your stank ass. I don't care what you two bitches had going. Yaw fucked up coming for mine."

"Fuck you! Get the fuck away from here!" I slammed the door and began to cry.

My mind began to race as I thought about what the other officers had said. What if they were in on this shit with him? I had to think of something and quick. I needed someone to protect me. I looked over at my cell phone and decided to call the only person I knew a motherfucker wouldn't fuck with. Tokyo.

"You going to let me see the twins?" she spoke as soon as she picked up.

"Yeah, yeah, sure. But I need a huge favor. I know you want nothing to do with me, but I need you. And this will be the only way you can see them or be around them as much as you want. Peters is dead, and I need somewhere to stay, and whoever did it said they coming for me next. Tokyo, please help me. I'm scared."

"Don't worry about it. Yaw can come stay with me and Python. I'll protect you. I wish a motherfucker would. I mean, after all, we are still sisters."

"Thank you so much." I sniffled.

"You good, now bring yaw asses on. I'll text the address to you."

"Okay." I hung up the phone and threw my and my kids' shit into duffle bags as quickly as I could.

I had a feeling that Buckey would be back later that night or the next day. I figured if I could get back into my sister's good graces, she would protect me from him. I ran all of our bags down to the car and then went back up for the babies. Once I had them strapped in, I peeled the fuck out and thanked the Father above for people who forgave.

CHAPTER SEVENTY-TWO

TOKYO

"Told you that shit would be easy. That girl too damn soft. Until a dick telling her what to do. Then she full-blown crazy and in GI Jane mode!" I sat back on the bed, shaking my head.

"So, how we gonna handle it when she get here?" Python walked out of the bathroom, brushing his teeth.

"Ain't no handling anything. I want to slowly make her miserable, get threatening notes and shit sent to her. Make her feel like a motherfucker is following her. Toy with her a little bit."

"You real deal petty."

"No, what she did was petty. She knew before she called that bitch and the folks that she couldn't take care of them kids anyways. Now, she wanna call me because she scared. We'll help her though. But believe you me when I say I got something for her ass. Has your mom reached here yet?"

"Yeah, she at the airport."

"You not going to get her?"

"Nah, Jaheim on his way to get her now. Plus, she still isn't too happy with me after the shit I did."

"I'm not either, but we will all get over it soon enough."

"If you say so. Have you contacted a priest or anything?"

"Not really, baby, this takes time."

"No, it don't. Buy all the shit, get the invitations out, get a preacher and shit. Damn, that do sound like a lot." He laughed and walked back into the bathroom.

I texted Cynthia and told her what was all going on, and she called me a crazy motherfucker for even thinking to let India come here, but it was all a part of my plan. I just wanted the twins back with us where they belonged even if that meant having her around for the time being.

An hour later, there was a lot of commotion downstairs. Me and Python rushed down to see what the fuck was going on. His mother and India were arguing in the living room.

"What the fuck is she doing here?" She pointed at my sister.

"Look, we will discuss that later. For the time being, everyone under this roof needs to get the fuck along, for the kids anyways, since nobody seems to want to let them go!" Python yelled. The room stayed quiet for a while. It was times like that that turned me on. His mother threw her hand on her hip and walked off into the kitchen to go hug her sister. India sat the twins down, and they instantly started crawling toward me and Python.

"I still don't want that bitch here!" his mom shouted. We all looked into the kitchen as she flipped India the bird. She hadn't seen her since the night that everything happened.

"Ma, chill out with that shit, please!" He picked up baby Ryan. "What's Daddy's man been up to?" He tickled him. India shot him a dirty look. Then she walked over to me.

"Tokyo, can you help me bring our things in, please? I need to talk to you."

"Sure." I followed her back out to the car. "What's up?"

"Thank you. Tokyo, look, I seriously don't wanna beef with anyone in here. I just need you to help me with them and look out for me because . . ." She trailed off.

"'Cause what?"

"Because I think Buckey killed Mrs. Peters, and I think he is going to kill me too."

"Now, why the hell would he be after you?" I laughed.

"Because he knows that Mrs. Peters had his mom shot in the face so she wouldn't show up to court and I could get out."

"Well, is it true?"

"Yeah, but I didn't know that's what she was talking about when she said she would take care of it."

"Well, I'm sure he's understanding, and if you tell him that, we can squash the shit."

"You know it's not that simple."

"So, you want me to play security?"

"Exactly, if that's what you wanna call it. Please?"

"Okay, cool." I grabbed a bag, and then she hugged me tight.

"Can we just do things the way we used to? It is a Friday after all. Can we just kick back with some drinks and movies, please? I need something familiar in my life right now."

"Yeah, that would be pretty nice."

I was going to play nice, and I was going to be Captain Save-a-ho, too. Little did she know, the next time she left for good, those babies weren't going with her. I had grown too attached to them and so did my man. And seeing that I believed I couldn't conceive, that was as close as I was going to get with raising blood of my own. Me and Python had never used protection, and still I hadn't gotten pregnant yet.

When everyone had settled in for the night, Python and his mother went into the den to talk, and me and India sat in the living room with some coolers and pizza. It kind of felt good doing this again. I glanced at my cell, thinking I would get a call. That was something I often found myself doing sometimes on a late night, expecting to hear my father's voice. I still hadn't gotten over that either. I mean, it was still pretty fresh.

The next morning, I got up early and went downstairs to cook a big breakfast for everyone. I had plans for me, Cynthia, Sherryl, and India to start planning my wedding. I didn't want something small, but nothing majorly big. I had already called Cynthia and her daughter to invite them over for breakfast. As I set plates out along with glasses, everyone started coming into the kitchen.

"Well, I can't say I don't like the way this feels." Python kissed me on the cheek. There was a knock on the door and then Cynthia and Susan walked in.

"Damn, you got it smelling great in here!" She danced around with bags in her hands.

"You know I can kill anything."

"Literally." India busted out laughing, and we all just looked at her. "Damn, my bad."

"You good." I smiled, hugging her. "Get the twins set up in their highchairs, please." I felt everyone's eyes on us.

"So, what's up with this big-ass breakfast?" Sherryl asked.

"Weeee"—I pointed at all the women—"are all about to start planning my wedding."

"Today? Well, hell ain't shit else to do." She shrugged.

"Is something wrong, Mrs. Sherryl?" I looked over my shoulder.

"Hell, yeah, it is! I don't understand why—"

"Because she is whether you want her to be or not!" Python interjected.

"Please, just try to bear with us, please?"

"I don't think I like staying where the hell I clearly ain't wanted. Maybe me and the twins should just go so she'll feel better." India stood up.

"No! You're going to stay right where you are!"

Breakfast was awkward as hell. I didn't know what the hell I was thinking trying to pull this off. After we all ate, Sherryl made us all mimosas, and we started flipping through magazines and calling different numbers. It felt weird but kind of good that I was planning my wedding, seeing that I'd always said I would never get married.

I ended up deciding on white and yellow colors for everything. Every time India tried to suggest something, Mrs. Sherryl and Cynthia would talk over her or just flat-out disagree. I still had to contact a reverend or something. I was more excited to just start shopping for everything.

"Babe, you're rushing me to get things in order and you ain't even set a date yet." I walked into our den and sat on Python's lap.

"It'll happen as soon as you get everything together."

"So just like that you expect . . ." Out of nowhere, I felt this uneasy feeling and threw up right on the floor.

"What the fuck?" Python jumped up and ran after me to the bathroom. "Babe, you good?" He stood in the doorway.

"I think it was the mimosas. I'm straight." I wiped my mouth and did a quick rinse and spit with the mouthwash. I went and sat back down on the couch when Cynthia walked in.

"Python, I like Buckey, and I think you need to set that up for me." She threw her hand on her hip.

"Well, damn, ain't yo' ass demanding?" He laughed.

"I'm serious. He knows I like him, but he won't bite. I mean, sometimes he flirts, and then sometimes it's just weird. That's yo' homie."

"No offense, but you older than him by far. What you gonna do with him?"

"Turn his ass out, of course. I know how to take care of a man and please one. Plus, I'm fun. Do that for me."

"Ehh, I'll see what's up, but I ain't making no promises, woman."

"Fine, enough for me. Hey, Tokyo, you wanna come stay with me and Susan tonight? Do a little girls' night or something?"

"Yeah, baby, go ahead and go do that. Take ya mind off everything or get more finished. Plus, me and Buckey gotta go handle something anyways."

"You sure? Well, what about India and the twins?"

"She's their mother, and besides, my mom and aunt are here. They'll be fine."

"That's the problem, your mom and aunt might try to fuck her ass up."

"Nah, shit is smooth."

"Hey, son, me and ya aunt going back to her house tonight to catch up on some things. You all are going to behave while I'm gone, right?" She smiled.

"Well, shit, I guess everyone is leaving. I'll let India know she will have the house to herself tonight, then. I'm sure she'll appreciate that."

CHAPTER SEVENTY-THREE

BUCKEY

"Mom, I handled Mrs. Peters for you." I sat back in the chair in her room as she ate her dinner.

"What does that mean, you arrested her?"

"You know what it means. She tried to have you killed. I'm going to handle India's ass, too, soon enough."

"This is all too crazy. I guess, I really can't be upset because what you put into the universe is always guaranteed to come back around tenfold. And Lord knows I have done a lot of fucked-up shit to people." She began to sob with her mouth full of food.

"Damn, Buckey, what you do now?" Python walked in, eating a bag of chips.

"She's all right. She'll be fine. Let's go handle that situation with Tristan." I stood up, ready to leave.

"What? What's wrong with Tristan?" My mother looked up, wiping her nose.

"Ma, Peters told me he been working for you and her for a while. We ain't got room for moles in our shit. Why would you do that?"

"That boy has helped a lot. Made my job and hers easier."

"I can only imagine. That's exactly how you were building a case on me, right?" Python finished off the rest of his bag.

"It was nothing personal, Desmond." She shot him a dirty look.

"Yeah, you say that now, but did you ever think that if I went down, your son would too? It would've looked bad on your part, also."

"I would have kept him out of it, unless you were going to snitch once caught."

"Not at all. But one thing I don't do is get caught. I kill any- and everything in my way before shit like that happens." He walked out of the room. I was upset with my mother because she really hadn't thought any of that through, and if she did, her ass was most definitely not worried about my well-being.

"Well, something else you can think about while you're still in here is that you just got that boy killed," I said before walking out myself.

When we pulled up to one of Python's many trap houses, the guys were just all out reckless with the way they were serving right out in the open. A few of them looked at the truck, waiting to see who would step out. I got out first and then Python.

"Oh, shit!" one of the young boys yelled and froze up. Another one ran in the crib, I'm sure to get Tristan.

Me and Python both stepped in and were met with a face full of smoke. A couple of females were walking around naked, there was music going, and I was sure there was a bitch sucking dick in one of the corners. Python pulled his gun out and let off a few shots in the air. The girls started screaming and ducking and a few dudes jumped up and froze once they laid eyes on him.

"So, is this what we doing?" He looked around. "Where the fuck is Tristan?" Python walked around, looking at all his product scattered all over the tables. The shit was a mess, and he hated that shit. A dude tried to ease past me, and I punched him in the face as hard as I could, sending him flying back onto the couch.

"Ain't none of that. Your ass wasn't trying to leave when shit was just poppin' in here." I spat my gum out on the floor and kept eyes on everyone. Me and Python always handled shit on our own.

"Tell Tristan's snake ass to get the fuck down here now!" Python ordered. Everyone sat around quiet as Tristan came down the stairs like he was the boss of it all without a care in the world.

"What's up, boss man?" He smiled.

"The fuck is all this shit, yo?" Python looked around.

"Man, you know, just having a little fun handling business at the same. I got this bad little broad upstairs right now—"

Python socked him in the mouth, instantly knocking his two front teeth out.

"What the fuck, man?" His eyes widened with terror as he looked up at Python.

"Aye yo, go up there and get them hoes. Bring them down here now."

I walked up the stairs where three rooms were. I pulled my gun out and checked every room until I got to the one in the far back. This nigga had actually decked out a room in the trap house. The two females were lying in the bed, kissing and sucking on each other.

"Looks like he sent someone else up to handle his nasty work." She smiled and flicked her tongue at me.

"You two bitches ain't hear them gunshots down there?" I watched the smaller one as she caressed her breast.

"Hell, that happens all the time. Them niggas be acting a fool."

"You say that like you be here a lot or something." I walked closer to them.

"I'm always here. Hell, I cut the shit, bag the shit, and sometimes snort the shit." She giggled. No wonder they weren't fazed by anything going on. These two bitches were high as a giraffe's pussy on mars.

"Yeah, well, get the fuck up and come with me." I cocked my gun so they knew I was serious. They quietly got dressed and walked in front of me as I watched their asses jiggle and bounce with every step.

When we reached the bottom of the stairs, Python grabbed the first one he could by the hair and threw her on the floor next to Tristan.

"You know, you've always been a breast man, so I know this one is yours. What's up, li'l momma?" He squatted down in front of her.

"Tristan, who the fuck is this? What, we being robbed or something?" She glanced at him, scared to take her eyes off Python.

"No, I can't rob my own shit, now can I?"

"The fuck you mean your shit? This my man's shit, motherfucker!"

"Oh, really? Is that what the fuck he been telling you?"

"He run all these trap spots on this side!" She rolled her neck. All I could think was this bitch was half retarded.

"You a jazzy, slick-mouth-ass bitch, and let's see how slick that motherfucker really is." Python stood up. "Suck his dick."

"What? No! I ain't doing that in front of all these people, nigga!"

"You really ain't got a choice." He aimed his gun at her friend and blew the side of her head smooth off.

"Oh, my God, Whitney!" The girl started screaming and backing away from the dead body.

"Now get to sucking, li'l momma." Python stepped back and grabbed a chair to sit down. "Yaw ready for a show?" He grinned.

"Come on, man, why you doing this?" Tristan asked with tear-filled eyes.

"'Cause you a fucking snake. You think you hot shit now, huh? Thought I wouldn't be coming back to the 'ville, my nigga? You guessed wrong. You fucking sloppy! Got all these motherfuckers in my shit and just doing as they please outside like the fuck shit can't get robbed or ran in by the Feds or some shit! That ain't how the fuck a boss operates, my nigga. Now, drop ya shit and let that bitch get to work."

Everyone sat around quiet as she slowly sucked his dick, crying and snotting everywhere. One dude had the nerve to pull his cell phone out and try to record on the low. That was a big mistake on him. I pointed my gun at him and shot him in the face twice.

"Record that, motherfucker!" I kicked the phone away from him and stomped it to pieces.

"You got all that mouth for a nigga who dick won't even get hard." Python laughed.

"That's because he scared as fuck right now." I laughed.

"Shit, even under pressure my shit still get hard as brick, my nigga." Python grabbed himself. "Call the cleanup crew, Buckey. It's about to get messy in this motherfucker." And with that said, me and Python started shooting everyone in the house. All that could be heard was screams and gunshots and people outside yelling, "Oh, fuck!"

CHAPTER SEVENTY-FOUR

PYTHON

I was glad as fuck that I had a pair of extra clothes in the truck. While the crew cleaned up the mess in the spot, I showered and changed clothes. When I was done, Buckey did the same. I didn't have to worry about the police showing up anytime soon because that neighborhood was just too ruthless for anyone to actually give a fuck about the mess that always went down there.

When the crew was done, we wiped off the drugs that were already bagged up and left. I had told the crew they could take whatever they wanted out of there, including the money and all that was on the niggas I'd killed. Now I had to find someone else to be in charge. I looked over at Buckey.

"How you feel about running all the spots now?"

"Shit, that's more work and more money for me." He smiled.

"Myyy nigga. The only motherfucker who ain't switched up on me. I got another thing for you too."

"Damn, don't overwork a brotha now."

"How you feel about being my best man?"

"Nigga, what?" He smirked. "Who the fuck else gonna do it?" He punched me in the arm.

"Silly motherfucka. That's what's up. I can't believe I'm actually about to marry the crazy-ass, sexy motherfucking killa I've always wanted." I had to shake my head.

"I'm happy for you and her. Yaw both deserve it. Shit happened all fast and whatnot, but I know you been having your eye on her for the longest and yaw love is real. I don't know too many people who will ride for each other right off the humble like yaw did."

"Shit, did start out kind of crazy, huh? But that's why I love that woman. It's always a thrill with her."

"Well, you know they say that once you tie the knot, shit kind of falls off."

"Who is they?"

"Shit, I don't know, people do. I be reading and shit you know. Plus, the guys at the office and station say that shit all the time."

"Well, they ain't fucking with a chick like Tokyo."

"Yeah, you right about that," Buckey said, causing us both to laugh.

"Let's go out for some drinks or some shit."

"Well, the women ain't at the crib anyways. Tokyo went to go stay the night with Cynthia. I think she just wanted to get her away from India for real. Which I'm glad she did because I don't think I could've comfortably left knowing that she still got an ill feeling toward her." When I mentioned India, Buckey turned his nose up. I know what he wanted to do to her, but things just couldn't happen like that. Not on my watch.

We went and hit up a couple of different bars until we found one with a cool enough atmosphere for us to kick back. We ended up getting so fucked up that I had to call my brother to catch an Uber for us to drive us back to the house. When we got there, he left my and Buckey's drunk asses in the living room. I had told him that he could stay the night because I dead serious didn't want my best friend putting his life in any more danger trying to drive home drunk.

I told him where the blankets were and that he could sleep in the den since the guest room was occupied with India and the babies. I passed out after he said he was straight. Sometime around six that morning, I got up and finally took my ass to bed. I was sleeping like a baby until I heard Ryan screaming and crying. I jumped up to check on him. When I walked into the room, India was nowhere in sight. There was a letter on the twins' dresser.

Python, sorry I didn't wake you. I had to run to the old house real quick. I'll be back shortly.

I shook my head and picked him up. He was soaking wet. I took his clothes off him and changed him. I checked Rya'Lynn, and she was fine. Walking into their bathroom, I ran some warm water and went to wash him up. After I got him dressed, we went downstairs so I could make some breakfast and call Tokyo.

"That don't make no fucking sense for her to have done that shit. I told your ass she ain't ready to have them. Who the fuck does that? And what if you wouldn't have been there?"

"Yeah, I know, but she said she would be back shortly, so I don't know. We'll see, I guess."

"Well, either way, I'm on my way back now. Need anything before I get there?"

"Yeah, some Tylenol. I got one hell of a hangover."

"Awww, does my baby want Mommy to come home and take care of him?" she teased.

"Yeah, I got something you can take care of all right."

"Smart ass. Well, I'll see you when I get there." She hung up.

After I was done making me and Ryan some eggs and bacon, I went back upstairs to check on Rya, and she was still sleeping. I assumed it was from the Children's

Tylenol that was sitting on the dresser. I went back downstairs and flipped on some football. Not long after that, Tokyo came through the door with my mother on her heels.

"Hey, Ma, what's up?"

"Not much, but look, I got an old dress."

"Nope!" Tokyo threw her hand up. "No, ma'am. No disrespect, but I will be getting a custom-made wedding dress and it probably won't even be white."

"Well, damn! Rude-ass heifer!" She laughed while following Tokyo into the kitchen.

CHAPTER SEVENTY-FIVE

INDIA

When I pulled up to the house, there was a for sale sign in the front yard. I shook my head and continued on in. Everything looked as it did when I had left a year ago. The furniture and all was still inside. Someone had obviously been there because there was a drink and some sandwiches on the table in the kitchen along with some old mail. I walked down to the basement where I knew Tokyo had a vault. It was partially cracked open.

I stepped in to find that it was empty. That girl moved pretty fucking fast. As I was about to leave, I noticed a ring that I knew all too well in one of the corners. I picked it up, and my heart cracked into a thousand pieces. It was a ring I had bought for Bryson a couple of months into our relationship. It cost a pretty penny, too. I shed a few tears as I could only imagine what she had done to him down there for all that time.

I walked out and went to go to my room where my money was stashed away in my closet. When I got up there, my bed was still made and all with the exception of some of my clothes still thrown around and spread out from when I had left. I sat down and thought about all the good memories me and my sister had in that house, none bad at all. Standing up, I walked into my walk-in closet where some of my things were missing.

"Guess I'll have to buy some new shit as usual." Scooting some boxes around, I pulled up a piece of the floor where my money was. When I opened it, I almost screamed at the top of my lungs when I saw that it was empty. My money was fucking gone, and there was a piece of paper. I snatched it out and read it.

Got'cha!

I grew so fucking furious as I snatched shit down and tossed it around. Tokyo had got my ass. It had to have been her. She was the only one who knew where my money was besides Bryson, but he was dead. I ran down the steps and started breaking shit left and right. If she thought she was going to sell that house, it was going to need some work before she did so.

When I was finished, I went outside and started the car. The only thing that was keeping me from driving it through that fucking house was the fact that it belonged to my now deceased attorney/lover. I pulled off like a bat out of hell. She had fucking gotten me, and there wasn't shit I could do about it because I needed her for security reasons. I could get her back and hit her ass where it hurt. I stopped by the liquor store on my way back to the house. Getting the largest bottle of 1800 they had to sell, I wasted no time cracking it open and guzzling some.

When I pulled up in front of the house, I sat in the driveway for a moment thinking my plan through. She might've been the killer, but I was the smart and sneaky one. I pulled my cell phone out and called JC Penney.

"Hello, do you all still do photos?"

"Yes, ma'am, we do. Would you like to schedule a date to come in for a photoshoot?" the lady on the other end asked.

"Yes, when is the earliest that I can schedule it?"

"Well, we have a lot of openings for every day this week and Monday through Thursday of next week."

"I'll take Monday of next week please." After handling all that, I got out and walked into the house.

"Hey, sis." Tokyo looked up at me as she sat on the couch next to Python.

"What's up? Sorry I took so long getting back."

"It's cool, next time just wake me up. Can't be leaving them like that and Ryan was pissy wet." Python sat up.

"My bad. I had checked them before I left. Hey, Tokyo, I was thinking maybe we could go do a family photoshoot together next week? You know, just me, you, and the twins if you don't mind."

"That sounds nice."

"Yeah, I want some pictures to hang up when I get my new home. I want me and you to dress alike and the twins to dress alike. I'm talking having the same hairstyle and all. You know, the whole thing." I gave a fake smile.

"That does sound fun, and I wouldn't mind going to a salon. I ain't did that in forever."

"Yeah, I can get my hair cut like yours and everything."

"Girl, you mean to tell me that you want your head half shaved like mine?"

"Hell yeah! You are rocking that shit, so I know I can too. I mean, hello!" I outlined my face as we all laughed.

We all sat around talking and watching movies until Buckey showed up. He looked like he had been drinking. Every time I looked up, he was giving me a side-eye look. I felt so uncomfortable with him being around. It made me have a queasy feeling in my stomach, and I seriously had to go shit. When I was done using the bathroom, I washed my hands and walked out.

Buckey was coming up the stairs. I backed into the room and tried to shut the door, but he put his foot right there, blocking me from doing so.

"What is it, Buckey?"

"Count your days, bitch. Tokyo won't be able to protect you for long. If I wanted to get your ass, I could have my man take her out of town and then murk you."

"Well, then what's stopping you from doing it?" I folded my arms. I was getting tired of him already.

"Just know it's coming."

"Keep acting like I can't go to the cops if I want to!"

"Try it and watch your ass get locked up right there. You had a motive to have my mother shot. You think I didn't record that bitch before I killed her? She told everything. You know how much time your ass could get for shooting someone of the law? That's if they don't give your ass the death penalty." He kissed me on the cheek and walked off.

"Just like a bitch!" I mumbled and followed behind him.

When I got downstairs, me and Tokyo called our old hairstylist to set up an appointment. Then, we planned her miniature bachelorette party and Python's bachelor party. I just couldn't shake the fact that this bitch had taken my money. I kept faking my smiles and laughter as the night went on.

It was a couple of days later when I was sitting in the living room and got a phone call from the community college telling me when I could start my classes and asking if I needed financial aid and all that other mess. It felt good because that was at least something positive that was going for me. After that phone call, I called around looking for some apartment openings. I wasn't going to tell anyone where I was going either. Although Tokyo had taken all my money, I had some of the money that Jacob had left behind. A motherfucker could only think of how happy I was when I looked through those duffle bags and saw that. It was at least $50,000 in cash. I guess you could say things were kind of looking up for ya girl.

All through the weekend, Cynthia and her daughter and Python's mother were in and out of the house always in Tokyo's face. I got annoyed and would just go into my room whenever they did come through.

Monday morning, we got up early and left to go get our hair done. The hair salon was jam-packed, and I was glad we had appointments. When we walked in, some of the females became quiet while others continued their conversations quietly.

"Damn, I know yaw ain't still fucked up about that little dispute over a year ago?" Tokyo walked over and sat in the chair that belonged to Alice. She had been the only one to touch our hair besides ourselves for the last six years.

"Girl, don't you come in here on that foolishness! She don't even work here no more." She walked up and gave us both hugs.

"That bitch had a bath mouth. It wasn't my fault she ain't have no fucking edges."

"Okay, so what am I doing for you two ladies today?" She whipped an apron out and tied it around Tokyo's neck.

"We are both getting a wash, a cut, and a style done. We want the same hairstyle. So we can look exactly alike." I smiled.

"Then that means someone is about to have to get a dye done also." She pointed at Tokyo.

"I'm all for it. A new color would be nice I think."

She was about to get her hair dyed blond just like mine.

"Also, we need our lashes done if you don't mind when you are finished." I picked up a magazine and flipped through it.

The whole process took about four hours. Our photo-shoot appointment was at three in the afternoon, and it was going on one thirty. We got to the house and both took showers and got dressed. Mrs. Sherryl had already gotten the twins ready. Python had left with Buckey to go make some runs around the city.

The photoshoot went amazing, and the twins had a ball. We couldn't get Rya to smile as much as her brother though. She had an attitude and personality like her aunt Tokyo. When we were finished, we went to Applebee's to get something to eat. People kept complimenting how pretty we were and how adorable the babies were. A couple of people kept asking to take photos with us. It was all so funny and very much needed, besides a chick who made me feel uneasy the way she kept her eyes glued on the twins and kept asking questions about them in particular.

Around seven thirty, we all got back into the car and left to go home. When I finally checked my messages, there were a few from different landlords returning my calls. One even said I could move in as soon as tomorrow. That was the last place I wanted to go to though. I decided to decline the offer and wait on something better since I had the money for better.

When Python came in, he had to do a double take when he saw how Tokyo's hair was.

"Damn, you look good as fuck with blond hair, girl!" He grabbed her by the hand and twirled her around, making her dress flare a little.

CHAPTER SEVENTY-SIX

TOKYO

Python couldn't keep his eyes off me that night. It made me feel sexy as hell that he liked my new look so much. I decided that when it was time for bed, I would dress up in something sexy for him. I knew he would really like that, seeing the fact that he was going strong on this whole baby-making thing.

"I don't care what you're talking about, my soldiers gon' step! You poppin' out a baby soon enough. Believe that shit, baby." He caressed my ass and kissed me softly.

"Speaking of, uhm, I'm officially almost a week late." I smiled. "But let's not get carried away because it could just be my cycle changing up."

"You a goddamn liar! I'm getting you a pregnancy test tomorrow morning!"

"Seriously though? I can guarantee it's going to be negative, sir." I giggled.

"In due time she will have a baby." India walked into the kitchen to fill the twin's sippy cups.

"I know she will."

"Besides, you don't want her sick and throwing up on your wedding day."

"Speaking of that, I go Wednesday to get fitted for my dress. Cynthia found a preacher to marry us, too, and a church. It's a pretty nice size."

"Aye, make sure he legit. We ain't got time for her crazy-ass ghetto shit. Plus, one of us is going to have to go get the marriage license at least seventy-two hours before the wedding."

"Well, then, why don't we just have the wedding next Monday? We can do our parties this weekend."

"I call dibs on the house. I'll buy you and the ladies a suite to do your bachelorette party."

"Damn, how you gonna just jack the crib like that?"

"Hold on, you gonna be fine with him having half-naked women in here?" India turned around.

"I'm secure in my spot, li'l baby. Besides I'm the one about to marry him." I walked off.

Getting back into the living room, I noticed that India's cell was going off. I walked over to pick it up. I slid the lock screen over and decided to meddle a little. Making sure that she couldn't see me, I walked right into the bathroom. I scrolled through her call log and found nothing but some 800 numbers that I assumed was the college or some shit. When I got to the text messages though, I read one that had just been sent to her phone saying, The money I took was only the beginning, bitch. What the hell other type of shit did this girl have going on? I walked out of the bathroom and went straight to her.

"Aye, sis, someone texted your phone." I handed it to her.

She looked at me, then at it. "What the fuck?" She sat down, looking confused.

"What you got going on? What money are they talking about? And who is that?"

"I actually don't fucking know. What I do know is that all my money that I had stashed in my closet at the house is gone."

"What the fuck you mean it's gone?"

"In all honesty, I thought you took it."

"Why the hell would I take it? I got my own bread."

"We the only ones who . . ." Her voice trailed off.

"What?" I leaned against the wall.

"The only person besides me who knew where my money was, was Bryson. And since you said he's dead, I can only assume that he had to tell someone. But who?"

"More bullshit coming our way. That was clearly a threat."

"Yeah, but what else could they possibly take? My money and my babies is all I have."

We all looked over at the twins who were crawling around on the living room floor.

"I wish the fuck a motherfucker would." I switched off to go sit with my babies.

CHAPTER SEVENTY-SEVEN

BIANCA

"I been trying to find this bitch for a year now! Glad your ass was able to help." I smiled and passed my girl, Rachel, the blunt.

"It ain't nothing, boo. I just wanted to get them bitches back for tearing up my damn shop with that ghetto-ass hood-rat shit." She spoke of India and Tokyo.

She had too much mouth, always calling and harassing me. Bryson was the only thing we had in common. I knew of India, but coming from Bryson, he was just using her for her money. I ain't have a problem with that. I was straight and so were our children. But since he was dead and gone now, my money was seriously looking funny. When he was dealing with her, he had told me about how her and her sister kept their money in their house somewhere. I took it upon myself to finally go there after hearing about one of their arrests.

When I did get there, no one was there. Looked like no one had been there in a long while. So, I searched the place top to bottom until I came across her closet. I started to take all the clothes, but as I went through that motherfucker, the floorboard under my damn foot almost fell through. That's what caught my attention. When I raised it and saw the money, I instantly sucked my teeth, smiling. *Jackpot!* I snatched up the money, some of the things in her room, and dipped out. I had to admit, sister girl had some expensive taste.

Sitting in Rachel's shop under the dryer, I watched the two walk in and be seated. They had no idea what I looked like, so I was on the safe side. Bryson had always had a thing for thick women, but the way these two were stacked it looked like they were handcrafted by God through every stage of their damn life. I crossed my legs and flipped open a magazine, occasionally glancing at the two. I could tell which one was India. She seemed a little more calm in the face. Tokyo was most definitely the one who kept side-eyeing different females when they would walk by or get too loud.

After a while, it was time for me to get my rollers snatched out and styled. They were just being seated under the dryer. When I was finished getting slayed, I paid my stylist and walked out, throwing my shades on. I could feel their eyes on me. When I stepped out, I looked both ways and then crossed the street to get into my car. I sat in there, listening to music and texting on my phone while waiting on them to come out. After about an hour and a half, they finally did so. I cut my car on and followed them to a nice-ass, big house.

I sat and watched them until they both came walking out, dressed alike and carrying a car seat. I followed them to JC Penny and watched as they took their little family photos. When that was over, I followed them to the restaurant. It was there that I noticed the twins' babies, and they belonged to India. My stomach started to do flips as I thought about how old they looked. I almost bent my damn menu and threw it. Instead, after ordering, I walked over to them and asked if I could get a picture. We talked a little until my waiter approached my table, setting my food down.

Those damn babies most definitely belonged to Bryson's lying ass. This bitch had just gone up on my "get fucked up" radar. I knew she had something to do with my man's disappearance. I could feel it in my gut. There was only enough room on this earth for the babies I had with him. That was it. No more! I was going to take this bitch's babies and get rid of them if it was the last thing I did. She was going to hurt like I was. When they were done eating, I followed them back to the house I had earlier that day. That was where they were staying, and I was about to shake that motherfucker up.

CHAPTER SEVENTY-EIGHT

TOKYO

It was the night of my bachelorette party, and I was kind of geeked about it. Of course, India opted to stay at the house with the twins. I really didn't protest it because there was still some tension between her and Cynthia. I just didn't want the negativity ruining this night for me. The music was going, and we were dancing all over the place. Cynthia had a pole set up and was showing us some tricks she could do. I had to say, at the age of 50, she was talented on that pole. No wonder guys loved her all over. She had two tables being set up after a while. We were about to get massaged from head to toe and get our feet and hands done.

The massage therapist cut off the rap music we were listening to and put on calming nature sounds.

"What in the hell!" I busted out laughing.

"This is just to relax you all while you get your kinks and whatnot worked out." She started to light some candles.

Cynthia spun in a circle in her robe with her wine. "Hell, Python done worked out every kink she got before we got here. I'm sure." We all fell out laughing.

"Oh, is he a massage therapist too?" The poor woman looked around at us. That made us laugh even more.

"If that's what you wanna call it! Only thing is he uses his dick, not his hands, Miss Thang!" she snapped.

I removed my robe and lay on the table naked. Mrs. Luci put a towel over my lower half and grabbed a bottle of oil she had sitting by the candles. When she poured it onto my back, it was cold. But as she began to rub it in, it started to heat up. I heard someone knocking on the door.

"I got it!" Cynthia jumped up and ran to answer it.

"Who is it?" I tried to lift my head up, but Mrs. Luci forced it back down.

"Just room service. How did the dress fitting go by the way?"

"It went well. I think my damn titties are going to be lifted to the moon in it, though." I laughed, "Plus, we need to go to the church Sunday night and start decorating."

"Okay, just call me and let me know when we need to be there or when you're leaving." She opened the door.

I relaxed a bit more and closed my eyes, tired of looking at the floor. The feel of her warm, soft hands soon changed and were a little firm. I heard Cynthia and Susan giggling.

"What the hell you wenches laughing at?" I lifted my head and saw a damned fine-ass man standing next to me.

He continued to rub my back. I didn't even feel bad when my pussy started to throb from the sight of him. I just shook my head and put it back down. I tensed up a little bit when I felt his hands glide over my ass. He rubbed and gripped and rubbed and gripped it, then went farther down to my legs. Once he got to my feet, he stopped.

Hearing a belt buckle be undone, my head shot up, and I looked behind me. He was undressed already and rubbing his body down in a shit ton of oil.

"Whoa! Wait a damn minute, playa! This ain't that type of party!" I sat up.

"Girl! He ain't about to fuck you! Lay ya ass back down and enjoy this shit. I can bet Python is enjoying himself right now, not thinking about you." Cynthia sipped her glass.

"Well, what the fuck is he naked for?"

"He is about to massage your naked-ass body with his naked-ass body," Susan slurred.

"How the hell does that work?"

Cynthia walked over and made me lie back on the table. "Girl, look, basically all he is going to be doing is rubbing his body against yours. Then after that, his fine ass is going to strip for us." She rubbed her hand over his chest.

I tried my best to contain myself, but once I felt his hard dick slide over my ass and drop on my back, that was it! I jumped off the table and snatched my robe up off the couch.

"Girl, what's wrong with you!" Cynthia had spilled her drink on herself.

"I can't do this shit. Bitch, if Python found out, he would fucking kill all of us!"

"Aw, nah, li'l momma. I get paid to do this, not be killed." The guy rubbed his chest.

"What she meant was her man would not be happy with you on her, but that doesn't mean you can't strip for us though!" Susan ran over and turned the music up and back to some shit he could dance to.

I sat back in the chair she had decorated for me that said BACHELORETTE and grabbed a bottle of wine. "Fuck it, he's enjoying himself. So, I'm going to do the same. Come swing that dick in my pretty-ass face, baby boy!"

The dancer slowly walked over and started to grind on me. I couldn't take my eyes off that massive-ass muscle swinging back and forth. He reached for my hand, making me caress it while looking me in the eyes.

"Yesssss, bitch!" Cynthia started throwing ones and dancing around us. Susan stood up and threw her whole wad at him, smacking him in the back of the head with it. We both started laughing. After about an hour, the three of us sat around talking and painting each other's toenails and whatnot. I didn't know how the fuck Susan was still hanging in there, but she was. I guess that's why she was a great bartender. Not to mention, shorty was making us some nice-ass drinks all damn night.

My mind wandered to my man and the kids. I wanted to call my sister and check on her, but I knew she probably was online or asleep by now. We started watching *Jason's Lyric* and eating the pizza I had ordered.

Cynthia lit up a blunt and passed it to me. "I don't understand how your ass is so forgiving with that girl even though that's your blood. She has done some mighty shady shit to you. Some snake shit for real."

"Well, what can I say, we share the same DNA. I've done my fair share of things to her also."

"You did your shit out of love for her. She did hers out of spite and jealousy to you. There's a major difference. baby girl."

"It really is!" Susan fell off the couch.

"Lord, let me go lay this damn girl down before we end up making a trip to the emergency room." She giggled.

"I'm okay, Momma! I got this!" She pulled herself up using the table, reaching for her glass that was almost empty.

"Your ass is more fucked-up than we are!" She sat back down next to me. "All I'm saying is, be careful. I got a feeling that girl got something else up her sleeve, baby. She ain't just letting this shit ride like that. And I know you. She can't live with yaw forever, and you most definitely are not about to let her leave with those babies."

"Trust me, she isn't taking them anywhere with the way she chooses men over family. I guess I'm not the only one like our mother." I sipped my glass. "But I got a plan. Might not be right, but I have one."

"Do I even want to know what that is?"

"Even if you did, I wouldn't tell you." I smirked and turned the TV up. We both laughed.

CHAPTER SEVENTY-NINE

PYTHON

To say my mans had gone all out for my bachelor party was an understatement! From the food to the DJ to the damn fine-ass honeys who were prancing around naked and getting their paper. Every time I turned around, someone was handing me a drink and a stripper was trying to rub their titties, ass, or bare pussy on me. I loved this shit. This was shit we did anyways before I got with Tokyo, but the meaning behind it held something different for me.

Every now and then though, I went up to check on the kids and India, taking her a drink. I was glad my house was big enough to do the party and not disturb the twins as they slept. Every time I came in the room, India looked like something was bothering her or that she was worried about something. It wasn't my place to pick at her for info, though. That was between her and her sister. I did, however, let her know that if she needed me to handle someone, I would.

Walking back down the stairs, I saw one of the girls in the middle of the floor putting a flame to her pussy. When that motherfucker caught fire, my eyes grew as wide as her big-ass titties that were bouncing around as she pussy popped on a handstand. Now I had heard of females doing this in the club, but I had never witnessed it with my own eyes.

"Nigga, you see that shit! Shorty is wild!" One of the younger guys of my clique grabbed my shoulder.

"Yeah, that shit is amazing. I see yaw balling on these bitches. Probably the most they done made in a night ever." I laughed and took a drag on my cigar.

"Man, I can't believe yo' ass is getting married, OG!" Another one walked up, eating some fried chicken.

"And why is that?" I continued to watch the girl in the middle of the room.

"Because, nigga! You too damn mean and evil for a bitch to wanna be with you forever!" he laughed.

"Call my shorty a bitch again and your ass is going to eat ya fucking tongue off the floor." I glared at him.

"My bad, boss man, I didn't mean it like that."

"I'm just fucking with you. I know you aren't that stupid."

"So, when do we get to meet the boss lady?" He took another bite.

"You won't. Now, go enjoy this shit like I am," I dismissed his ass. I don't know why, but his presence irritated the hell out of me. Probably because I hated to see a motherfucker talking with their mouth full.

"Why you so tense, Python, what's bothering you?" Buckey stood next to me.

"Is it fucked-up that I dead-ass just want to kill something? I feel like I'm getting too soft or some shit. Man, I don't know." I kept my voice low, watching the guy who was hanging on to me earlier walk off when he heard what I said.

"Nigga, what are you going through, a midlife crisis?" Buckey laughed at me. "You got niggas to do that for you. Niggas like me."

"Nah, I feel like it's just something I need to get out of my system. I'm getting married, and I already got two kids even though they aren't really mine. Is the husband thing really in me? Or am I just doing this because I don't want her to ever leave?"

"Let me tell you this as a best friend and brother whether you marry her or not, bro. If she didn't want to be here, she wouldn't be. You can't be getting cold feet, Python. That would break that woman's heart. You two are perfect for each other in every sense of the word. What you gonna do without her?"

I had to laugh at myself. My best friend was absolutely right. I think it was more so that I was nervous I wouldn't be able to be everything she expected of me as a husband. I knew that sometimes when people got married is when shit started to go bad. Everything wasn't perfect with me and her all the time, but somehow at the end of it all, we always managed to come out on top smiling and standing beside each other.

"Okay, motherfuckas, it's time for yaw to sit the fuck down somewhere so my mans can receive his damn near final lap dance!" Buckey walked to the center of the room and looked around. He motioned for me to come take a seat. When I did, the music started back up. Three dancers seductively walked over to me and started freaking on each other. I leaned back, relaxing a little more.

Buckey leaned down and whispered in my ear, "Wait until you see the main dancer I got for you." He patted my shoulder and walked away. I had to admit, with the drinks and the way these females looked, my dick started to grow a little hard. *Thank God for blue jeans and briefs,* was all I could think when one of the girls sat on my lap and ground her ass just the right way all over my mans.

CHAPTER EIGHTY

INDIA

I stood at the top of the stairs, smiling as I watched the strippers dance all over Python. I looked to my left up the hall where I had the main dancer Buckey had mentioned tied and gagged in the closet. When the three ladies were finished and the lights dimmed, I fixed my mask and pushed my breasts up higher in the dark blue, sparkly lace I had on. When Willie Taylor's song "Music" started, I walked down the steps with all eyes on me. I smiled hard when I saw Buckey mouth, "What the fuck?" I slowly walked over to Python, rubbing my breast and swaying my hips to the rhythm. He started blushing as I rolled my body in front of him.

"So, this was ya main dancer for me, my soon-to-be wife?" he asked Buckey, keeping his eyes on me and rubbing my legs.

"Not really, but enjoy." He scratched his beard and backed up.

I took Python's hands and had him rub my ass and thighs as I continued to dance. I could tell by the look in his eyes that he was far beyond drunk and high as he tried to focus on me in the dimly lit room. When I turned around, he gently bit me on my ass. I spun back around to face him, throwing my leg over his shoulder and still grinding. He gripped my ass and put his head in between my legs, kissing my lace-covered pussy. I threw my head back because it felt so damn good to feel a man's mouth down there after all this time. When the song was over, I leaned down and kissed him deeply in the mouth. All the men in the room cheered and clapped and threw money as I switched my ass hard, heading back toward the stairs. The applause was greatly appreciated because the show had just begun for me and him.

When I got back up there, I quickly changed out of the lace fit I had on, throwing my pajamas on. I ran over to my computer and logged into it. I clicked on the camera footage I had and skipped past the part of me lying in their bed and talking about the stripper I'd tied up. I sat back and smiled as I watched myself interact with my sister's man and dancing on him. Payback was a bitch. She had taken two men I loved away from me, and I was going to ruin her shit for her. When I walked back out into the hallway and looked over the railing, the atmosphere had totally changed. There was so much tension downstairs a motherfucker would've passed out walking in, and it was for them.

Python was removing his shirt and rolling his head around as if trying to sober himself up a little. My eyes darted in Buckey's direction as he held some chick by the hair.

"Bitch, how the fuck did you get in here and what the fuck do you want?" he barked and threw her to the ground.

I squinted, my eyes trying to get a better look at her. She looked familiar, I just didn't know where I knew her from. I walked toward the stairs, about to head down, when I made eye contact with Python. He threw his hand up for me to stop, and I did.

"Where is that funky-ass bitch, India!" she shouted, looking around. "I'm going to kill that bitch and her damn babies!"

When her ass said that, I didn't give a fuck what Python didn't want me to do! I ran my ass down the stairs and got straight in her face. I grabbed her by the chin, trying to get a good look at her.

"India, you know this bitch?" Python took a long swig from his champagne bottle.

"She looks familiar, but I honestly can't recall." I pushed her head back and backed up.

"Bitch, you know who I am! I'm Bryson's wife, whore!" She spat at my feet.

I shook my head and had to laugh. "How the fuck did you know where to find me? I mean, what's your issue with me?"

"I know it was you who had him come up missing! Bitch, you did something to him when he ain't wanna be with you no more! He told me shit had gone sour between yaw when you found out about me! Told me what type of bitches you and your sister are!"

"I could honestly give two fucks about you. Why are you here?" I cocked my head.

"Because like I said, I'm going to kill you and those damn babies of yours! Only kids need to be walking this earth with his DNA is mine! Not some fucking bastards he had on the side because he was using they mammie for money!"

When she said that, Python ran up and kicked her in the chin hard, knocking her out. A couple of her teeth fell to the floor when her face hit it, along with a long, slobbery line of blood.

"She must be the one who's been texting me that bullshit and who stole my money. Fuck that bitch. He's dead, and neither one of us can have him from the grave I'm sure my sister put him in."

"You niggas ready to have a good time?" He walked over and poured the rest of the bottle all over her. The rest of the guys in the room started barking like dogs and growling.

"Yeah, fresh meat! Yaw know what to do!" Buckey smiled the most sinister smile I had ever seen on a man.

"Wake that bitch up, first!" Python pointed to one of the guys and snapped. He ran over and grabbed a big bowl of punch and walked back over, throwing it onto her. She quickly sat up, taking a big deep breath and looking around.

"What the fuck?" She grabbed her face, crying.

"Record this shit. I'm sure Tokyo would like to enjoy this. Where her ass go at anyways?"

"She'll be back," I blurted out. "Said she had to go let Cynthia in at the hotel because her daughter went to sleep drunk." I shrugged, asking more of a question than giving an actual answer.

Python nodded his head and pulled his phone out, cutting the flash on for the camera. The first guy walked up and started unbuckling his pants. The girl's eyes grew big as she watched his pants hit the floor.

"I know your short-dick ass is not thinking about doing what I think you are!" Everyone busted out laughing as she looked him up and down. He backhanded her so hard it dazed the shit out of her. Walking over, he grabbed her by the hair and put her face right in his dick area. After three quick pumps, he let out a bloodcurdling scream.

"This bitch bit me!" His fat ass stumbled back and fell to the ground, holding himself. Everyone busted out laughing in the room.

Some tall guy walked up, smiling. "Bet she can't bite this motherfucka." He smirked as he got down on the ground and made her flip over on her stomach. He damn near ripped off her leggings, exposing her petite, smooth ass. When he got his own pants down, he started stroking himself until he was hard. Pushing her face down into the floor so she couldn't move, he rammed his dick straight into her asshole.

"Ahhhhhh! Somebody help me, please!" she screamed at the top of her lungs. "Please God, don't do this! Help meeeee!" She continued to scream as he continued to pump harder and harder. After about a good five minutes of that, he jumped up and busted all over her back and hair. There was cum, shit, and blood covering his dick. I shook my head and sat back as Python and I watched each guy in the party take turns violating and mutilating that poor, dumb-ass bitch. When they were finished after about three hours, that girl was a nut-covered, bloody, shitty, unconscious mess. She had broken into a damn snake pit and didn't even know it.

Buckey walked out the door and returned with a tarp. Python walked over and looked down at her.

"I don't like baby killers, little bitch!" He spat on her and started stomping her head repeatedly. When he was sure she was dead, he kneeled down and actually started running his hand through the mess while puffing on a cigar. This dude was sick, and I could see why my sister's sick ass loved him.

While they were cutting her body up, I walked into the kitchen to fix Python and the rest of the fellas a drink. When I was done, I dropped two roofies into the cup I was going to give to Python. They bagged up the parts, and two of the guys left with them.

"Now that that's over with, let's get back to drinking! After all, this is your bachelor party, brother-in-law!" I laughed, holding my cup up and handing him his. The other men in the room started grabbing cups as me and Python downed ours. I looked up to the stairs, thinking I'd heard one of the twins crying.

"Are you getting that or am I getting that?" Python pointed up the stairs, smiling.

"I got it, and Tokyo said she'll be back in a few."

"Cool, it's late as fuck, and I need to get these niggas up and out so I can fuck the shit out of my wife. Damn, what the hell you put in this shit? It's good." He swallowed the rest.

"If I told you, I would have to kill ya ass." I turned to walk away, laughing my way up the stairs.

After I changed Ryan, I put my contacts back in and changed into some more lace lingerie. Walking into Python and Tokyo's room, I did a double check to make sure the camera was still going. It was, with a full battery. I looked around and smiled to myself. I was about to find out what the hype was about and why that dick had my sister on her best behavior. I looked at my watch and saw it had been about twenty minutes. Taking my watch off, I placed it on the dresser and turned the camera on. I quickly walked back to the kids' room and checked my laptop to make sure it was connected.

When I was done with that, I walked out into the hall and looked over the banister. The men were filing out, and Buckey was lying across the couch. I should've put something in his drink too. That's when it hit me. I was going to in fact put something into Buckey's drink. The pills I had given Python should have been kicking in by now. I walked down the stairs and into the kitchen, fixing a drink for his best friend. When I walked into the living room, I could tell Python's head was spinning. He was trying to compose himself and couldn't.

"Damn, this nigga wasted." Buckey laughed and stopped smiling when he laid eyes on me. "What the hell, Tokyo!" He covered his eyes.

"Boy, it's okay. All this is for my man. I fixed you a drink, and you can crash here for the night, okay?" I handed him the cup. Call me a bitch, but I put three in his cup hoping it would kill his ass while I was doing what

I was doing. He wasted no time guzzling that shit down. *Fucking alcoholic.*

"I'm gonna need me another one of these." He looked into the cup.

"Well, first, help me get his big ass up the stairs, and then I can fix you another."

When I say that goddamn man was heavy as fuck, that shit was just an understatement! We struggled like hell trying to get him up the steps. When we did reach the top, his legs were like noodles, literally.

"Tokyo" he mumbled, and I rolled my eyes.

"Yes, baby?"

"I don't think I can do this tonight. I had too much I think." His head dropped back down. Damn near stumbling through the bedroom door, we almost dropped his ass. Buckey's drink was kicking in. I needed his ass back down the steps before I could do anything. Throwing Python onto the bed, I started undressing him.

"Gat damn!" I said out of shock when I saw the sleeping monster that lay under his briefs. I looked over, and Buckey was slowly making his way out the door. I tugged and pulled on Python's briefs until they were off.

"Damn, baby, I told you I don't think I can." He raised his head, then dropped it like dead weight back onto the pillow.

"It's okay, I got you. I can handle this all on my own." I grinned.

Once he was naked, I walked out of the room to see where the hell Buckey was. This nigga was passed out at the top of the stairs. I shook my head and debated whether I wanted to drag or just flat-out push his ass down the stairs. But with the way he was, I was sure he would break his fucking neck if I did. I said fuck it and left his ass right where he was.

Going back to the room, I climbed on top of Python and started kissing and sucking on his chest. He wasn't completely out, but I knew I had nothing to worry about. His body was too heavy for his own good. He opened his eyes and looked me dead in mine as I began to stroke his dick and lick the head.

"Damn," he mumbled and fell back out.

Once he was hard, I wasted no time sliding down on him. It was kind of difficult because I wasn't wet enough. I raised up a little and spit on my hand and wiped it on his dick head, then tried again. He felt so good to me. I bounced, ground, and twerked on his dick until I felt myself building up to my climax. Slowing down, I leaned forward and kissed him. It shocked the shit out of me when he actually kissed me back. As I started to ride him again, he started fucking me back.

I had kind of forgotten why I was doing this in the first place. I was lost and didn't want this to stop. When he tried to raise up, I forced him back down, and this time, I didn't stop when I felt myself about to cum all over him. He pushed me off him and slowly climbed on top of me, kissing me hard in the mouth. I rolled over so he could fuck me from the back. I started to get nervous as he seemed to be coming down off the pills I had given him. He wasn't gentle with me at all as he stroked me long and hard from the back. When he snatched me by the top of my hair, I got an instant migraine. Was this the type of shit my sister liked? He got a little more aggressive and rough as he wrapped his big-ass hands around my throat and fucked me even harder.

"Python, baby, it's starting to hurt." I tried to get out. That's when he slowed down and soon stopped. I looked behind me and almost pissed on myself when I saw the look on his face. He shook his head and rolled off the bed. I sat up and watched him. He was making his way to the dresser. Pulling himself up, he faced me again.

"What . . . what the fuck?" He tried to focus on me. "Tok . . . India?" He tried to shake his head.

"It's me, Tokyo, baby." I grabbed the sheet, trying to cover my body.

"Nah, nah, Tokyo, she got my name tatted on her lower back. Tokyo likes for me to fuck her hard from the back, but she hates me pulling her hair."

The shit pissed me off how well he knew her ass. I shrugged and stood up on the opposite side of the bed.

"Fuck it, either way, we just fucked. You felt good as hell, too." I laughed hard, almost falling into the nightstand.

"You are fucking sick! Get the fuck out of here!" His voice boomed throughout the room, "I should fucking kill your ass." He slumped back against the dresser.

"Well, I highly doubt that. Plus, I recorded this little fiasco between us. So, if I were you, I'd be a little more careful on how you speak to me, bitch." I snatched my panties up off the floor and walked out, slamming the bedroom door behind me. As I stood outside the door listening to his movements, I heard his body drop hard to the floor. I cracked the door and saw him knocked out on the side of the bed. I eased my way in and grabbed the recorder.

"Got ya, bitch!" I clutched it and switched my thick ass right back out. Heading to my room, I kicked Buckey hard in the ribs as he lay at the top of the stairs.

I looked back down at him. "Fuck it!" I bent down and rolled his ass down the stairs. As I watched him hit each one and hit his head a few times, I prayed like hell he was dead. As he landed at the bottom with his head turned in a fucked-up position, I shrugged and went into my room so I could shower and go to bed.

CHAPTER EIGHTY-ONE

TOKYO

When I got home the next afternoon, my head was banging something fierce. I walked in and plopped down on the couch, kicking my shoes off right there.

"Did you have fun?" Python asked groggily as he came down and sat next to me.

"I sure did. Did you have fun?"

"From the little bit that I can remember, I did."

"Damn, was it like that in here?" I looked around.

"Yeah, I'm assuming it was, seeing I had to pay the crew to come clean up."

"That's good. Anything you wanna tell me?'

"What does that mean?"

"I wanna know what happened. Or at least how you felt." I looked up at him.

"Well, to be honest, I don't too much remember anything after we killed some bitch."

"Shit, I do," India said as she sat down on the other side of the living room, staring Python down.

"And what exactly might that be, and killed who?" My head darted back and forth between the two.

"He had some dudes dancing on him." She busted out laughing.

"Oh, you a real piece of shit." We all laughed as Python threw his head into his hands.

"What the hell, baby? I know you ain't have one of those types of parties." I couldn't contain my laughter.

"Hell nah! Don't do that shit yo." He leaned back and gripped himself, licking his lips at me.

"Well, I can tell you what, I missed the hell out of you while I was at mine."

"Awww, big momma got drunk and missed this dick is what it sounds like."

"Boy, fuck you." I stood up to go to the kitchen to fix us some coffee because we most definitely needed it.

"So, what do you have planned for the day?" Python came in the kitchen and sat down. It looked like he was struggling to remember his night.

"I don't know yet, but more about this bitch yaw fucked-up last night. Who was she, one of the dancers?"

"Nah, she broke in here. I think. I just don't know why she would do that shit like she didn't see all the cars outside or some shit. You have got to be one bold-ass motherfucker to do that with a house full of people. Especially at my fucking house."

"It was the bitch who stole my money and was sending threatening texts to my phone. Also known as Bryson's wife! Plus, it kind of makes sense. I mean, there's a large party going on, so I'm sure she believed nobody would hear her ass while she was attempting to get the twins." India shrugged, opening the fridge.

"The hell you say?" I spun around to focus on her.

"Yeah, she was here to kill me and the twins. But Buckey got her ass, and let's just say the shit I witnessed them men doing last night to her I wouldn't wish on my worst enemy."

"You a damn liar because I sure would."

"That's why we are different, big sister." She poured some apple juice into a cup.

"Well, anyways, anything else happen?"

"Hey, Tokyo, did you come here last night?" Buckey walked in, scratching his head. India jumped and dropped her cup all over the floor.

"You okay, sis? And no, why would I be here? I was at my own shit."

"Nah, I thought you . . . Man, what the fuck? My goddamn body hurts. Feels like I got thrown off a fucking building!" He popped his neck and stretched.

"If only God were that good," India mumbled.

"Yeah, yaw asses had a damn good time. He can't remember shit, yo' ass is hurt, a bitch broke in, and even my sister doesn't wanna say what yaw did to her? Like damn, even mine wasn't that lit. I should've partied with yaw instead." I laughed, pouring some coffee into mugs.

As we stood around in the kitchen, there was an awkward silence. I looked up and watched everyone over the rim of my mug. I don't know why, but the way India was staring Python down made me feel uneasy. Or like someone wasn't telling me everything. It was crazy how her ass was able to remember shit and witness things when she was supposed to be upstairs with the twins the whole time.

"You okay, sis?" I looked back and forth between her and my man as I leaned forward on the table.

"Yeah, why do you keep asking that?"

"No reason. Baby, I'm about to go lie down for a little bit. You wanna join me?"

"Hell yeah." He jumped up and placed his mug into the sink.

"Yaw mind if I crash here for a little while longer? I need some more sleep." Buckey stood up.

"You know that's not an issue." I walked out of the kitchen and went upstairs with Python close on my heels.

When we got into the room, I turned around to face him.

"Baby, you sure everything was okay last night? 'Cause I don't like the way shorty acting down there in that kitchen all jumpy and shit!"

"I really can't remember, but I'm sure yo' ass was here last night. Well, at least I think you were." He looked down at the floor, then up at the ceiling.

"Well, I know one thing for sure and two things for certain. For one, I wasn't here last night, and for two, something more than what yaw can remember most definitely happened. But for you and Buckey to both believe that I was here is mind-blowing, don't you think?"

"I mean, it could just be because India was here."

"Yeah, could be." I walked over to the dresser and picked up a watch that I knew belonged to her and not anyone else. "Babe, if I was here last night, what is it that you remember me doing?" I stood in front of him.

"I don't know, baby, what are you getting at?"

"This is India's watch. Did anyone record the party last night?"

"I don't know. I doubt it. What the fuck is her watch doing in our room?" He barely got it out as he stood up and looked back at the bed. "I'm about to hit up the crew. Even though I told them niggas no phones out, I'm sure somebody got something or remembers something."

"That's my man." I smiled as I walked up to him.

"You think your sister did some shady shit last night?"

"I don't know, and I wouldn't put it past her either. But the way she keeps watching you, I know something isn't right at all. And if I am tripping, I still want to know what business she had in our room. For all we know, she could've set that shit up last night." I tossed the watch around in my hand.

"But what reason would she have to do that?" Python took his phone out and dialed.

"I don't know, I'm just going with my gut and twin instinct."

"Hey yo, you remember anything from my party last night?" He placed the phone on speaker.

"Awww, man, hell yeah! Shit was lit, and you need to do more parties like that from now on in the future."

"Yeah, but did anything in particular happen?"

"I mean, like what? You talkin' about us having fun with that chick or yo' soon-to-be wife dancing for you? I hope my shorty do some surprise shit like—"

Python hung up the phone, cutting the guy off.

"I fucking knew it! India!" I shouted.

Python grabbed me by the arms, trying to shush me. "No! Don't call her up here. Call Buckey up here real quick. Eventually, we gonna start to remember some shit or something."

"The fuck I need to do that for when the source is down there in the kitchen?"

"Because we both know she is going to lie!"

I had to admit, he had a point. I sat down on the bed and thought about the shit. Then, it slapped me hard in the face.

"Python, she danced on you?"

"I guess."

"But you don't remember, right?"

"Nah."

"Okay, bet. When her ass leaves today, I'm checking that fucking laptop and that room. I got a good feeling about this shit. I'm telling you, baby."

"If you say so. In the meantime, why don't you come show me how much you missed me last night." He began to grin. And I did just that. I climbed on top of him, and we kissed like teenagers who had snuck away to see each other. Python undid his pants and slid under the covers. I rolled off the bed and did the same. When I joined him back in bed, I leaned over to kiss him again. Making my way to his spot on his neck, I snatched the covers back off him.

"You know damn well I love to see your body, baby." I smiled, looking down at his dick. That's when I felt like I had to throw up. My fucking heart shattered into a million pieces, and I could feel the rage building up inside of me.

"Python, what the fuck is that?" I pointed to his pelvic area.

"What's what, baby?" He looked down.

"You don't see that big-ass hickey? Because I know damn well that ain't no bruise!" I almost yelled at him.

"Baby, look, I don't know how that shit got there, and I'm being a thousand percent honest!"

"You can't remember shit from last night and got a big-ass hickey by your dick! What, you fuck one of the stripper bitches or something!" I jumped out of the bed and frantically looked around the room.

"Man, you fucking tripping! Even I know I ain't do that bullshit!" he said as I looked at the watch I'd put back on the dresser.

With tears in my eyes about to stain my cheeks, I asked him, "Python, did you fuck my sister last night? I mean, after all, she did dance on you!"

CHAPTER EIGHTY-TWO

INDIA

I stood in the doorway of my room, giggling my ass off as I listened to Tokyo and Python go back and forth. She could be upset and accuse all she wanted to, but she had no solid evidence, only I did. Yes, it was petty, and as if the video of us fucking wasn't going to be enough to get shit rolling, I'd left a few a hickeys here and there last night. I jumped back and quickly shut my door a little as their bedroom door swung open, and Python stormed out.

"Really, motherfucker! Your ass is just going to leave like that? Your tough ass can't own up to the truth, huh?" Tokyo shouted, following him down the stairs. I slid back out into the hallway and continued to silently laugh to myself about it all.

"The fuck you find so funny about that shit?" Buckey stepped out of the room next to mine and the twins'.

"Nigga, what?" I damn near jumped out of my skin as I mean mugged him.

"Yo' ass heard me. The fuck is so funny about them arguing like that two days before they are supposed to get married?"

"Boy, whatever, they asses will be all right." I rolled my eyes and was about to shut my door.

"I know your snake ass had something to do with something that happened last night, bitch." He glared at me.

"Sure, like I said, whatever." I slammed the door and cursed myself when baby Rya popped her head up and frowned her face up as if she was about to cry.

I flew over to her and popped her pacifier into her mouth and patted Ryan on his butt as he began to move around. Once she lay back down and dozed off, I locked the door and sat down in front of my laptop. As I watched myself fucking Python, I reached in my sweats and started to rub on my pussy. Tilting my head back, I imagined how he felt in me last night. As I was about to cum and start rocking on my own fingers, there was a knock at the door.

"Damn!" I said, getting up to open it. "What's up, sis?" I tried to get my breathing under control.

"Did I interrupt you or something?" She barged her way in.

"Uh, no, why? What's wrong?" I almost yelled as she glanced at the laptop. I rushed over and shut it.

"Did a bitch stay here last night with him?" She folded her arms.

"With who?"

"You know damn well who! You heard us arguing, I know you did!"

"Well, for one, calm down and tone it down before you wake the twins, and for two, not to my knowledge, babes. He got drunk and went up to your room and fell asleep." I smacked my lips.

"Speaking of our room, your watch was in there on my dresser."

"Oh, yeah, me and Buckey helped him up to your room. After he was in the bed, I looked in there for Rya's pacifier and probably set it there and forgot about it."

"And did you find it?" She threw one hand on her hip.

"Clearly, you see it in her mouth. If you don't believe me, you can ask Buckey. I'm sure he'll back me up on us helping him—"

"No need for all that." She threw up a hand, cutting me off, and left the room.

When the coast was clear, I laughed some more and sat back down. Pulling out a USB, I loaded the video to it and snatched it back out after saving it. Sliding it into the desk drawer, I patted it as I knew it would be safe there for the time being. Call it fucked up, but I was going to figure out a way to get it played at their wedding or during the reception, ruin her whole damn day, and embarrass her. By the time that would happen, though, me and the babies would be long gone!

CHAPTER EIGHTY-THREE

BUCKEY

As I lay in bed, I tossed and turned but couldn't get comfortable. My body was aching bad as fuck. I knew whatever we'd done last night, it shouldn't have left me in pain and me and my boy with a fucking memory loss. I couldn't shake the ill feeling that India had played a part in whatever may have happened. I guess you could say it was the detective in me because I lay there just thinking and racking my brain with possibilities.

That's when I heard all the commotion coming from Python and Tokyo's room. I got up and peeked out the door to see what was going on when I spotted India laughing at the shit. After confronting her, I went back into the room and threw my shit on. If my boy was leaving, then so was I. Besides, I was going to have to talk some sense into him or his wife. I was going to try with him first.

Rushing down the steps and out the door, I threw my shirt on and didn't give a damn if it was backward. When I got outside, I yelled for Python before he could pull off.

"Aye yo, Python! Wait up, nigga! Damn!" I ran to the passenger seat and jumped in after he stopped backing out.

"Man, I know you heard that shit, dude. Tokyo straight tripping! I don't know what happened last night," he said as he finished backing out of the driveway, "but I'm telling you, bro, I didn't fuck no bitch last night!" He sped off.

"I know you didn't, but at the end of the day, we gotta figure out what the fuck happened. You hungry? 'Cause I am." I buckled my seat belt.

"And she knows it was India who danced on me last night. I called Austin and asked him a few questions. He confirmed that shit!"

"Do what?" I sat back, thinking. "That explains why we both feel like Tokyo was there at the party. But what the fuck would make her wanna do that shit?" I glanced over at him.

"Man, I don't know. I'll figure this shit out after I get something on my stomach."

He gripped the wheel as he swerved left onto the expressway. When we got to Dizzy Wizz, a burger and fry joint in the east, we ordered our food and sat down and started smashing. With a mouthful of food, I looked at my boy. He looked sad as fuck like he was hurting. The shit sure didn't stop him from damn near swallowing the whole burger though.

"Aye, man, it's going to be all right. Let her calm down and clear her head, and we'll all figure this shit out. In the meantime, what started the argument?"

"Man, we was about to fuck, and when she looked down at my shit, there was a hickey right there. I mean a big-ass hickey. A bitch did that shit on purpose, bruh. But I'm fucking confused because I ain't do shit with nobody last night!" He dipped some fries into his ketchup and shoved them into his mouth.

"I find it funny how we can't remember shit, but India can."

"Yeah, and her ass was drinking just as much as we were last night! I was taking her drinks back-to-back last night."

"Yeah, I remember that shit. I remember them good-ass drinks she made for us, too." I laughed, thinking about them, and then my smile dropped as me and Python locked eyes.

"That dirty-ass bitch! She did make us all drinks!"

"That's the thing though, she made everyone drinks. Why them niggas ain't like us?"

"Nigga, 'cause them fools wasn't the ones staying at my house. Now granted, I don't know why she would put something in our shit, but I'm going to make that bitch talk!" He pounded his fist on the table, drinking some of his Sprite as others in the restaurant looked at us.

"Nah, nah, nah. Before we spazz out and do anything, we have to be sure, bro. At the end of the day, she is your girl's sister, and we gotta give her the benefit of the doubt because anyone could've drugged us. You had more niggas around you last night than ever before."

"You right, but she made the drinks. You a damn detective, fool, think, nigga." He smirked at me.

"Well, to keep it a buck, when you and Tokyo were arguing, she was in the hall laughing her ass off. If she really gave a fuck about yaw getting married in two days, she would've tried to talk her sister into calming down."

"You right, and not only that, but her watch was in our room."

"That might've fallen off when we tried to carry your big ass and put you in the bed." I laughed.

"Nope, that motherfucker was placed on the dresser. It wasn't on the floor or anything, so I know it ain't fall off or break."

"Fuck it, let's go back to the house and search her fucking room then." I laughed, taking a big bite of my burger. Python didn't break eye contact with me when I said that. "Aw, come on, man, you really wanna go search her room?" I lifted a brow.

"Nigga, let's roll. She ain't about to fuck shit up for me and my wife!"

"Them wedding bells sure are ringing now." I stood up, slurped some of my milkshake, stuffed my mouth with fries, and wiped it. We rushed out and jumped back into the truck. The whole way there, Python kept trying to call Tokyo. She was clearly still mad because she kept sending him to voicemail. Shorty had been mad hormonal here lately. I knew with as emotional as she was, that girl was for sure pregnant. As evil as she was, if shorty was to shed a tear at any time, it would confirm it.

When we pulled into the driveway twenty minutes later, India was leaving with the twins. We both bumped shoulders when we realized this would be easier than we'd thought. Walking into the house, Python called out to Tokyo. She didn't answer. Guessing she was still mad in the room, we both rushed up the stairs to India's room. Busting in the door, we scared the shit out of Tokyo, who was going through her closet.

"The fuck is wrong with you niggas?" She clutched her chest, falling against the wall.

"Naw, what yo' ass doing in here since you didn't fucking believe me?" Python smirked.

"Man, fuck all that. Search this shit while she gone! Evidently, yaw both got the same thing in mind!" I walked over and lifted her mattress, looking for the laptop.

"The fuck yaw looking for?" Tokyo continued.

"Anything that can explain what she did last night or if she had anything to do with it. Because we pretty certain she drugged our ass last night."

"Are you serious?" Tokyo smiled with interest.

"I'm sure she did." Python opened a duffle bag that was under the bed. "Look at this bullshit!" He held up a pill bottle. When he opened it, he dumped the rest onto the bed.

"Those are most deff roofies, playa." I shook my head.

"The fuck is she doing with that shit?" Tokyo walked over. "Damn, this is cute." She held up a lace bra in one hand and the bottom in the other. She had a weird look on her face.

"What's wrong, baby?"

"When I came in here earlier, she was watching some video of herself on her laptop, and I'm sure she had this on!"

"Well, where is the laptop?" I opened a drawer.

"She took it with her. Damn, that little bitch is slick." Tokyo bit down on her knuckle.

"She gets it honest." Python smiled at Tokyo, who rolled her eyes.

"But not slick enough. Let's see what's on this." I smiled, holding the USB up.

"Come on! Mine is downstairs!" Tokyo flew out of the room with us right behind her.

CHAPTER EIGHTY-FOUR

PYTHON

We all sat around the laptop in the living room and waited on Tokyo to plug in the USB. I grew kind of nervous when she unlocked it and opened the tab.

"So, where did India go anyways?" I watched as she pulled up a video. After all, that was the only thing on there. That motherfucker was mad long, too.

"Something about an appointment for an apartment or something." She waved me off. When the video started, you could see India setting the recorder up in our room. She stuck her tongue out, smiled, and made a few funny faces. We continued to watch her as she lay on our bed and rubbed herself and twerked. Then, she walked back up to the camera and positioned it to a better angle.

Tokyo turned the volume up so we could hear better and skipped through a little. She stopped when India sat in the camera and was talking. She was real deal crazy as she talked about the stripper she had tied up in the hallway closet and how she was going to do a special dance for me and make me wish I was with her instead of Tokyo.

"I got a special dance for her all right with my foot up her fucking ass!" Tokyo sucked her tongue.

"She tied up a stripper in the closet?" Buckey laughed.

Tokyo skipped through some more. India was back in front of the camera, except this time she took it and positioned it at the top of the stairs. When the song started, she walked down to me and began to dance on me. As we watched the video, Tokyo glanced over at me and shook her head.

"Come on now, sis, it was his bachelor party," Buckey tried to reason.

"It's not about the other girls, it's about my sister. How did you of all people not know that she wasn't me? Our eyes are different colors, Python!" She focused back on the video.

"I was drunk or drugged up! How was I supposed to be able to tell the difference?"

"You should have remembered that I was at my party!" She paused it.

"She lied really good and made us all believe she was you, though!" I tried to defend myself.

"I mean, she really did, sis."

"Shut up, Buckey!" me and her said in unison.

He threw his hands up in defense. "My bad! Can we get back to the video though?"

"I'm not sure I want to. I can't stomach this shit." She folded her arms.

"Man, we got a fucking point to prove. And I wanna fucking know what the fuck went on last night!" I pushed the play button.

Then, that's when the worst part started. You could see her and Buckey helping me to the bed. I could barely walk, and he could barely make it out of the room. As I lay there on the bed, looking a hot damn drunken, drugged-up mess, she walked over to the dresser and set something down, then came back to me and started sucking my dick after getting me undressed. We watched in awe as it all went on. Tokyo started breathing harder and harder as the video went on.

At some point, I started fucking her from behind, and that didn't last long. Soon, you heard us arguing, and then she called herself trying to blackmail me. When she left, I passed out on the floor next to the bed. Then, she came back moments later and took the camera. As she exited the room, she walked over to the steps. We all had to turn our heads with the way she was holding the camera to get a good view. We could see Buckey lying at the top of the steps. She set the camera down and then walked over to him and rolled his ass down the steps.

"That dirty-ass bitch! She could've killed me! Funky bitch!" He almost jumped up.

Tokyo jumped up and threw up in her hands as tears ran down her face.

"Baby, calm down, please." I tried to grab her, and she snatched away, running to the downstairs bathroom.

"Man, what the fuck?" Buckey's eyes were big as saucers.

"Dude, I don't fucking remember doing that shit. And clearly, she planned this shit. I didn't lie!" I threw my hands up.

"I know, bruh, but dammmmn." He looked back at the video then back at me.

"What the fuck am I gonna do about her?" I pointed to the bathroom.

"First, let her process this shit and calm down. She will talk to you when she's ready."

"I'm good." Tokyo came out of the bathroom, wiping her face. "I got something for her ass though, and I'm so serious." She shook her head and looked up at the ceiling.

"Baby, I swear, I didn't know anything about that shit." I walked over to her and grabbed her hands.

"I know, we are over that. I just need to handle her though." She stood up on her tippy toes and kissed me, then walked away and into the kitchen.

CHAPTER EIGHTY-FIVE

INDIA

I rocked the twins back and forth in their stroller with my foot as I signed my new lease for our new home an hour away from where Tokyo lived. I was proud of myself about the house I had just gotten. It was a nice-sized three-bedroom and was in an even better neighborhood than I thought it would be. I smiled to myself and dashed the date dramatically as I looked up to my landlord.

"Thank you so much, sir. This is a really big step for me and my babies." I handed the pen back to him.

"Oh, you are very welcome with your beautiful self."

I blushed and grabbed the keys, then got my babies and left. He was giving me weirdo vibes the whole time by looking at my cleavage and licking his lips, but that didn't take away from the joy I felt at the moment! I was ready to go buy a bottle then head back to the house to do a lot of online shopping for our new beginning.

When I had left earlier, it looked like Python and Buckey were on a mission and eager to get back. I paid them no mind and minded my own business because my laptop was safe with me. I ran into the liquor store as quickly as I could and purchased what I wanted, then made it back out quicker before anyone could notice I'd left the twins in the car alone.

"Dirty bitch! Next time, take them babies with you, or someone might take them!" some stranger shouted across the street.

I shrugged and hopped in my car and pulled off. I felt like going for ice cream with my babies. When I got to the parlor, I ordered myself some vanilla ice cream and the twins some Popsicles. As I sat at the table and locked the wheels on their stroller, I checked my phone. When I saw how dry it was, I wished that I could've met someone at Python's bachelor party like I had hoped. But then again, I was glad I didn't because once I got my belongings, there was no looking back after the wedding.

As me and my babies enjoyed our treat, I pulled my laptop out while smiling. I was about to watch the video in peace while I didn't have someone breathing down my neck or in my space.

"Damn! Where is that USB?" I checked my pockets and then my purse, hoping I was tripping because I thought I'd grabbed it when I left.

"Fuck!" I gritted my teeth as I emptied all the contents in my purse onto the table. When it finally hit me that I had in fact left it at home, I took a deep breath and gathered my babies. I damn near did one hundred all the way back to the house. Quickly getting the twins out of the car when I pulled up, I didn't even bother grabbing car seats. I threw one on each hip and rushed up to the door, damn near falling through.

"Damn, girl! You okay?" Tokyo rushed over to me, grabbing Ryan.

"Yeah, what yaw doing?" I looked around to check out the vibe.

"What, was somebody chasing you?" Python gripped the strap on his hip.

"Nope, I just forgot extra diapers is all." I smiled and let Rya down onto the floor.

"Aw, well, don't be scaring us like that."

"Sorry, but I'll be right back! I gotta pee, too." I ran up to my room and snatched the door open. Going over to my desk drawer, I pulled it open and was relieved when I saw the USB was still there. I snatched it up and shoved it into my back pocket. I went into the bathroom and ran some cold water, splashing it on my face.

CHAPTER EIGHTY-SIX

TOKYO

This bitch really had the game shook if she thought I was that dumb. We all knew why she had come back in such a hurry. Her ass had tucked that laptop and left with it like it was one of the twins. Yeah, me and Python had made amends and I'd apologized for getting upset the way that I did. But she really had herself fooled before anyone else. Every time I laid eyes on her or every time she spoke, I wanted to go grab my gun and blow her fucking brains out of her skull. As a sister, how in the fuck could you do something like that? Like, I had seen this shit on talk shows and whatnot, but to actually go through it was a different story.

I sat back on the couch, laughing while me and her watched Eddie Murphy's *Delirious*. Python and Buckey had left to go get some pregnancy tests after Buckey tried to convince us all that I was pregnant. Don't get me wrong, I was showing symptoms, and I was late, but after all the evil shit I had done in my life, would God really bless me enough with some babies?

I looked over at my vibrating cell phone on the coffee table. Snatching it up, I smiled hard because I hadn't talked to Cynthia in a few days.

"Hey, girl, what's up? Where the hell you been?" I beamed through the phone.

"Decorating this goddamned church! What the hell, Tokyo?"

"I'm so sorry! There's a lot that's happened since the bachelorette party. We have seriously got to talk. Like dead-ass one-on-one." I glanced over at India, who was paying me no mind as she surfed on her laptop. While me and Cynthia were on the phone, we agreed to meet up at the church so I could help her finish decorating for the wedding day.

When I arrived at the church, after walking in, I had to admit that she had done a great job so far.

"So what is the gossip? Spill the shit, girl." She took my coat and laid it over one of the pews.

"So, check this shit out. Python's party was more lit than mine, no offense."

"None taken." She side-eyed me.

"I'm serious. The bitch who had been texting India and threatening her ass broke into the house!"

"Say what now?" She whipped around in my direction from pinning a flower up on the wall.

"Yeah! And they killed her. Did some real nasty-ass shit, too, from what I'm assuming."

"Damn."

"But you wanna hear the real good shit?" I asked, about to tear up all over again.

"Awww hell."

"India pretended to be me, and she danced for him."

"See! I knew that bitch was on some more snake shit!" Cynthia threw her hands on her hips.

"You wanna hear the worst part?" It was over, and the waterworks started. Cynthia rushed over and hugged me.

"I'm not sure. If it's making you cry, I'm sure it's going to make me wanna kick her ass even more."

"She drugged Python and Buckey and fucked him!" I broke down. "How could she do that shit!"

Cynthia let me go and backed up. "The fuck you mean, Tokyo? And you still allowing that bitch to breathe?"

"What the fuck can I do? I will be married after tomorrow!"

"You can do a lot!"

"And I'm pretty sure I'm pregnant." I tried to calm myself down.

"Well, shit, I been called that right along with everyone else. But just because you're knocked up don't mean you can't still handle your business. Shit, me and Susan can do it for you."

"I know, but this shit is real personal now. I don't know what I want to do, but something has to be done."

"It has to be done, and it will be. It needs to finally be ended! All this back-and-forth shit is a goddamned headache!"

"Tell me about it."

"Naw, you tell me about it. Tell me what you gonna do. Tell me how Tokyo is going to end this shit." She held me by the shoulders, looking me dead in the eyes.

"I don't know yet." I looked off to the side, not wanting to make eye contact with her.

"Well, all I'm going to say is don't let this baby make you soft, and don't let it stop you from being who you have always been."

We finished what little bit of decorating we had left to do and then we left. Cynthia agreed to go back to my house with me, saying Susan wouldn't be coming out tonight because she had to work late. I was glad she did because I just wanted to be around Cynthia. Besides, I needed the extra support and backup. I knew once I got in, Python would be on edge. I had just up and left while he and Buckey were out getting the test.

Parking in the driveway, I noticed that they hadn't gotten back yet. I was more than relieved until I shut off the truck and noticed him pulling in behind me. Stepping out, I took a deep breath of fresh air. Watching him get out of that truck, I was instantly turned on, and I didn't know why.

"Where was you about to go?" He shut the door.

"Well, if I was going anywhere, your ass just blocked me in. I just got back from getting Cynthia." I smiled.

"Well, here you go, let's go." He smiled back at me.

Cynthia got out and instantly started blushing when she saw Buckey. We all sat outside talking about the shit that happened before we went in the house. Walking into the living room, India was nowhere in sight.

"Thank God, because I might fuck around and smack the shit out of that bitch." Cynthia placed her jacket on the coat hanger.

"Be quiet yo, you so damn evil. I see why yaw get along." Buckey pointed between me and her.

"Yeah, well, I'm just saying. You all are handling this bullshit a lot better than me."

"Well, it is what it is." I walked up and smelled Python. He smelled so fucking good. What the fuck was going on with me? I mean, I had always been attracted to him, but this time around the shit had gone into overdrive.

"Girl, what you doing?" He stepped back.

"Nothing." I inhaled deeply.

"Well, get to it. Go take the test. We'll all sit in here and wait." He shooed me off, placing the bag back in my hand.

I walked into the bathroom and braced myself. I took the tests out and placed all five of them on the counter. Looking into the mirror, I really didn't recognize myself. Something about me was different. Everything felt different. Then there was a knock on the door. I opened it and there was India, grinning and holding a bottle of water.

"Hey, drink this and run the water in the sink if it's hard for you to pee. It helps."

I put on the fakest genuine smile and took it from her, shutting the door.

"Hormonal already," I heard her say from the other side.

I opened the boxes and placed them all down, then read one. I grew nervous while tearing open the little stick packet. I grabbed a plastic mouthwash cup out of the cabinet and pulled my pants down. When I was done peeing in two of them, I took a test and dipped it in the urine. Lord knows I needed to drink more water. I was slipping already. I waited two minutes and looked at the test. I was confused as I held it up to the light like a fake hundred.

"This can't be right," I said to myself.

"What can't be right?" I heard from the other side of the door.

"Seriously, you guys!" I shouted, opening the door.

"What? What happened? What does it say?" Cynthia smiled.

"I'm sure it says negative."

"Nope, that ain't right. Take another, because you got 'I'm pregnant' written all over your face." She shut me back in the bathroom.

I took a deep breath and decided to use all the tests with the same urine. As I sat on the toilet seat waiting, it seemed like the five minutes were more like five hours. I looked at all the tests and then read the boxes separately. I felt a little rush and sigh of relief. Opening the bathroom door, I was actually kind of happy.

"Okay, talk." Python jumped up.

"I'm not one of your do boys. Don't tell me what to do."

"Come on, Tokyo, quit playing with this man and us!" Buckey backed him up.

"I'm pregnant, I think." I smiled hard.

"Girl, you are! That first one was most definitely a false negative!" Cynthia ran over and hugged me.

"Aw, hell yeah!" Python pumped his fist.

"Well, I guess your soldiers do march!" India joked.

We all laughed except Cynthia, who sucked her teeth and rolled her eyes.

"Well, congrats, boo! Looks like we'll be planning a baby shower soon after the wedding also."

"Looks like." Everyone agreed.

CHAPTER EIGHTY-SEVEN

PYTHON

To say I was excited was a fucking understatement. I was about to marry the woman I loved and finally have a baby. I sat down on the edge of the bed as Tokyo was taking a shower. I grabbed my cell phone and texted my mother, letting her know. No more than two minutes later, she was calling.

"Yes, Ma?" I shook my head, smiling.

"What?" she shrieked through the phone.

"Yeah, she took more than a few tests, too."

"I knew it! I thought it was just your brother's girlfriend who was pregnant! But all them fish me and ya aunt kept dreaming about here lately confirmed it!" she shouted. "I finally get me some grandbabies! Took yaw stubborn asses long enough!"

"Wait, what? Bro having a baby too?"

"Yes, but his will be here within the next couple of days!"

"Okay, Ma, now I'm really confused. How come he ain't told me? How come you ain't told me?"

"Because something about he wasn't sure if it was his, because the girl gets around a lot or some mess like that. They did one of them DNA tests you can get done when you so far along or something."

"He always had a thing for fast girls though. Next time you talk to him, tell him I said congratulations, and he needs to hurry and get back for the wedding."

"I will, baby, but in the meantime, me and your aunt will be there by morning. What time is the wedding rehearsal dinner tomorrow?"

"At six, Ma."

"Okay, baby, see you all then."

We hung up with each other. Finally, Tokyo had come out of the bathroom. As I watched her walk across the room with a towel on, I admired the young woman before me. When she dropped the towel and began to oil her body down, I tried to imagine her with a big pregnant belly.

"What are you looking at, boy?" She grinned.

"Yo' fine ass."

"Well, my ass won't be fine looking in a few months when I'm all big and bumping into everything."

"You still gonna be the finest pregnant thing walking, you know that." I caught the oil bottle she'd tossed me to rub her back down. When I was finished, I lay in bed with her, watching *Orange is the New Black* until my phone rang.

"Talk fast," I answered.

"Man, you ain't gonna believe this shit, boss man! Some girl showed up to the trap talking about she had a baby with Leo and wanted to talk to him."

"And?"

"Leo who you got rid of," he whispered into the phone.

"And?" I said again.

"Well, we told her she couldn't talk to him, and her ass called the police! Nigga, they done shut the whole shit down. Now there's cops everywhere and shit, and they tearing shit up and locking motherfuckers up!"

"Nigga, what?" I jumped up, startling Tokyo.

"Baby, what's the matter?" She watched my every move as I got my shoes and things back on. Soon, Buckey came walking into our room.

"Bruh, turn on the fucking news! Our shit all over that shit!" He grabbed the remote and turned the TV on.

I instantly felt my blood beginning to boil. "Even from the dirt, this nigga still causing problems." I gritted my teeth. "I'll be there shortly. Find out who the mother-fucker in charge is right now and keep they ass there until I get there. Don't mention my fucking name or nothing." I hung up, frustrated.

"So, what we gonna do?" Buckey muted the TV.

"I'm about to pay off whoever I need to so I can get my shit back. Them fucking pigs know that's my shit there. I know they do!"

"Something ain't right about this, Python. I'll go over there. You need to keep your ass here just in case.

"And why is that?"

"Because I can find out more than you and get shit worked out better than you can in that field." He waved his badge around.

I shook my head and stood there, thinking he was right, and I couldn't risk anything else at the moment with everything going on. I nodded my head for him to go. In the meantime, I was about to find out how to get ahold of that bitch of Leo's. If there was one thing I hated more than a disrespectful motherfucker, it was a snitch fucking with my money!

"Make sure you find out who shorty is and see where her ass lives at. I'm gonna pay her ass a visit tomorrow."

"Cool." He left with a quickness.

"Baby, we have the dinner tomorrow. I don't want you there all stressed and upset." Tokyo looked up at me.

"I won't be. I'll handle it all first thing in the morning. Then, we'll bounce back to us like nothing ever hap-pened." I lay back down with her.

"We have to start making better decisions, babes. We have our own bundle of joy on the way, you know?"

"Yeah, I know, but that don't mean the way that I handle things is going to change or stop."

"If you say so." She shrugged and snuggled up under me about to fall asleep.

CHAPTER EIGHTY-EIGHT

PYTHON

When I got up the next morning, my mother and aunt were already down in the kitchen fixing a large breakfast. It smelled hella good, but I was hell-bent on a mission. I had tossed and turned all fucking night while Buckey was gone. I was too pissed off to sleep. When I finally did doze off, I found myself right back up. The spot that had been raided was the main one. Where a majority of the money and drugs were. And now, my shit was gone because of the bitter baby-momma drama bullshit of a nigga who no longer even walked this earth.

"Hey, baby, good morning," my mother greeted me.

"Hey, Ma, hey, Auntie. Good morning." I gave them both hugs and sat down. They fixed my plate and set it in front of me.

"Eat up, breakfast is the most important meal of the day, and today and tomorrow will be a long one." My aunt set a large cup of orange juice in front of me. I really didn't have an appetite as I scooted the eggs around on my plate.

"Boy, go ahead and eat that food before it gets cold." My mother looked over her shoulder. "Everything will work out fine. I know that was your spot that got hit last night." She continued cooking.

"The news does tell all, and so do facial expressions," my aunt chimed in.

"Yeah, well, you both know how I afford everything for everyone, so we need that shit back."

"Hey, everyone." Buckey walked in the kitchen and took a seat next to me.

"What happened?" I watched him anxiously.

"Damn, can I eat first? You done had me out all night trying to get shit right." He grabbed the plate my aunt fixed him and started throwing it all down like he was never going to eat again. I waited as patiently as I could for him to finish.

"Come on, man, quit playing." I stood up.

"Man, damn." He wiped his mouth and stood up, pushing his chair back in. "Come on so we can go talk about this shit because it ain't looking good." He sucked his teeth.

I followed him outside and then out to the back of my house where there was a black van parked.

"The fuck is this shit?" I grew nervous. "I know you ain't bring a Fed van to my shit! This shit is trackable or something!"

"Man, shut up." He opened the back doors to it. "I got this."

My fucking jaw dropped when I laid eyes on all my product and the money.

"The fuck? How you do this shit?"

"Told you, I got you. Especially as your best man it's my job to make sure you don't stress about shit before the big day!" He laughed, punching me in the arm.

"Nigga, thanks, but I'm serious. How did you do this?" I grabbed one of the packs.

"No lie, I had to give the chief of police sixty thousand to give it back and leave your shit alone. Hey, at least now he's on your payroll and we ain't gotta pay the motherfuckers below him." He shrugged.

"Fuck it, more money for us and him. And fewer fucking problems, too."

"Right, now let's go handle that bitch of Leo's."

"You got an address?"

"Yeap, she lives with an aunt or some shit in the west end."

"I don't give a damn. She just put them all in danger and on my fucking radar with that weak-ass shit."

"Cool, well, let's head to the west then."

"Give me a few to get ready."

"I'm about to get me another plate anyways. Take your time." He rubbed his stomach, laughing.

Parking a few houses down from the address Buckey put into the GPS, I watched the surroundings. It was still pretty early in the day. I had no clue what the girl looked like, but Buckey did. Didn't take long for me to notice her when I saw a girl who had to be in her late twenties, early thirties come out of the small blue house, packing a baby.

"Well, I'm sure that's her." Buckey put his mask on and so did I as we watched her hand the baby to someone in a white van.

"Day care, I'm assuming?" We looked at each other.

"That makes it even better. I don't hurt kids. Not physically anyways." I made sure the machine gun in my hand was ready.

"You are a fucked-up piece of shit." Buckey laughed while doing the same.

"Well, she fucked with me first." I got out and walked in her direction as the van pulled off. When it got around the corner, I waited on her to turn her back before I let the gun go the fuck off. Thank God it looked like it was about to storm out because no one was outside. She never even noticed as me and Buckey crept up behind her.

"Snitches end up dead around my parts, bitch!" I yelled and held the trigger down as bullets ripped through her chest and midsection when she spun around. We continued shooting the house up, leaving it looking like it had been dropped into a big-ass shredder. We then took off running and jumped into the black van Buckey had used before we came peeling out.

We pulled up to the warehouse where I usually had my guns disposed of. We cleared the van out and threw them into the acid barrel. Then, we took all the drugs and money out and loaded them into my truck. I was going to keep my shit at home. It would be safer anyways. Nowadays, motherfuckers were making too many mistakes with my shit.

I didn't normally like to shit where I laid my head, but for the time being, I just couldn't have any more fuckups happening. Everything had happened so fast within the past year. Hell, even within the past month. If this shit stayed up, I was sure to go bald or gray soon.

When I got back to the house, the girls had already left. We had three hours until the dinner, and I was more than ready to get this over with. I just wanted one good night of rest. Peaceful rest at that, with no fucking bullshit.

CHAPTER EIGHTY-NINE

TOKYO

I was excited as I looked at everyone all dressed up. The twins were especially adorable in their all red and black. A part of me was sad because I kept thinking about my father. Seeing Python interact with his mother and aunt and Cynthia with her daughter, and India with the twins, I was proud of our own little family. The fire engine red dress that was hugging my body made all my curves show off majorly. Python kept touching me every time I moved damned near. Call me crazy, but this pregnancy already had me glowing and feeling silly.

"So, you two ready for tomorrow?" Buckey stuffed his mouth full of broccoli.

"More than. Is this how everyone feels when this happens?" I sat back down and sipped from my champagne glass.

"How the hell we supposed to know? Ain't none of us married," India chimed in.

"Well, I was married, and Cynthia was once upon a time too." Mrs. Sherryl picked around at the food on her plate.

"Ma, what's wrong? Why you not eating your food?" Python looked over after I bumped him.

"Because your brother was supposed to be here tonight. He said he would." Her eyes watered up.

"Ma, it's cool, he will be here for the wedding and that's all that matters." Python grabbed her hand.

"But this is a special time for you. He needs to be here as your big brother for it all. He already missed the party, now the dinner!" She got even more upset.

We all started smiling as he stood behind her with roses.

"Ma, sometimes you act like I ain't talked to you in years or seen you in forever for that matter." Jaheim smiled. Mrs. Sherryl jumped up and hugged him like I had never seen before.

"Boy, what took you so long?" She released him as he went to hug Python and hand us our roses.

"Well, I told you I was coming. Sorry I was late, little brother. How has everything been?"

"It's been cool. You know me and Buckey keep shit tight."

We all sat around drinking, eating, and laughing. We made the agreement that after the wedding, this would be something we would do all the time at least once a month. I got annoyed as the night went on because Python wouldn't let me have more than two glasses. I guess he was right because of the whole baby thing. But with everything going on, it had honestly slipped my mind. Python told his brother about the soon-to-be baby, and they both—along with Buckey—started talking boy names and what they were going to do with him if it was to be a boy. I enjoyed every minute of it. Who would have thought it would be me of all people about to be a mother? When we got home, everyone decided to stay. They would get dressed there, whereas me and Python would get ready at the church. I was so nervous I'd thrown up three times before bed. Tomorrow was going to be a big, crazy, and amazing day for everyone. Even a crazy day for my sister, who just clearly didn't care to be a part of anything socially. I lay in bed tossing and turning until Python grabbed me and cuddled me. We fell asleep not long after a good lovemaking session.

When I got up the next morning, I felt like I hadn't gotten enough sleep and just wanted to throw the cover back over my fucking head. Cynthia, Susan, Mrs. Sherryl, and India all came busting in the room.

"Come on, get up, bride-to-be!" Cynthia danced around. "Time to get your hair and makeup done!"

I rolled over and looked at all of them and flicked them off.

"Told you, moody already." India folded her arms. "Come on, sis, get up, baby. It's you and my . . . I mean, Python's big day."

That little slip-up she had just made instantly lit a fire under my ass on what today was and what I had to do. I was most definitely about to get ready to walk down the aisle with my man, and I hoped that it would tear her soul apart that it could've been her, but her men and woman were fucking rotting away somewhere.

Cynthia and Susan had gotten me a professional hair-stylist and makeup artist. When they were done, I had to admit I looked fucking amazing. Not that I never did, but they had beat my face to the gods. Not too much makeup, but enough to make Python drop his jaw on the fucking ground.

When that was all done, the other ladies got dressed, and we all left after snatching up my wedding dress. It was sleeveless, and the chest part was lace and outlined around the neck with diamonds. The middle hugged my belly just right with tiny little flowers. The waist was outlined with diamonds and from there on down was more lace, diamonds, and silk, with a slit that went all the way up my thigh. It was classy, elegant, and sexy all in one.

When we got to the church, the outside was so beautifully decorated with white and yellow flowers and streamers everywhere. The girls' yellow and white dresses were eye-catching as hell. Mrs. Sherryl looked hella sexy in hers too. The men were eyeing them as we all walked up. Especially Buckey who couldn't take his eyes off of Cynthia. She flipped her hair and kept walking past, throwing her ass extra hard as she passed him up.

India decided because the twins were so messy, she would get them ready right before. Rya still hadn't decided to fully walk yet, so we decided to decorate their stroller and push them both down the aisle. As I sat in my dressing room in front of the vanity, I said a silent long prayer to my father, asking him to look over me and to guide me in this marriage. I also prayed to my mother, telling her that although I still hated her, I forgave her. I felt like I needed to do that in order to be better to my man and my children.

Before getting dressed, I reached into my purse and pulled out a small blunt that Cynthia had rolled for me just in case I got nervous again. She said it would help calm me down and keep from throwing up all over myself or my groom. I opened the window and leaned my head out, lighting the blunt. I almost choked on the smoke when I noticed Cynthia and Buckey getting down on the side of the building.

"Oh, shit!" Buckey snatched his pants back up with a quickness.

"Well, shit." Cynthia rolled her eyes and walked closer to the window. "Hand me that damn blunt! Least I can be high since you ruined my nut." She laughed.

"Uhh, I'm just going to head back in real quick." Buckey cleared his throat and walked off.

"I knew yaw asses were going to hook up. We all noticed the way he looked at yo' ass when we all first came in." I had to laugh myself.

"You know even stubborn men can't hold out for long with me." She did a slow turn in her dress.

"Yeah, sure, crazy lady."

"So, you decided what you gonna do about your sister? She's outta here as soon as this day is over. She ain't even told you where she gonna be moving to. How you gonna see the twins?"

"Don't worry, I got that shit under control." I sucked my teeth. "I'm going to take her ass to court."

"If you say so. Well, let me get back in there. We'll talk more about this after everything is finished. I don't want you upset."

"I'm okay." I took the blunt back, hit it again, then ashed and put it out.

CHAPTER NINETY

TOKYO

As I took my dress out of the suitcase, there was a knock on the dressing room door. I glanced at it, then back at my dress. They continued to knock. I didn't know why it was so important for them to keep bothering me when I was trying to get my head together, seeing there was still an hour and a half until the wedding started. I snatched the door open, and there stood India with a smug look on her face.

"What's up, sis?"

"Nothing much, how you doing?" She walked past me and set her laptop down. I felt my blood beginning to boil.

"Where are the twins?"

"Around. Anyways, I had something to show you before you walked down the aisle." She opened it up and plugged a USB into it. I was about to stab this bitch all in her face and neck if she thought she was going to ruin my day by showing me the video of her and Python.

"You must be out your rabbit-ass mind for real!" I said, then quickly shut up when the video started. When the song, our favorite song, "Pocket Full of Sunshine," started playing, it hurt my heart. She had put together a video of pics of me, her, and our father. From the time that we were babies, all the way up until we had taken pics for the family photos of me, her, and the twins. I shook my head at myself.

"Nice, right?" She smiled at me. "I just wanted you to never forget: before there was anyone else, it was always me and you. I also wanted you to see how we have grown up and changed, too. And that everything we have been through is okay because we are sisters, and I love you." She turned around in the chair to face me.

"Sis, I'm sorry." I barely got it out before the laptop continued to play. The video of her and Python started. My mood instantly changed right then and there.

"Oh, shit! Oh, fuck!" She whipped back around and slammed the laptop shut.

"Bitch, I've known about what you did." I shook my head.

"What you talking about?"

"You really gonna sit here and play me stupid? Me of all people, India. How the fuck could you do some grimy shit like that to me?" I walked up on her.

She stood up and walked toward the window, looking out of it like I had just said nothing to her.

"It really wasn't that hard once you think about it. Everyone who loved me or thought they would have a future with me, you took away from me. By either killing them or running them off. Including our parents!"

"What you mean? Daddy died from fucking cancer!"

"And by himself because your stupid, selfish ass couldn't ever do right! He was too sweet to say it, but, bitch, you broke that man's heart repeatedly! So, fuck you and how you feel!"

"Yeah, bitch, you gotta be on drugs to say that shit to me!"

"Not like your man was when I fucked him a few nights ago. The fuck you gonna do, Tokyo? In a church full of people? While you're pregnant? You gonna shoot me? Fight me? What? Don't forget I have one up on you, ma'am. You do want to be a part of the twins' lives, right?

Let the hurt and pain of me fucking your man eat your ass up every night and day! Every time you see me just like the hurt and the pain you caused me does to me day in and out." She looked back out the window.

"Bitch!" A gun cocked, and we both jumped when we turned around to see Cynthia, Susan, and Mrs. Sherryl standing in the doorway. "She may not touch your ass because you her sister and it's her wedding day, but you better believe your snake, slimy, dusty, wack, pussy ass that I will. And that I am going to," Cynthia continued.

"Tokyo, you take your dress and go get ready right now, baby. Time's winding down, and we got this." Mrs. Sherryl stepped forward.

"And don't forget to apply some lip gloss, too, boo." Susan picked up a snow globe off one of the tables and threw it dead at India's head, causing her forehead to instantly split open, making her fall over.

"You stupid, crazy bitch!" India held her head, dazed.

"Remember you abducted my mother and spat on her? Bitch, nobody touches her and gets away with that shit!" She pulled a knife from under her dress. Cynthia pulled a blade out of her mouth while Mrs. Sherryl escorted me out of the room. I was finished with that chapter of my life. And good riddance to her ass. It was time for a new beginning for me, my husband, the twins, and everyone else.

I felt proud as hell standing in front of my man with my girls behind me. In so little time, they had shown me more love, care, and loyalty than India. I don't know what they did with her or to her, but she sure wasn't up there with us. After me and Python kissed and said, "I do," we jumped the broom. To say my baby had showed out with the actual ring was an understatement! It was a silver waterfall ring that had over thirty diamonds in it.

On the ride in the limo on the way to the reception, I held my man's hand and said another prayer, asking the Lord to forgive us all and to not take anything out on my baby or the twins because I knew karma could be a bitch. Python repeatedly asked me what happened to India until I finally told him that she would never come around again. He then decided to leave it at that, saying, "Well, I hope yaw didn't hide her ass in that church."

The reception was even better than the wedding. We ate and danced our asses off until we couldn't dance anymore. Python had decided that for our honeymoon, we all would go to the Bahamas for two weeks. That would be fun since Cynthia and Buckey were clearly going to be a thing. How it was going to go would be crazy, I was sure.

Nobody bothered to look for my sister after I said that she'd run off, leaving a note saying she couldn't do the whole mommy thing. Buckey, of course, backed me up on that, and everything was smooth sailing in court when me and Python signed the papers, officially adopting the twins.

They deserved us, and we deserved them. They deserved a better and good life far more than what my sister could have given them. I loved those babies, and soon, I was going to be loving on my own just the same. Everything was going to be great because if anyone tried to prove otherwise, they would find out just how much me and my husband would risk it all to get their ass gone. I couldn't wait to start living my life as Tokyo Philips. I finally had a real deal solid and loving family with a mother I had always prayed for.